DON'T BE CRUEL

A novel by Ray Zacek

Florida is fatal. Living in Florida can kill you. That's no joke. Random horrors proliferate in the Sunshine State.

Hurricane season is often cataclysmic. Hurricanes rip through the state, spinning off tornadoes. The torrential rain, storm surges, and wind damage result in astronomical property losses. And people die.

Frequency of thunderstorms crowns Florida the Lightning Capital of the United States, leading the nation in deaths by lightning strike. Statistically, of course, injury or death by lightning is rare; but if you are one of the unlucky ones fried by a bolt of lightning, the stats don't mean a thing.

Summer is a hot and sticky hell that few tourists or snowbirds choose to endure. From June through September, suffocating, drenching humidity can peak at 90 percent. The blistering Florida summers precipitate fatal heat stroke and dehydration that lead to agonizing kidney failure and death. During winter in south Florida, when temperatures drop, frozen iguanas fall out of trees, injuring passerby, and damaging cars.

The Florida peninsula is a sponge. Under a thin veneer of sandy soil sits a vast porous plateau of limestone with a fractal Swiss cheese structure that soaks up rainfall. Water filters through vast underground caves and these occasionally collapse. Sinkholes gape open without warning like terrestrial vore, swallowing whole houses and anybody who happens to be inside.

With over twelve thousand miles of coastline, Florida ranks number one in the world for shark bites, with more than double the incidents of second ranked Australia.

Seaweed in the warm, shallow coastal waters of Florida contains a flesh-necrotizing bacteria that can kill a human being within a day or two of infection.

And alligators! Over a million inhabit the state, lurking in every lake, pond, and canal, occasionally popping out of storm drains or climbing chain link fences and invading residential yards. Florida leads the nation in fatal gator encounters. A gator snatched a toddler playing in about a foot of water on a beach area at Disney's Grand Floridian Resort & Spa. An 85-year-old woman walking her dog in a Fort Pierce retirement community was attacked by a 10-foot alligator that emerged from a placid lake like a primitive, prediluvian monster and dragged her under the dark water, never to be seen again. At least not whole.

Invasive, hungry, and voracious, Burmese pythons proliferate in south Florida and are migrating north. Every species of venomous snake native to North America slithers through Florida, lurking in the grasses and rocks of rest areas along the interstate. Not to mention black widow and recluse spiders, swarming fire ants whose stinging bites leave ugly pustules prone to infection, and toxic bufo toads. An invasive, parasite-carrying species of giant African snail, the size of a catcher's mitt, infests south Florida like a Biblical plague.

While getting into her car in a Publix supermarket parking lot, an elderly Sun City Center woman felt something strike her arm. She didn't see what it was and didn't register any alarm. But returning home she went into the bathroom and discovered a tiny bat clinging to the flesh of her arm and a patch of her skin turning purple. The horrified woman squished the creature with a towel. Blood dripped from the perforation on her arm. She contacted the Florida Department of Health. The bat tested positive for rabies.

In another documented incident, a vicious rabid otter attacked a woman kayaking on the

Suwanee River. Her nose and cheek gnawed, an ear partly ripped off, the woman required reconstructive surgery and, like the woman in Sun City Center, a series of painful rabies shots.

Jason Root knew all this and more from doom-scrolling the internet and chose to reside in Florida anyway. But as he ran down a rural Florida highway at dusk on a Saturday night, with demonic rednecks chasing him, Jason wished he'd never left the tranquil suburbs of New Jersey for the crazy, lurid carnival of Florida.

Oh, Jesus oh Jeeze save my ass! He panted and muttered. Pain in his side spiked. Blood stained his shirt. Pink and black Nike sneakers, a size too small, pinched his feet. A pair of slinky pink shorts borrowed from a teenage masseuse hugged his hips. Behind him, angry shouting echoed in the pine woods that sheltered Ococonee Spring and the abomination that lurked there.

Jason sprinted down the road in the fading light. Sheer terror and survival instinct compelled him. Killers and hellhounds pursued him. Escape remained his only thought.

The darkening road curved. Ahead lay Hygeia, Florida, the scrap of a town on Highway 19. Ramshackle houses hidden under the pines, a convenience store, and an abandoned white stucco church tucked amid the oaks. A tall, dark, and sinister figure emerged from the church, waving his arms, and shouting but Jason recoiled from him and plodded toward the X-press convenience store, the stitch in his side like a dagger.

To the west the sky rippled purple and yellow, and the light turned blue, color draining, the air humid and oppressive. Jason's lungs ached. He stumbled over the gravel and past the gas pumps and lumbered inside the X-Press store. Struggling for breath, he flopped over the ice cream cooler. He slid the door open, cold air gushing, beads of sweat dripping on the Klondike bars.

"Are you alright, hon?" The obese woman behind the counter wore a green smock. Name tag on the smock read Ardell. She pursed her lips, concern written on her plump face, her eyes fixed on Jason.

"Do you have a phone? A landline?"

"Who you gonna call? Ghostbusters?" Ardell's raucous laughter echoed.

"This is serious! People are trying to kill me!"

"Are they?" Ardell crushed out her menthol cigarette. "Sugar, you got something coming, and I am going to deliver it."

"Deliver what?" Jason said.

"Comeuppance." She glided from behind the counter and grabbed an ax from the shelf, its price sticker still attached.

"What the fuck!" Jason backed away from her. "What're you doing? Put that down! Stop!"

Ardell raised the axe over her head with thick, adipose-flapping arms and approached him on tiptoes like a mad elephantine ballerina. She shrieked, her face contorted, a demonic mask, lips stretched, serpentine red tongue wriggling, eyes wild and protruding from sockets.

The axe blade came hurling down like doom.

***

Over a year earlier at Ococonee Spring, Elvis ascended from the chilly water and floated in the pale, predawn light. The water percolated beneath him. Leaving the spring, Elvis skimmed through the slash pines and palmetto. Stiff coontie fronds rustled as Elvis breezed by, aiming for the ramshackle Victorian house with rotting grey gingerbread trim. Feral cats hissed, snarled, and arched their backs as Elvis approached, then scattered.

On the sagging porch, Shire, the younger Fenner brother, curled in a fetal ball on a threadbare sofa, mouth-breathing, drooling, and sleeping off an alcohol and chemical binge. Elvis glided past, through the tattered screen door, into the house. Elvis didn't bother with runty Shire who couldn't sense Elvis' presence passing through; for only Edgar Fenner had *The Gift*. Born with it. Raw talent that Elvis had shaped over the years since Elvis put out his first tentative feelers to Edgar Fenner, then a chubby child anchored in front of the television set. And the distraught had child received him with joy and wonder.

Billowing up the creaking staircase, Elvis swept down the dark hall to the corner bedroom where he found Edgar fast asleep. Edgar's bulk strained the bedsprings. Squealing springs and Edgar's snoring blended into an awful cacophony.

Elvis hovered over Edgar, getting a taste of his dreams, like a mosquito drawing blood. Edgar Fenner's mind had remained open to Elvis since the first magical moment they had met.

What did Edgar dream of? Pussy, of course. Girls with soft, doe-like eyes, their skinny, sun-washed bodies shining as they swam in cool, clear water of Ococonee Spring. Girls lolled in the sand, playing with red coonhound puppies. Pretty naked girls and playful puppies. Edgar was all about yearning. Elvis smilesmirked approval. Yearning was one of the keys to the soul, and Edgar's soul was his. Signed, sealed, and delivered.

Wake up, Edgar, Elvis said. *Boy, wake up!*

Of course, Elvis did not 'say' anything, didn't make a sound, and didn't need to. Edgar served as his Receiver. He and Elvis parlayed on a psychical level. But this morning the loyal Receiver failed to respond. Edgar remained mired in sleep, clinging to his dreams.

Edgar, hey! I'm talking to you, boy! Wake up!

Edgar mumbled but didn't open his eyes. He snorted. He farted. A foul vapor mingled with Elvis' ectoplasmic essence. Elvis seethed.

Boy, set your fucker to receive! Dammit, lard

ass, I'm talking to you! Wake up! The King is present in the building. Hup, two, three, four. Atten-SHUN!

Edgar shot up straight in bed, banging his head on the low slant of the ceiling in the corner of the bedroom. His eyes popped open. He rolled out of bed, plopping on the floor, tangled in the sheet. He wore a t-shirt and white boxer shorts, size XXL.

"Yessir, I'm awake!" Edgar Fenner stared into the roiling blue-green mist that filled the bedroom. Elvis, Almighty Elvis, the Once and Future King. Edgar's skin tingled and hair stood up on his arms.

You got wood there, Edgar. Whoa, the cat couldn't scratch that!

"Sorry 'bout that." Abashed, Edgar covered his erection with the sheet.

Don't be sorry. Nothing to be ashamed of. A stiff prick is the most natural thing in the world. Be proud of it.

"Thank you, Elvis." Edgar grinned at ease now as well as at attention.

Elvis shimmered, a coruscating cloud, sparkling like Christmas lights. Then, as Edgar gawped in open-mouthed awe, Elvis condensed into form. Ectoplasm shaped a body. The Rockabilly Elvis in pink blazer, pink slacks, the wave of jet-black hair; the piercing blue-grey eyes, flashing a radiant smile upon Edgar Fenner. His hips swiveled and he crooned.

Yaaaaaw-uh! Yeah! Hunka hunka burnin' love. Got to find you a girl, Edgar. Yes, we do, oh yes, we do. To satisfy your natural urges. You're too pent up. Got to let your juices flow.

"For sure, that would be nice," said Edgar, his head bobbing. He added, "You *did* promise me that."

I know what I promised. No need to remind me.

"Well, I've been waiting and waiting on that," said Edgar in a plaintive voice, thinking aw heck, it's a sore subject, but Elvis brought it up, not me, so, I'll take that plunge, "Can't help but wonder when."

Don't bug me about it. I will get around to it when I get around to it. Some things can't be rushed.

"Tell me when," said Edgar.

You got a problem? Turbulent clouds formed in the misty room. *You're bugging me like some kid. What did I say, Edgar? Didn't I say I will deliver? And when I say I will deliver ... I WILL DELIVER!*

Edgar realized he'd pushed a little too far. Elvis'

rage crumpled him. Throat and facial muscles tightened and burned, as if Elvis would peel his face right off. Agony! But Elvis relented and released His grip on Edgar. Edgar caught his breath, cowered and steepled his hands in supplication. "Sorry, sorry, sorry, I didn't mean anything by it."

A soothing cloud like balm covered Edgar and wiped away his pain and Elvis spoke gently *I'm sorry for having to do that, Edgar. I really am. I hate losing my temper, I really do. Hurts me to have to do that. So, don't make me. Don't you get cocky with me. And never doubt my word.*

"My mistake! My mistake, a weak moment."

Alright, cool it. Let's move on to business. I got you up early for a reason. Trouble is heading our way. Something wicked is coming to Ococonee Spring.

"Wicked?" Edgar gasped. "Another enemy? Darn!"

Threats always lurked. Enemies plotted; perverse creatures in the gross, material world vied to drag down and trample Elvis. He made Ococonee Spring his sanctuary to regain strength for the Coming Battle, the final battle, like Armageddon in the Bible. Elvis charged the Fenner brothers with keeping secrecy and guarding Ococonee Spring. Like the Knights of Medieval Times or the Guardians of the Galaxy or the Magnificent Seven, only minus five.

It's not clear yet. Don't fail me, Edgar. You and the Diddler have to be on guard.

Elvis referred to Shire Fenner as Diddler because, according to Elvis, Shire diddled around and had to be kept on a short leash. Another of Edgar's responsibilities.

I know I can count on you, Edgar. You're true blue and that's why I love you.

"I love you too," Edgar replied.

Edgar's eyes watered. Elvis' love was a powerful thing, swallowed you whole.

I've told you how it was. I wandered in misery between worlds before I came to Ococonee Spring. Wandering, lost, wandering, and wandering. It was an ordeal. I got so lonely, I got so lonely, I got so lonely worse than death. But then I found a new place to dwell. A sanctuary, a resting place, where all is well. It's not the heartbreak hotel. No, it's Ococonee Spring. Ococonee Spring is where I dwell.

He swaddled Edgar in a glittering blue-green

mist that made Edgar feel as comfortable and secure as when he had cuddled upon his Gamaw's bosom as a child.

When the time comes, Edgar. When time comes …

The magic words, the promise. When Time Comes signified that future date when Elvis broke out of the worldly domain and ascended to the next plane of existence, called Graceland. Not Graceland physically located in Memphis, Tennessee, for that was a discarded shell, a mere glimmer of the true Graceland to come, which would prove grander than anything on earth, a spiritual and eternal Paradise, Elvis-style. The exact date of the ascension remained indeterminate. Elvis did not fill in the details. He hinted, he cajoled, he dangled Graceland like a shimmering trout lure. When Time Comes, always imminent, finally arrived, with great clamor and convulsion and fire in the sky, Elvis promised that his loyal guardians would march along with Him like Pharoah's retinue. Forever after to dwell in Graceland.

Hand in hand, Edgar, we'll march to that golden land and go to Graceland together. Don't never doubt it. Never.

"I don't doubt you. I don't, I don't!"

Guard my sanctuary. You know how to deal with intruders.

He faded. The blue-green shimmer dimmed and receded, shrinking, flowing out the window, streaming down the side of the old ramshackle house, wafting through the palmetto, back to Ococonee Spring, cutting like a knife into the chilly water. Elvis plunged to the depths of the spring, where he abided, his refuge. And there the scaly primeval alligator-snouted beast with whom he communed stirred in the pure artesian water, a small chamber in the vast mysterious limestone catacombs of subsurface Florida.

***

That same morning, fifty miles from Ococonee Spring, in Gainesville, Florida, Kat Condon heard the juicer roaring like a turbojet engine. Her head ached. She wrapped herself in herself in a sheet, a bleary-eyed mummy with tangled magenta hair.

Josh Quinnell walked into the bedroom, already dressed. "Kat, get up."

"*Nooooo.*" Kat moaned.

"We're going canoeing."

"Changed my mind." She plopped a pillow over

her head.

"You said you'd be thrilled to see primeval Florida. Can't renege."

"Ugh. Primeval, my whitegirl ass," said Kat from under the pillow. "That was Pernod talking." The empty green liquor bottle stood on the bedside table. Pernod, a recent discovery of hers. A wicked kick-ass French confection, great going down, for sure, but the morning-after proved dire.

Kat lifted the pillow. "I dreamed I was drowning. Bad omen. But then a sketchy Black man gave me a bag of money, a good omen. I guess it balances out."

"Dreams are mental barf," declared Josh.

"Whatev, let me sleep." She clutched the sweat stained pillow.

Josh pulled the sheet. Tug-of-war ensued. Kat snarled and hissed but Josh won, unraveling her, and snapping the sheet from the bed. He held the twisted sheet like a captured banner.

Oh, fuck you, Kat thought. Why had she ever hooked up with him? He was awesome at oral, okay, there was that. Josh hovered over her in his black antifa t-shirt, its red flag waving. Joshua

Quinnell with scraggly goatee and perpetual smarty-pants smirk. Anarcho-Man, Anti-Capitalist and Antifascist, former freelance writer and blogger for Creative Loafing in Tampa, former adjunct professor of Poly Sci at a community college, a gig he quit. Or was fired from. They shared a cramped, off-campus apartment. Her apartment, her name on the lease. She paid the rent from student loans and generous cash infusions from her stepfather who lived, ugh, in *The Villages*. Josh crashed at her apartment, temporarily, he said, until another full-time gig came available, possibly organizing in DC. He made sporadic contributions toward the costs. This relationship, Kat decided, had run its course. His butt had to go. Like when they came back from this canoeing trip. Of course, no man she'd ever met rated as a keeper; they were all, in various ways, damaged. Broken units.

"Bring me juice," she said.

Josh fetched her fresh-squeezed pear and guava juice, green and foamy in a plastic tumbler, lumpy with scoops of protein powder added. Kat sat on the edge of the bed wearing only thin panties and sipped the concoction. Daylight filled the room as Josh flung the heavy curtains open and Kat shielded her eyes from the glare.

"Have a *sun-gasm*!" Josh said.

Kat recoiled like a vampire.

"Want an egg?"

"I don't eat eggs," replied Kat. "I'm a vegan, remember."

"For, what, a whole week now?"

"It's a *commitment*." She slurped juice. "Cigarette me."

"Vegans don't smoke," said Josh.

"This one does."

"Filthy habit I refuse to enable."

"Fuck you." Kat fishfaced him and crawled over the disheveled bed to grab her black pebble leather bag. She fished out a pack of American Spirit, lighted one with a Bic, wincing at the flame, and puffed. She exhaled a long sinuous stream of smoke toward the ceiling.

"Nicotine is poison."

Kat brandished the pack. "Look, see, all natural." She deposited the cig in the empty Pernod bottle. "I want to take a shower."

She hopped off the bed and locked herself in

the bathroom. She peed copiously, swallowed four orange-flavored baby aspirin, then pulled back the dingy polyester curtain and tortured the shower knobs until they confessed to water. Adjusting the water temp proved tricky. The knobs squeaked. They stuck. Cold water gushed, dousing her shoulder; Kat shrieked. When she adjusted the temp and pressure where she wanted Kat stripped off her panties and luxuriated in the warm spray of the round daisy shower head. This delighted her. Pores opened; water rippled on her rinsing away all the overnight blahs. Kat cooed with delight.

"Where's this place we're going to?" Kat emerged from the shower and toweled herself. Stepping out of the steamy bathroom she found Josh looking at her phone. "What the fuck, Josh? Why're you spying on my phone?"

"Not spying," he replied. "It dinged. I glanced. You got mail. Couldn't help but see some amazing photos from Harve, your stepfather."

She grabbed the phone. Yeah, amazing pics alright. Monumental photos of ancient stone temples, and selfies from a skinny bearded man bare-chested and gaunt in brown khaki shirt and shorts and fedora, like an emaciated Indiana Jones.

"That's not my stepfather Harve," she told Josh. "That's Harve my step*brother*. I have two; the other one, Jason, he's an asshole but that's a story and I don't want to go there. Harve's the weirdly interesting stepbrother who lives in Cambodia. We stay in touch." She scrolled through the photos. "He says the food is awful in Cambodia and he's living on cheap white wine and bananas. That's Angkor Wat."

"I assumed it was," said Josh.

Oh, like he'd traveled there extensively and could write the guidebook. She wriggled, pulling a jersey over her upper body. "This canoe excursion. Tell me again where we're going?"

"Down the Lacoochee River," said Josh. "To Ococonee Spring."

***

"What's he done *for us* lately?" Shire said over breakfast.

Edgar almost spilled his coffee. After taking breakfast to elderly aunt Katie, who lived in the attic and never left her room, Edgar had waddled downstairs to the kitchen and sat across from Shire at the wobbly kitchen table and discussed guard duty.

"What's he *done for us*? How can you talk that way, Shire?"

"Oh, sure, Edgar. Coddles you. Gives you hugs n' kisses and shiny lights. Me? Gives me *nothing*. Won't even show himself to me."

"Dive in Ococonee Spring, and you *will* see him."

A dare Shire would never accept. He said nothing. Wielding his fork like a backhoe, Shire attacked the sausage biscuits on his plate, stuffed a heap in his mouth, and chewed with his mouth open. White gravy dribbled from the corners of his mouth. He heaped tablespoons of sugar into his mug of inky black coffee.

Edgar took a conciliatory tone. "We do these things for him, and he's promised to take us to Graceland."

"Promises'rrrr issy t'mkkkkk," Shire said.

"Don't talk with food in your mouth, Shire. That's uncouth. Elvis will keep his promises. What Elvis requires of us is, um." He searched the cubbyholes in his brain for the word. "Fortitude. Holding down the fort. We got to guard his sanctuary real close today because some wickedness is headed this way."

"I got other plans today."

"Oh, bull … *stuff!*"

"Don't get mad, Edgar. Your blood pressure goes sky high, and you'll keel over with a heart attack and you're too big to catch."

Pinched arteries in Edgar's burly chest throbbed. Shire liked to pester people, like a kid sticking pins in a helpless creature to make it squirm and suffer, which Shire had used to do to small animals when a child. "Darn it, Shire, you're just being ornery. You got no other plans and even if you did, there is nothing is more important than guarding Ococonee Spring. Because Elvis sees trouble coming. T-R-U-B-B-L-E."

"You can't spell for shit, Edgar."

"Watch your language, Shire."

"The fuck you gonna do about if I don't?"

Edgar counted to ten; the good Gamaw who raised him had always told him to do that. Never give in to wrath, she had counseled, and don't never covet nor be uncouth. Words Edgar took to heart. He took a deep breath. Then another. The ache in his head subsided. Finally, Edgar said, "Elvis gave us a task to do, and we are going to do it. Or do you want to get on his bad side?"

Invoking the wrath of Elvis always caused Shire to get that scared, contrite look. Shire was no Receiver, but when Elvis chose to, he could materialize to Shire. When Elvis manifested around Shire, the sizzling blue-green shimmy in the air made Shire tingle all over. Once, when he had aroused Elvis' wrath by misdeed, Shire had trembled, convulsed, and pissed and shat himself.

"We'll take turns," Edgar said. "Fair and square. You go on down there for two hours and I will stay here and keep an eye on the house and auntie Katie and then I will spell you. We take turns through the day until Elvis says the danger is passed."

"I got a better idea," said Shire. "I'll stay down there the morning, and you take the afternoon."

"All morning?" Edgar eyed Shire with suspicion.

"Yeah, the whole fuck'n morning, Edgar."

"Stop talking that way."

"Stop being a big fat old bully and do things my way for a change."

"Okay, alright," replied Edgar with an exasperated sigh. Had to admit Shire's plan was better than them traipsing back and forth all day from spring to house and giving in to Shire was better than wrangling all morning. "But no diddling."

"I don't diddle."

"Yes, you do, Shire. You diddle like nobody's business."

"That's a double-D damn lie!"

"Stop it, Shire! Let's stop butting heads and do this. For Elvis."

Shire grinned, his amiable aw-shucks grin. "Okay, Edgar. No diddling. I will stay on top of things. Promise."

But Shire made promises, discarded them for no good reason, and then denied he ever made any such promise. Edgar invested all the elder brother's authority he could muster into his voice. "You got to stick to the task, Shire. I mean it!"

"On it like white on rice."

Shire stuffed the last sopping dripping bits of biscuit and gravy into his mouth, made a ravenous sucking sound, and swallowed. He stood, his chair scraping the drab grey linoleum. "And bring me my lunch when you come down, Edgar. I want a baloney and cheese sandwich and don't forget to cut the bread crusts. And tater salad. Bring me some Little Debbie cakes too." He took one last quick slurp of coffee and stuffed his pack of Marlboros and matches in the breast pocket of his chambray shirt. From under the table Shire picked up the pump shotgun; he already had a .22LR pistol tucked under his belt. He removed a 2-liter plastic jug of ginger ale from the fridge to take with him too. He swaggered toward the screen door.

"To Ococonee Spring! On my fuck'n way!"

The screen door slammed as he exited.

***

The Gourds blasted from the speakers, *goin' to El Paso, chicken blood on my pants, gonna dance with a Strawberry girl, aaaaarrrrrrrr!* Bobbing to the music, Josh hunched over the steering wheel of his Toyota Tacoma. He had secured the canoe in the truck bed with a spider web of bungees. Before leaving Gainesville, he had switched his antifa shirt for one featuring a country western singer. A tattered copy of the Florida Atlas and Gazetteer, pages dogeared and red Sharpie marked, lay on the seat. Josh careened west on State Road 26, weaving in and out of lanes.

"Slow down, bitch!" She shouted over the music. "Stay in one lane!" Kat dialed down the volume. "You're driving *like reckless.*"

"Not reckless," Josh replied. "Counterintuitively. Vast difference."

Kat cinched her seat belt tighter. "How far is this boat launch?"

"Not far."

"In actual drive time when do we get there?"

"Time, time, time," Josh said, annoyed. "Time's an illusion, a human construct, like gender. There is no time, only *moments*. To be experienced to the fullest."

"Where's the fucking boat launch?"

"In a county park under an old train trestle. Deep in rectalbilly country."

"*The fuck* ... deep in what?"

"Rectalbilly," said Josh, with a professorial air, "is a subspecies of hillbilly. Stupid, head thrust up ass. Rural redstate rethugs are obsessed with guns and conspiracy theories. Proven statistic, the most violent people in the country. That is why I put on a Travis Tritt t-shirt. Deceptive coloration.

Travis Tritt's a total MAGA asshat but, in all fairness, Eagle fans have him to thank for reuniting Don and Glen."

All Kat heard was blah blah blah. Tritt, Eagles, Don, Glen blah blah blah. Country music guys with big hats and drawls, and old rockers and their perpetual farewell tours and reunions and sky-high ticket prices. Countryside inhabited by rectalbillies with guns alarmed her. "This trip sounds sketchy and sketchier."

"Not to worry! Ococonee Spring is unspoiled and uncommodified, unlike most of fascist Florida. It is pristine, a first magnitude spring."

"But, but, but," said Kat. "You said this spring is on private property."

Josh dismissed her misgivings with a wave of his hand. "No worry. I was there before and left on excellent terms with the he/him who dwells there. He's red of neck, of course, but he's cool, has a kind heart, exceptional among that ilk. A Florida Man named Edgar Fenner."

"What a derp name!"

"A gentle giant," Josh said. "Banal as that sounds. Edgar Fenner told me *y'all come back* to Ococonee any time. Lonely guy, craves company."

"But did you tell him we're coming *today*?"

"Not exactly, no."

This sounded wishy-washy to Kat, and totally unacceptable. "What does 'not exactly no' mean?"

"Edgar Fenner isn't connected," said Josh. "No phone, no internet. I tried to contact him. I wrote to him."

"And?"

"The postcard came back return to sender."

***

Guard duty, as usual, proved boring. Warm breezes rustled the palmetto, water percolated in the spring, and Elvis remained dormant, hidden in the depths. Maybe, thought Shire, this was another false alarm. Elvis got edgy at times. Made demands.

Shire yawned. He slouched in a canvas camp chair, almost dozing in the heat and humidity. The 12-gauge Mossberg lay across his lap. He admired his .22 pistol; he had retrofitted a homemade silencer and prided himself on his ingenuity. Using only a 2-liter plastic soda bottle, after he drank the ginger ale, some duct tape, and a hose clamp from the red toolbox he kept at the spring, he converted a small caliber Ruger pistol, good only for plinking and varmint elimination, into a stealth killing machine. That was cool. Shire swelled with pride. But it needed a field test.

Armadillos are stupid. Shire chuckled when he saw one of those long-headed, peg-toothed, sticky tongue-flicking 'dillos scrambling about amid the palmetto in its slinky armor. Scratching its tiny claws in the dirt, bustling along, looking for bugs to eat, its tail dragging.

Shire scanned all around Ococonee Spring; he shielded his eyes from the sun and gazed down at the run to the Lacoochee River, looking for any movement, listening for any sound.

Nothin'.

Stupid, vulnerable creatures appealed to Shire's predatory instincts. Okay, he thought, a little diversion might be in order. Uh-huh, shouldn't begrudge a man a little relief. Only fair. Elvis was prob'ly asleep anyway and dreaming in the depths, whatever Elvis dreamed about. Shire picked up his pistol. Maybe, he figured, smoke a jay, and jerk off in the woods for that kind of relief. Edgar might call it diddling, but Shire planned to be back before fat old fingerwagging Edgar discovered he was gone.

The armadillo sensed a threat. As soon as Shire began stalking, tiptoeing around the edge of the spring, the armadillo raised its snout, and ambled away. Shire tagged along after it, amused, in no hurry, keeping the critter in sight. He emptied his ginger ale swollen bladder, paused to light a jay, took a hit, breathed deep, held the pungent burning smoke, then exhaled languorously, feeling an immediate buzz and head spin. He coughed, hocked, spat, and scuttled into the pines. On the hunt.

As Shire Fenner skulked into the woods after the armadillo, Josh and Kat caught sight of a heavy metal cable strung across the banks of the Lacoochee, impeding their approach to Ococonee Spring.

***

Turtles sunning on tree trunks plopped into the river as the canoe approached. The Lacoochee river snaked through flat Florida countryside, a narrow stream the color of tea. A sluggish current carried the canoe. Paddle splashed, branches cracked. Cicadas buzzed. Dragonflies flitted. Fallen trees and cypress stumps presented obstacles. Spider webs in the branches caught Kat's hair and hideous green flies buzzed around her head. She cursed. Her arms and shoulders ached. She pulled icky strands of moss from her hair.

"Canoeing is fucking work," said Kat. She pulled sticky spider web and bits of Spanish moss from her hair. "Fuck! Keep us out of the branches!"

"Let me steer, okay?" said Josh.

"Fine! You steer! How much further?"

"Not much further." Josh surveyed the shoreline.

"You said not much further half an hour ago!"

"Be chill. It's coming."

"What's coming?" Kat feared some new, dread obstacle. More fallen oaks, a curtain of nasty moss, a slimy gathering of hungry chomping gators …

"The spring," said Josh.

In a few minutes they rounded a bend and reached the channel that fed into the river from the spring, but another impediment greeted them. Steel cable strung attached to wooden posts blocked the passage. A hand-lettered wooden sign swung on the cable. *Private Property Ari Ver Deechee.*

"Huh," said Josh, chagrined. He laid his paddle

across the thwart of the canoe. "That cable wasn't here before."

"Who the fuck is Ari Verdeechee?"

Josh shook his head. "No idea."

"No idea? Great! You're sure this is the place?"

"Am I sure? Absolutely positive," he replied in an aggrieved tone of voice. "Can't you feel the current coming from the spring? It's pushing our canoe. Yeah, Ococonee Spring is that way." The canoe swept about in a circle.

"Okay," said Kat. Exasperated, hot, sweat soaked, itchy, bugbit, and achy, she wanted to bash Josh's head and see blood and mucky grey matter spurt and then toss his body in the river for the alligators who would surely materialize because Florida. "But what if your red of neck gentle giant pal Edgar sold out to some guy named Ari Verdeechee, and he doesn't want visitors?"

"Edgar bragged his family owned the land since before the Civil War and selling was unthinkable. He's got to be there."

"Nobody has *got to be* any fucking place," Kat replied, reflecting for a moment on the arbitrariness and futility of existence and then absent-mindedly swatted a mosquito insect that lighted on her shoulder, leaving a blot of blood on her fingers. They both stared at the sagging steel cable. Then Kat said, "Oh, fuck it! Let's go! I didn't come all this way to turn back."

"That's the spirit of Murrica."

"That's the spirit of a pissed off whitegirl," said Kat.

Josh steered, turning the canoe into the channel. Kat, crouching in the bow of the canoe, lifted the cable and they scraped underneath. Unlike the tannin-stained river, the run to Ococonee Spring remained crystalline. They paddled against a swift current, the freshwater pumping out of the spring as if from a beating heart. Pebbles and rocks lined the sandy bottom like a mosaic and clumps of grass danced with the current. On either bank the woods gave way to open pasture, replete with bovine creatures, and rolling hills. A cool breeze rippled across the water. Paddling ceased to be a chore for Kat.

At last, they found themselves in a huge circular pool, hidden among huge old mossy oaks and cypresses and rimmed by sugar white sand. The azure water sparkled, percolating from a cumulus of mossy green-gray rock. Under a crude lean-to they spied a folding canvas camp chair and a red toolbox, but no one was around, not a soul. They ceased paddling and bobbed in the canoe, passing a bottle of energy drink back and forth, slurping. Kat popped berry-flavored CBD gummies in her mouth.

"Ococonee Spring," announced Josh. "In all its pristine splendor."

"Awesome." Kat, elated now, dipped her hand, and reveled in the chilly water.

"Seventy-two degrees," said Josh. "Scrotum-shrinking cold."

"What effect on vaginas?" said Kat.

"Jump in and find out."

"I have goose bumps. A feeling like electricity all over." She opened her top to peek down. "My nips are big as cherries. Gawd, this place is so sexy."

"Ococonee Spring is a vortex," said Josh.

Kat leaned over the gunwale and splashed herself with spring water. She wanted to chirp like a bird, shuck off her clothes and dive in, swimming and frolicking like a frisky she-otter. Glancing at the mossy green rocks below she saw something deep in the water. At first, only a shadow. It moved, rising toward the surface. An elongated and misshapen creature emerged from the rocks and waggled toward the surface.

"What's that?" Kat said, alarmed.

Josh peered into the water. The creature swam along the bottom of the pool, long and dark, its movement deliberate.

"Catfish," said Josh. "See the whiskers. *Monster* catfish. Wow."

"It's fucking enormous! And all scaly and has nasty-looking blades on its back. Like a steampunk fish. I'm not getting out of the canoe!" She was a few clicks short of panic but moving in that direction on a steady course.

"Probably, it's just checking us out."

"It's circling us." Kat tensed. Memories of Animal Planet and Nature episodes she had watched on cable came flooding back into consciousness. "It's acting like it's going to attack."

"Oh, come on!" said Josh. "Not likely."

Then the creature surged toward the surface and leaped. A huge, armor-plated fish broke the water, soaring over the canoe and bringing a wall of water in its wake. Kat screamed. She saw a blur: *a monstrous thing.* Dark slimy brown with a silvery white underbelly; a long pulpy, wriggling, tentacled snout and stubby whiskers; dorsal and pectora fins that opened like bat wings; a twisting, scimitar-like tail that slashed at them.

Blood spurted.

Cold water cascaded over them. The canoe tipped.

Kat found herself struggling in the water, immersed under the capsized canoe. She flailed, kicking her legs, holding her breath, gripped by terror. She saw nothing but foam, beads of bright blood, and churning water. The huge dark creature glided by beneath her like a torpedo, diving, retreating amid the porous rocks. Kat gulped water and kicked her legs, frantic to escape. After an eternity, Kat broke the surface again and gulped air. The canoe floated half submerged in the water. She heard men's voices, angry shouting, and the roar of an engine as a green truck rolled over the palmetto along the edge of the pond. She saw Josh, bleeding as he crawled over the sand, sprang to his feet, and dashed away through the palmetto.

"Come back!" She yelled at him, but her mouth filled with water, and she choked. Her feet found the sandy bottom. Coughing, dazed, bleeding from an abrasion on her forehead, Kat struggled to the sandy rim of the pool. She stood, unsteady on her feet, staggering. A giant in overalls stood there, obese, ogre-like, and staring at her slack jawed with amazement as she emerged from the water.

"Help me," Kat said. "Please."

"Hold still," the giant said. He reached out with his huge hand and lifted her face, then landed his fist squarely on her chin, knocking her unconscious. Edgar Fenner, the gentle giant no longer.

***

Shire emerged from the palmetto holding a dead armadillo by its tail, the Ruger in his other hand. He surveyed the scene coolly and clicked his tongue. "What's going down, Edgar?"

"It's a gosh awful mess!" Edgar flailed his arms over the canoe capsized in the spring and the unconscious girl in the sand. He wanted to throttle Shire for dereliction of duty but movement across the spring caught his eye. The other intruder fled through the palmetto. "He's getting away! Get him, Shire! Don't let him escape!"

"I'm on it." Tossing the armadillo at Edgar's

feet, Shire darted off in pursuit.

Edgar kicked the dead armadillo into the brush. Elvis was not going to be happy about this, not happy at all. Edgar fretted as he waded into the spring. Elvis' wrath was going to be terrible to behold and his judgment severe. Edgar's shuffling feet conjured a cloud of sand. He dragged the canoe to the shore and then collected the items floating in the water for an impromptu probate. A small cooler, empty plastic bottles, paddles, fanny pack, her purse, inventoried and piled into a heap under the lean-to.

Then, with a groan, Edgar lifted the unconscious girl. His hand felt the cool, bare skin of her thigh. Edgar lingered, holding her in his arms, as if he were trying to guess her weight, and gawking at her purple-red hair and the soaked T-shirt clinging to her unbra'd breasts. His lower lip trembled, and a vein pulsed in his neck. He plopped her down like a sack of oranges in the cargo box of the John Deere Gator he had driven to the spring. She lay supine beside the picnic basket that held Shire's lunch. Barely breathing. Eyes closed like Sleeping Beauty, or a mythical she-spirit plucked from magical waters like in a fairy tale. A ribbon of bright blood trickled from her nose. With care, delicately, almost reverently, Edgar wiped away the blood with his balled-up bandana and dried her face. He stood over her. Looking at her. Long limbs, pale skin, tattoo of a wispy feather and three tiny fork tailed sparrows in flight on her arm. Pretty she was, for sure.

Desire gurgled in his brain. *If only ...*

The muffled firecracker sound of gunshots in the distance popped his reverie like a soap bubble.

***

"Hey, hippie," said Shire. "Give it up. I see you hiding there."

The intruder cowered in the palmetto where he tried, futilely, to hide, his face a mask of fear and panic. Scrapes and slashes bloodied his face and arms. Shire had followed the blood trail toward the river.

"Let's be cool," he said, standing, unsteady on his feet.

"Did you fall down and hurt yourself?" Shire said, as if talking to a child.

"Sprained my ankle. Uh, dude, what is that thing you're pointing at me?"

"What's it look like?"

"Like a BB pistol with a ginger ale jug stuffed

with rags attached to it."

"This here," Shire brandished the Ruger, "is a lethal weapon with an improvised suppressor device. What you think of *that*?"

"Honestly, I'm scared shitless. Please don't shoot me, bro."

"Big fraidy cat, aren't you?"

"I don't want to get shot."

This tickled Shire. He liked to see this hippie fucktard squirm. Shire resented big guys, hated 'em. He had been bullied and pushed around all his life, taking his licks, and dreaming of giving back, in spades. In Raiford, serving time for burglary, a big guy named Darby Shupe, reeking with stinky breath and bad teeth, had taken a liking to Shire. Called him Shrimp, cute little Shrimp. Shupe wanted Shrimp's ass, that kind of liking. Shire obliged Shupe for a time, biding his time, then shanked him with a sharp plastic toothbrush shiv. Punctured both lungs and a kidney and getting away with it too. Nobody liked Shupe anyway.

"One," said Shire, " I ain't your bro and, two, you're trespassing. Didn't you see the fuck'n sign? Private property. Keep out, goodbye, *ari ver deechee.*"

"You mean *arrivederci*?"

"It means what it means! Means stay the fuck out!"

"Look, my name is Josh." He forced a smile but the fear in his eyes remained palpable. "I'm a good friend of Edgar Fenner. He still lives here, right?"

"He does." Shire feigned interest. He knew that was a lie; Edgar didn't have any friends. But Shire wanted to string the hippie along. He lowered the pistol to put his prey at ease.

"So, so, so," Josh said. "Let's talk to Edgar, okay? He'll remember me. I was at Ococonee Spring before."

"When?"

"A year ago, before —- uh, what is that … *thing* … that attacked us?"

"It lives here," said Shire. "You disturbed it. How did you get here?"

"In a canoe."

"I meant *besides* in a canoe."

"In a Toyota truck," said Josh. "From Gainesville."

Gainesville, well, that figured. Though Shire judged this one kind of old to still be in college. Prob'ly one of those deadbeat parasite perpetual student types racking up loans he'd never pay back and would get cancelled by the fuck'n gubmint. "Where's that Toyota truck at now?"

"The, uh, the park. Under the train trestle."

"Uh-huh." Shire knew where that was, the county park by the CSX rail line. Picnic sites, shelters, a shithouse, and a boat launch. He held out his hand, palm up, and gestured. "Gimme the keys."

Josh stared dumbly. "Keys? To my truck? Why?"

"Because I said to, that's why."

"No," said Josh.

"Hell with you, then." Shire leveled the muzzle of the Ruger and emptied the magazine into Josh's face and abdomen. Plastic melted.

***

"Where's my lunch?" Shire said, strolling back to the spring.

He ambled to the Gator where Edgar waited. The Ruger pistol, minus its bulky plastic jug suppressor, was tucked under his belt. He dug into the picnic basket, unwrapped the baloney and cheese sandwich, its crusts carefully excised, chomped, and glued his eyes on the unconscious girl in the truck bed.

"Never mind her," said Edgar. "What happened?"

"Taken care of. Stupid hippie tried to jump me, but I was too quick for him. He is double-D dead. Had to detach the silencer. The plastic melted."

He dug into his pants pocket. He dangled a key fob and tossed it to Edgar. Then Shire tossed Josh Quinnell's eco-friendly hemp wallet to Edgar, who fumbled, dropping the wallet and keys. He hunkered down to scoop the items out of the sand. Shire had emptied the wallet of cash.

"Bitch and her boyfriend come here from G-ville in a Toyota pick 'em-up truck that's sitting over at the county park off Joe Flagg Road. Got that much out of him before he croaked."

"Don't talk with food in your mouth," said Edgar. "Where were you when you were supposed to be guarding Ococonee Spring?"

Shire jutted his chin and got in Edgar's face. "Where were *you*?"

"I got here, and you were *gone*!"

"I heard some commotion and went to investigate," said Shire. "I suspect now that was a diversion to throw me off."

Edgar pointed at the animal carcass. "Dead armadillo says otherwise! Darn you, Shire, fess up! You were off diddling."

"Was not," said Shire. "This is all your fault, Edgar."

"*My fault*?"

"You were late! If you had got your big butt here when you were supposed to, none of this would have happened. This is all on you, Edgar!"

Edgar stood mouth agape, like a fish out of water, stunned and trying to breathe. He couldn't speak.

"Now that *that's* settled," said Shire.

"That's not settled!"

Shire ignored him. "We got to get rid of the canoe and the truck. The dead hippie we can plant with the others."

Edgar shuddered. The old Fenner homestead, over past the few months, included an ad hoc boneyard behind the shed with the corrugated tin roof. The Fenner brothers had interred other trespassers there, along with the dead hounds that Elvis had condemned for always barking and growling at his emanation. Any thought of the boneyard and dead things in it evoked dread in Edgar's soul. But he accepted the grim necessity.

Shire jerked his thumb at the body in the Gator. "What about her?"

"Elvis decides," said Edgar.

"You already know what he's going to decide."

"Until he does, you don't touch her."

"C'mon, Edgar," said Shire. He winked and pinched the girl's thigh and went into the grinning, wheedling mode that Edgar knew well. "I want some of that. You want that, I know you do. I figure, we're got it coming to us. One of the perks of guard duty."

"What did I say? Do not touch her." Edgar raised his voice. He would remain resolute and rein in Shire. *The girl would not be molested.* "It's for Elvis to decide what to do with her and I doubt he's going to be in a generous mood. Now take your lunch basket and go on up to the house. Go! I will wait here on Elvis."

Shire sulked like a puppy swatted with rolled up

newspaper. He wore his resentment but complied, knowing he could push Edgar only so far and eager to be gone before Elvis surfaced. He grabbed the picnic basket and turned toward the house, pausing, in small defiance, to slap the girl's thigh before hastening away from the spring along the path to the house.

Ominous silence and stillness descended upon Ococonee Spring like oppressive humidity. Edgar knew that deep down in the eldritch caverns of porous Florida limestone, Elvis seethed, his fury building.

Edgar waited. Half an hour? An hour? Elvis existed outside of time as measured on the earth. He'd appear when he was good and ready. The girl in the Gator remained unconscious, her breathing shallow. Edgar watched her.

Then a ripple ran through the pond. Then a shadow, a stirring. Elvis moved upon the water, rising from the slimy green rocks. As Edgar watched in trepidation, a blue-green haze swept over Ococonee Spring. It coiled like a serpent, turning purple and turbulent, churning waves. Elvis manifested, clad in a flowing, razor-creased black jumpsuit of pure wrath. He glowered at Edgar through chili pepper red aviator glasses.

What did I tell you, Edgar?

Edgar hung his head, hangdog. "Tried my best. I take responsibility. I'm sorry."

Sorry don't get it done, Edgar. Now, let's review the ABC's. What did I tell you about trespassers? Well? Answer me, Edgar.

"None is allowed."

That's right. None allowed. Or what?

"I can't say." Throat muscles tight.

You can't say? This isn't rocket science. You were supposed to keep 'em out. You failed. People penetrated my sanctuary. One remains alive. What are you going to do about it, Edgar?

"I don't know," said Edgar.

Don't play dumb! You know what must be done. Don't be a sissy. I hate sissies and fags and Robert Goulet. Do it, Edgar. You pick up that girl and hold her head under water until she stops breathing. Simple. Now do it. I'll watch.

Edgar Fenner raised his head, took a deep breath, and stared into the dark maw of Elvis' anger. He could hear his Gamaw's voice. *Got to have backbone, hon. Stand up for yourself. Nobody else will if you don't. Get courage at the getting place and stick that courage to the sticking place in your heart.*

"No," said Edgar.

What? Did I hear you right? Let's try that again.

"I said no." Startled to hear himself say the words. Shaking.

Elvis struck out, aiming a karate kick at Edgar's chest. Edgar doubled over in agony. Elvis gripped him, but after a few seconds, he relented, leaving Edgar prostrate in the sand and straining to breathe.

I hate it when you make me do that, Edgar. Never say no to me. You're in enough trouble already. Now pull yourself together and take care of business.

"I can't do it! I will not do it!" Edgar crawled on his knees, his chubby fingers grasping sand. "This once I *will not* do what you say. Do to me what you will but I won't budge."

Edgar shut his eyes tight as a dark, vengeful cloud enveloped him. Suffocating him. A huge weight pressed upon Edgar's heart.

Is that your final jeopardy answer, Edgar?

"You promised me a girlfriend."

You fail at guarding my sanctuary, then defy me, and expect a reward?

"If I'm gone, who're you going to talk to? You don't got another Receiver. Going to be lonesome tonight. You made me a promise. All I'm asking is you keep it. This could be fate, this girl coming here."

There, that was said, the words leaped out of his mouth in a burst of audacity Edgar never knew he could summon. Then Edgar cowered, his eyes closed, waiting for another burst of Elvis' divine wrath to unload upon him. But after a long and dreadful silence, Edgar heard Elvis laugh. Chuckle. Snort with jollity. A weight lifted from Edgar's shoulders. He opened his eyes and raised his head. The dark shroud over Ococonee Spring receded and turned reassuring blue green, sparkling like Christmas lights. Elvis' black jumpsuit had transformed to blazing white.

Maybe I let my temper bring out the beast in me. I am hard but I am fair.

Edgar's heart fluttered like a bird. "So, I can keep her?"

I will make good on my promise.

"You will?"

Elvis' radiant smile roasted Edgar with joy. *Just said so, didn't I?*

* * *

"What is she?" said Shire. "Dinner?"

Edgar had brought the girl to the house in the back of the John Deere Gator, carried her inside still unconscious, and flopped her on the kitchen table. Huffing from the exertion, he plopped down in a chair. He panted, his face red.

"Get those thoughts … out of your … head, Shire."

"What Elvis say?"

"To keep her." His stomach rumbled.

"I figured when I saw you bringing her to the house." Shire leered at the girl sprawled on the kitchen table. "Okay, then. Share and share alike."

"No," replied Edgar. "No such … does not work that way … keep your hands to yourself, Shire. Elvis made a promise to *me*. Not you. You best be real darn clear on that, Shire. Hands off!"

"Hardly seems fair."

"I don't care!" Edgar's stomach rumbled

again, and he stood, emitting a loud *ffffrrrrrfffffft* from his backside. As he scurried down the hall toward the downstairs bathroom, he told Shire to keep an eye on the girl and *not to touch her*.

"Won't lay a finger on her," said Shire. "Promise."

Uh-huh, thought Shire as soon as he heard the bathroom door close behind his brother. Edgar's trips to the throne usually took a while; Shire counted on that. The girl could wake up any second … there was something Shire had always wanted to try. Now as good a time as any. Perfect opportunity. From under the kitchen sink he fetched a bottle of chlorofornum dilution he'd bought at a homeopathic store in Gainesville, sold as a health tonic. A small bottle, not much to spare; he had to dole out the dosage with care. He'd previously only used it to put down feral cats but those were only experiments. He took a clean kitchen rag from the drawer and added a few drops. The stuff had a sweet, pungent smell. He added several streaming whiffs of aerosol spray cooking oil; he knew from experience inhalation induced a rapid high that numbed the brain after only a few seconds. Then Shire stood over the girl and pinched her cheek to wake her. She stirred. Foggy. Eyes barely open. Looking at him. Shire put his weight on her body and clamped the rag over her mouth and nose.

Umf ummmf ummf. Uummmf ummf unnnnnnn.

"Take it, girl," said Shire. "Suck it up."

She grabbed his wrists. Weakly. With his free hand Shire peeled her hands away. Her body twitched. Energy slow drained from her body like the stuffing from a rag doll. Her chest heaved, her arms flailed, she moaned, and then she was out. Shire tittered as he removed the rag. That was fun. Way better than the cats.

"Is everything okay out there, Shire?" Edgar called from behind the bathroom door. "I heard some commotion."

"Everything's okay." Shire tossed the rag in the sink and slid his hands under her T-shirt and squeezed a breast. "I didn't touch your girlfriend."

"You had better not," said Edgar. "You are still in the doghouse over abandoning your post to go off diddling."

Shire picked up the unconscious girl and heaved her over his shoulder, in a fireman's carry. Heavier than she looked, and Shire struggled to balance her weight on his small frame. He picked up her Florida DL and University of Florida student ID that Edgar left on the table. Not a bad photo on the DL.

"Kathleen Kay Condon," he said aloud but not loud enough for Edgar to hear. He whispered to the girl. "We are going to play hide-and-seek with Edgar. It'll be fun."

As silent and stealthy as he could manage, Shire slinked down the hall and up the creaking stairs. To the attic.

***

Kat Condon regained consciousness in stifling darkness and in a stuffy room that smelled of camphor, pee, and mildew. She lay supine on a scratchy bamboo mat, wearing only string panties. Her head throbbed. A sickly-sweet ether-like smell lingered in her nostrils and mouth. Her skin prickled, and she felt nauseous.

"Hello, dear," a kindly female voice said in the darkness.

Kat sat up. "Who's that?"

She heard someone breathing. Then a crackling sound, a tiny giggle. And creaky sounds, a rocking chair.

"Turn on the lights, hon." An old woman's whisper. "To your left. No, that's my left. Your right."

Kat ran her fingers on the floor and found a plastic power strip, cords sprouting out of it. She clicked the switch and lava lamps illuminated the cramped room in orange, yellow, and green. Kat discerned a wizened old woman perched in a rocking chair, wearing a ragged fleece robe and furry slippers. Long, white hair fell to her shoulders. Her kindly smile was reassuring.

"You poor thing," she said. "Those boys are mean. They took your clothes and locked you in here. Shames me to say I am their auntie." She clucked her tongue in disapproval. "Their poor old auntie Kate who lives in the attic. Tell me your name, hon."

"Kat."

The old woman cupped a hand to her ear. "Kathy?"

Kat raised her voice. "I go by *Kat*."

"Kat? Oh, my! We're namesakes! How delightful!" The glop in the lava lamps rose, fell, and dull green light reflected in Auntie Kate's eyes.

Kat reached under the heavy window curtains; the windows were fastened with sash locks that wouldn't budge, requiring a key to open. Even if she smashed the glass, the roof was too high to jump.

"I want to get out of here!"

"Well, so do I, hon," said auntie Kate. "And people in hell want ice water. I had me a room all to myself in the Memory Care in Gainesville and the boys brought me here to visit the spring and they locked me in here and won't let me leave."

"What boys? Who are they?"

"The Fenner boys, my nephews. The big one is Edgar, and the little one is Shire." Old Kate leaned forward in the rocker and whispered, as if to impart a secret. "You know why those nephews of mine are so cruel? Because they worship the Devil. Did you see him a-swimming there in Ococonee Spring?"

"All I saw," said Kat, "was a monster fish and a fat fuck who hit me."

"So, you didn't see *him*?"

"*Him* who? What're you talking about?"

"Do not marvel," said Kate. "Satan is transformed into an Angel of Light. That's in the Bible, hon. Apostle Paul's Epistle to the Aleutians. If you're familiar with Scripture. I guess you're not. Because you're a sinner. You fornicate, don't you, dear?"

Kat ignored the jabbering old woman, crawled toward the door on her knees, and rattled the doorknob. Futile, she knew. The door was locked.

"The Devil in Ococonee Spring has got those boys hornswoggled. But I got wise to his tricks, and that's why they keep me locked up. Want some rock and rye?" Auntie Kate held up a glass jar filled with an amber liquid with a chunk of rock candy settled at its bottom. She rattled it, twisted off the lid, gulped, and *ahhh'd* with satisfaction. "Come here, sweetie, and I'll give you some."

"I don't want any!" Dejected, dazed, fearful, her head still hurting, maybe a concussion. Purple bruises on her thigh. Kat retreated to a corner of the room and sat with her knees up. She stifled sobs.

"Want to know where the Devil in Ococonee Spring comes from? One day Jesus and the Apostles were in the Land of the Gadarenes and met a man possessed by an unclean spirit."

"Please, stop talking," said Kat.

"This man lived *among the tombs.* Amid the stink and rotting flesh of the dead. Jesus said, what is thy name? The demon answered, my name is Legion, and we are many, and Jesus said, come out of this man, unclean spirit. And out they came, the whole kit and kaboodle. But nothing comes out but goes somewhere else. *Are you listening?*"

"Please *shut up*," said Kat.

But auntie Kate continued, perched on the edge of her rocking chair, a maniacal grin stretching her face. "The unclean spirit went into a herd of swine and those piggies cried wee, wee, wee, all the way down a steep slope into the sea. And Jesus notched another miracle on his belt and the Apostles marveled, which they did a lot of, and said maybe we should take notes, so we get it right when we put together the gospels, but I'm getting off the subject. Piggies drowned but getting rid of evil isn't that easy. Cast it out here, it pops up there."

"Will you shut the fuck up!?"

"*Legion* … moved in the water. Most of the planet is water. That demon swims until it discovers a hidey-hole and waits for dumb unsuspecting souls. It assumes a pleasing shape and doesn't call itself Legion. Takes a new name. *Now* do you get it?"

"I don't get any of this!"

"You will get it, and get it good and hard, you little whore."

Old Kate lurched out of her rocker. Kat shrieked. The old crone yanked Kat's hair and pinned Kat's arms to the floor with her knees. Auntie's breath belched sulfuric, fetid, hot. Her face was red and incandescent, distorted. Eyes bulging. Limbs strong, hands like claws. She wrapped her fingers around Kat's neck and choked her.

"The boys will fuck the daylights out of you! And the demon in the spring will do to you what it did to me! You filthy little cunt, you are going to suffer and die!"

Door hinges squealed. Edgar Fenner rushed into the room. He grabbed the old woman and threw her back into the rocker. In an instant, Auntie Kate resumed her kind appearance. She patted her hair and smoothed the wrinkles in her flannel robe. She looked at Edgar with dismay.

"Spoilsport."

"Don't do bad things, auntie," Edgar said. "We talked about this."

"Bring me some kerosene and cotton balls and matches."

"No," said Edgar. "You don't play with

fire."

"Phooey on you, Edgar," replied Katie. She blew raspberries at him.

"Don't do that, auntie, that's rude and uncouth."

Kat, barely conscious, gasped for breath. Edgar picked her up and heaved her over his shoulder like a sack of oranges. Shire had locked the girl in the attic and made Edgar search for her and thought that was hilarious.

"At least you can bring me more whiskey," said old Kate.

"I will when I get around to it, but I'll be a busy bee for a while. This girl got to Come to Elvis."

"He's not Elvis," Kate said.

Edgar, in no mood for further mischief, shushed her. He balanced precariously at the top of the stairs and slammed the attic door shut. The lock clunked. He trundled down the stairs, carrying unconscious Kat. Her conversion was about to commence. Elvis had given him specific instructions.

***

"Ain't fair."

In the darkness, Shire dug another hole by the

shed with the corrugated tin roof. The dead body of the fat hippie, already stiff with rigor mortis, lay on a strip of black poly sheeting. The body smelled of dried blood and voided bladder and bowel. Shire, wads of cotton stuffed in his nostrils against the stench, worked under the dim yellow glow of the low wattage bulb in the shed. Moths fluttered. Shire heard the owls screech in the blackness of the slash pines.

"Ain't fuck'n fair, is it?" Shire said to the body of Josh Quinnell. Shire had stabbed both eyes of the corpse with a screwdriver because the dead stare irked him. "Edgar's in the Jungle Room canoodling with your naked girlfriend, and here I am digging another fuck'n hole. And here *you* are, sucker, going into the hole. Serves you right, by the way. What you get for trespassing at Ococonee Spring. Curiosity, cats, you never heard about that?"

Shire tossed the shovel, hunkered down, and rolled the body into the hole. Then he discarded the cotton and tied a bandanna around his mouth and nose and squeezed his hands into rubber gloves. From a shelf in the shed, he carried plastic jugs of Crystal Lye Drain Opener, 100% Lye, from Walmart. After disposal of the last trespasser at Ococonee Spring, Shire deemed it a smart move to keep a supply on hand, on the basis that failure to prepare is preparing to fail. He opened the jugs and began pouring them into the pit. His eyes stung.

"Fuck! One of these days, Shire Fenner will be on top and somebody else will do the digging."

***

"What the hell you and Edgar got going on at Ococonee Spring?" Palatka Red inquired as he and Shire Fenner ate breakfast at a Waffle House on Interstate 10, where they met up early the next morning. Shire grinned as he chewed a mouthful of waffle and bacon. Syrup dribbled from the corner of his mouth.

"Like they say. If I told you I'd have to kill you."

Red shrugged. Reliable Red, an old pal of Shire's. The kind of bro you wanted for an accomplice. Shire phoned, called in a favor, and Red showed up. He owed Shire. Several times over.

They finished breakfast, left money on the table, pushed out the front door and swaggered across the parking lot to their respective vehicles, Red's old Dodge with the tail pipe sagging and Shire driving the Toyota Tacoma pickup truck. They lingered by the Dodge. Red produced a bottle of Jack Daniels from the glove compartment. They alternated taking swigs from the bottle and smoking cigarettes.

"We leave here," said Red, "follow me close but not too close."

"I know how to fuck'n drive. This guy in Tally won't give us any shit?"

"Hundred bucks, and no questions," Red replied. "One more junk in the stack and he's got an acre of 'em. You got cash?"

"Yeah, I got cash," said Shire.

"Don't get hot under the collar, Shire. Moody son of a bitch, aren't ya."

"You'd be too if you had to put with the shit I got to put up with."

Before dawn Shire had hiked to the county park on Joe Flagg Road to retrieve the Toyota pickup truck. He hauled the canoe and sunk it in a creek. While Edgar played cozy in the Jungle Room with the girl that Shire wasn't allowed to touch. And tonight, on orders from Elvis relayed by Edgar, Shire had to comb a pasture hunting up giggle mushrooms growing in cow shit. Yeah, for sure, Shire thought, all that would make a man moody and sure as fuck all wasn't fair.

"I don't ask," said Red.

"Let's go." Shire flicked away the cigarette. "Get this over and done with."

***

"This is torture!" said Kat.

"No, it's not," Edgar said. "It's *Clambake.*"

Edgar achieved savant status; he possessed encyclopedic knowledge of every Elvis movie ever made. *Clambake* (1967), Elvis as the heir to an oil fortune who trades places with a water-ski instructor at a Miami hotel to see if girls will like him for his own lovable self and not for his crass daddy's (James Gregory) money. Elvis' leading lady in the movie was the beautiful Shelley Fabares, Elvis' favorite actress to work. She was with Elvis in *Spinout* and *Girl Happy* too. But she and Elvis never got married. Wasn't fate.

"You're torturing me!"

"No," replied Edgar, sitting in in the La-Z-Boy. "I am not. I am not that kind. I'm not cruel and I don't like hurting people."

"Liar!" Kat spat at him.

Edgar wiped the saliva from his cheek and nose. Strands of magenta hair fluttered over Kat's face. She struggled against the thick layers of green duct tape that bound her to the chair in front of the 55-inch HD TV. Edgar sat next to her in the Jungle Room with its soft green shag carpet, cypress stump table, and Henri Rousseau jungle prints that Edgar bought at a thrift store in Lake City. Kat was naked, like the wild girl with the outstretched arm on the couch in the Rousseau jungle picture. Edgar saw her second tattoo now, the pretty flower bordering her lady parts.

Kat squirmed. "Untie me! Let me go!"

"Sorry," Edgar said. "Can't do that. Watch the movie."

"Where's Josh?"

"Uh, he went away." Thinking about the shuddersome boneyard and dead things gave Edgar the heebie-jeebies.

"No, he didn't! You're lying! What did you do to him?"

"Nothing. Told you. He went away."

"You're a pig!" Spittle sprayed. "A sorry fucking redneck pig! You suck! Fuck your fat whiteboy ass! Fuck you!"

Edgar shook his head, appalled. "Do you

eat with that foul mouth, girl? Don't make me gag you again," thinking might have to again anyway.

Edgar did everything Elvis told him to do. The instructions were clear. She remained tied to the chair for days now, with no sleep or food or bathroom breaks. Edgar doled out water from a sippy cup to keep her hydrated. He poured caffeine drinks into her mouth, with crushed white pills from Shire's stash of drugs.

There was more. She had to be fed magic mushrooms plucked from the cow pies under bright moonlight. Velvet Elvises, the King called them, soft, conical-capped mushrooms, dark orange brown and velvety. Shire fetched, crawling through the cow pastures neighboring the Fenner property, and Edgar sliced and diced and crushed them with a dribble of tap water into a sticky brown paste that he fed the unwilling girl with a turkey baster, pinching her nose to force her mouth open for air. She had choked.

"Don't spit 'em out," Edgar had said.

"Go suck a bag of dicks."

Regardless of the abuse, Edgar stayed by her side to see her through her conversion and would stay for as long as it took. She had to be cocooned, Elvis said, like the caterpillar that breaks free as a butterfly. She had to be Brought to Elvis. Then and only then could Elvis give her to Edgar and the rest would be Happily Ever After. That was the bargain between Edgar Fenner and Elvis, all sales final. Elvis' plan required she bear witness to every Elvis movie ever made from *Love Me Tender,* 1956, through *Change of Habit,* 1969. Plus, the concert tapes, the outtakes, a couple of documentaries, and the '68 Comeback Special.

Edgar had inherited the complete Elvis library on DVD from his Gamaw, Becky Fenner. Edgar had grown up on those movies, watching them again and again with Gamaw who'd seen the real live Elvis in concert, back in his early days touring Florida, before he achieved superstardom and became a legend, before Elvis went to Hollywood and made those movies that Edgar loved. The girl would love them too, soon enough. For now, she resisted.

"Please, please, please," Kat said. Tears rolled down her cheeks. "Please, stop this, and let me go."

"Sorry, no. Watch the movies."

"If you let me go, I won't tell anybody what happened. I promise I won't!"

"The movies are, uh, like a *tapestry.*"

Her face contorted with rage. "I hate you!"

"You feel that way now but that'll change." Edgar wrapped his arms around her. She struggled but he tightened his grip. "Everything is going to work out for the best even if it don't seem that way now."

"Let me go!" Kat tried to bite him and then howled. Screamed like a banshee, ear piercing, and shook. The din made Edgar shudder.

"Stop that now! Stop it!"

She showered Edgar with fricatives and saliva, straining against her bonds, shaking, her limbs and breasts taut. Until Edgar's patience was exhausted. He grabbed a hank of her hair, jerking her head back and stuffing a ball of gauze in her mouth. He had strips of hurricane tape ready and plastered them over her mouth. With a sigh, he plopped again in the La-Z-Boy. His heart pounded from the exertion, beating against his ribcage like a bowling ball.

Ejecting *Clambake*, he inserted another DVD. *Follow that Dream.* The one filmed in Florida, at Crystal River and Ocala, not far away from Ococonee Spring. Gamaw had been there too, with auntie Katie. They were extras in the movie, but you couldn't see them in the crowd scenes. Gamaw had told Edgar how Elvis had arrived in Ocala with his Memphis mafia people in a fleet of white Cadillacs and his hair was so black the sunshine glowed off it like a halo. That was when a skinny, wormy kid from Gainesville named Tommy Petty, whose uncle Earl was working on the set and let the boy tagalong, had his own Come to Elvis moment, a life-changing moment. Tommy Petty vowed to become a rock n' roll star and traded his Wham-O slingshot for a dozen Elvis 45 records and the rest was history.

Mmmmmfffffffmmm said Kat. *Fffffkkkkrrrr!*

"I know it's an ordeal, and I am terribly sorry for it. But has to be this way. You will understand later, after you accept Elvis, and you'll be happy as a housecat, and we will love each other forever."

Kat's eyes widened like saucers. *Love ... forever?* She glared at him with cold fury that froze Edgar's heart. *Nvvvrrrrrrrrrrrrrrrr!*

Elvis had promised abiding love, an unchained melody of love but she wasn't there yet. Her palpable hatred made Edgar shiver. How could such hatred ever melt? Seemed an impossibility. But he'd trust Elvis. Had to trust Elvis. And wait. Because revelation was just around the corner.

***

Days went by. Days and long nights sequestered and isolated in the Jungle Room with the continual barrage of Elvis movies.

The lady loves me, but she doesn't know it, Elvis serenaded Ann-Margret poolside in *Viva Las Vegas*. The lyrics gave Edgar encouragement. He watched the movie for a while, sitting next to Kat while she stared blankly, oblivious to everything but the TV screen, and then he tiptoed out of the Jungle Room to empty the pee bucket while Elvis danced in the University of Nevada gym with gorgeous Ann-Marget, a real goddess. Edgar closed the door behind him and toddled to the kitchen. Daylight outside caught him unawares. Scrub jays queedled. Shadows looked like midday.

Shire slouched at the kitchen table, sullen. He smoked the remainder of the American Spirit cigarettes, in a waterproof container, that he'd filched from the items salvaged from the canoe.

"How long does this shit go on?"

"Language," said Edgar, his reproval automatic, listless. He emptied the bucket and rinsed the sponges in the sink, then plopped in a chair. Feeling weary, deep bags under his eyes. He poured himself a mug of coffee. He hadn't eaten, washed, or slept.

"Well, how long, Edgar?"

"Until Elvis says it's time," Edgar replied. "Don't ask me when that will be because I do not know. Didn't I tell you get rid of all their stuff?"

"I got rid of it. Canoe's in the swamp and the Toyota's in a junkyard outside Tally. No point in wasting a good pack of cigarettes. Smokes are expensive these days, Edgar."

"You ought to stop smoking, Shire. It is unhealthy."

"Yeah, Edgar, I know, it's *uncouth.*"

Shire took a long drag on the cigarette. He exhaled a tendril of smoke at Edgar and continued to eat his buttermilk biscuit with lumpy gravy the color and texture of tile grout. His fork clacked the plate hard enough to chip the edge. Shire sloshed Jack Daniels into his coffee. He offered the bottle to Edgar.

"You know I never touch that, Shire."

"When Elvis says enough, then what happens?"

"Same as what happened to Auntie Kate," said Edgar.

Shire's spit-take sprayed coffee. "That didn't work out so well! Just what we need. Another crazy female we got to keep locked up."

"This time will be different," said Edgar. "Even Elvis learns from mistakes."

***

Her new name is Ginger.

"Huh?" Edgar, dozing in the La-Z-Boy, woke with a start. Bright blue-green shimmer flooded the Jungle Room. Radiant, dazzling, benign, bathing the room in divine light. Rainbows arced over the dusty damask drapes on the window. The girl remained bound to the chair, listless, limp, as if melting. On the screen, outtakes from Elvis '68 Comeback Special held her attention. Elvis in black leather, the guitar man, cool and a killer, at top of his game again, jamming with Scotty and DJ, because Bill Black had died by 1968. Like the old days in Florida.

Wake up, Edgar. It's time. We're at the end of a beautiful beginning. Listen to me.

"Yessir!" Edgar snapped to attention. "I'm listening!"

Elvis manifested himself in a glittering white jumpsuit, with golden studs, red spangles and a flowing red silk scarf that billowed over his shoulders. He towered over Edgar, a nimbus of gold cloud adorning his head, and obsidian rings on his spidery fingers. The Divine Vegas Elvis. Smiling. He extended his hand toward Edgar.

I've decided her new name shall be Ginger.

"Why?"

Elvis looked askance. *Why? Because I said so. Get used to calling her that.*

"Okay, I sorta like the name. Good pick."

Kathleen Condon is no more. Like she never was. Now she is filled with My Spirit, and when you are filled with My Spirit, you are born anew. At sunrise, bring her to me and we will finish this. In a beautiful ceremony.

"Where at? The spring?"

Where else? Elvis faded in a brilliant shower of green and gold particulates, like dust motes that floated to the carpet and flickered and dissolved like dew. His parting words echoed, *Get a move on, Edgar. Get your love.*

* * *

Edgar fumbled through the cedar wardrobe in Gamaw's old bedroom. Ginger needed to be properly attired, clad in finery. Naked was not appropriate for a Come to Elvis ceremony in the spring. Edgar switched on the brass lamp in the room, examined clothing, and selected a lacy white sleeping gown with a flowing wedding cake frosting hem. An elegant garment. Beautiful. Edgar almost wept.

In the Jungle Room, Edgar untied the girl, sponge-bathed her, and dressed her. She barely breathed, with only a flicker of consciousness, and was weak as a kitten. Almost weightless now as Edgar lifted her. He carried her in his arms and plopped on an Adirondack chair on the porch in the Florida humidity, suffocating and unrelenting, waiting for the first light to dispel the darkness.

"It's going to be alright, Ginger. Trust in Elvis because he is the Way to Graceland. Sorry about what you had to go through. But it's all for the best."

"Uh-huh," Ginger replied. Her eyes open now but unfocused, like an infant's, blue blots floating in pallid sclera.

The eastern sky became white and hazy. Then fierce sunlight broke through the skinny pines. Edgar picked up the girl and ambled down the path away toward the shining spring and its promise of redemption. He waded into the spring until the chilly water was up to his waist. The girl remained limp, but her hair and the hem of her gown dipped into the water.

Water rippled. Elvis, his great spirit locked in its piscine confinement, ascended to the surface from the depths of the spring. His armored scutes heaving, his scimitar like tail swishing, his stubby whiskers twitching. Elvis came close, within a few feet of Edgar. Whiskers twitched. Someday, the endtime when Elvis and his entourage ascended to Graceland, this ugly fish form would burst, releasing the Divine Elvis Spirit within in radiant light like the Second Coming.

White creamy blobs erupted from the distended gray underbelly and drifted through the water, forming a cloud. An electric blue-green curtain fizzled upon the water. Elvis was there, in the water, in the air, in Edgar's soul, in the bulky, armored sturgeon and in its lumpy milt.

Straining his back, Edgar gently dipped the girl into the water and let the milky cloud and cold spring water envelope her head and shoulders. Bubbles rose to the surface as she exhaled. She struggled a bit, gasping, and trying to raise her face out of the water. But Edgar held her under the water until she ceased squirming and kicking and lay still in his arms. Then he lifted her.

"There you go," Edgar said.

Her face and hair glistened with beads of milt. Goops of it dripped from the corners of her mouth too and her nose clouded her eyes. Edgar wiped her face. For several scary moments she remained still and grey as a dead thing, and Edgar shuddered with fear he'd lost her. But then, awakening with a start, she took a deep breath of air. Choked, coughed, retched, spit. Edgar held her tight and let her breathe the fresh, piney-scented air.

Her eyes popped open. Wide open. Not fearful now. Looking, seeing everything as if for the first time. She looked at Edgar, studying his big smiling face. She blinked and smiled back at him. A vacant smile, her mind a clean slate ready to be written upon with a whole new lesson.

"Wasn't so bad, was it?" He carried her out of the water and sat her down in a folding chair. "What's your name, sweetheart?"

"Whaaaa?"

"Are you with me here, hon? Tell me your name. *Your name.*"

She had to think. Confused, her mind searching.

Finally, she said, with confidence, "Ginger."

Edgar rejoiced. "Uh-huh, uh-huh, you're Ginger. Love me, Ginger, love me tender like I love you." He moaned. Ginger touched his face, with her cold, moist hand. She gazed into his eyes. They kissed. Tongues swirled. Faces dripped with gooey white sturgeon milt. Edgar's heart, surging with inexpressible joy, almost leaped out of his chest. On this fine Florida morning, Elvis had kept his promise.

***

His Mama had died when Edgar was young, real young, and he hardly could remember her. But she had spoken to him once in a dream, many years after she died, and he remembered the dream. His Mama angelic all in white and kind of floating and she looked sad, so sad, tears streaking the mascara around her beautiful luminous eyes. She told Edgar she loved him and that, someday, Edgar would have an *epiphany*. She told him other things too, but all Edgar remembered was that one strange word, *epiphany*. It meant that something, a great truth, would somehow and someday be revealed to Edgar, open his eyes, and change his whole life. Boom, like that. Edgar thought when

Elvis first spoke to him, that was the epiphany, and that surely was one. An epiphany was hard to come by, but now Edgar had another. Love was an epiphany like no other. *I'm in love – uuuh! —- I'm all shook up …*

In the days that followed, a whole new world bloomed for Edgar Fenner, a world he never knew existed. He doted on Ginger, calling her his buttercup or his honeybun; Ginger clung to him, calling him her hunk and her Honeybear. They cuddled and canoodled. They locked lips and tongues squirmed. They giggled. They tumbled into Edgar's bed with the creaky springs and snuggled. Edgar exulted over every inch of her bare body, her curves and flat belly, long legs, flower tats, teeny armpit moles, soft pink buds on her titties, and the warm moist pink folds of skin between her legs. She fondled his stubby man parts, taking him into her mouth. Edgar, surprised and awed, yelped with pleasure he never dreamed of. She straddled him, or Edgar hunkered down behind her. Bedsprings screeched. The bed bounced and scraped along the floor. Some nights they didn't drift off to sleep until dawn.

Ginger smiled all the time. *All the time.* But Edgar liked that. Funny thing, though, the pupils of her eyes stayed dilated, and she couldn't seem to focus and bumped into things, or tripped, or got lost between the bedroom and the bathroom down the hall. Disoriented, she said, because the hall, like, telescoped.

They sat together on the love seat in the Jungle Room while *Wild in the Country* played on the DVD and Edgar showed her the Fenner family photo album.

"See here," said Edgar, pointing to an old sepia snapshot of two skinny young women in floral print dresses. "That's my Gamaw and auntie Kate when they went to see Elvis in concert in Jacksonville."

Ginger marveled. "They were so young!"

"Well, it was 1955 and they were young and wild back then." He pointed to other snapshots taped on the thick pages of the book. "That's my daddy Walt C. when he was young with his brother Jesse G. Uncle Jess died."

"How did he die?"

"I guess you'd call it a workplace accident. He was in what they called a one-pot meth lab, and it blew up."

"What was he doing in a meth lab?" said Ginger.

"Um, well, I guess, he was making that stuff."

This astonished Ginger. "Your uncle Jesse was a drug dealer?"

"Don't get the wrong idea. He was uh, he had this, uh, *knack* for chemistry. And needed money. So, he uh, cooked that stuff but he didn't *sell* it. To the public, no. No, he never did that. He sold it to other people, and *they* sold it. They were the culprits."

"But he cooked it for them," Ginger pointed out.

"He needed money." Edgar flipped the pages quickly to show other photos, which did not carry any opprobrium. Happy photos of himself as a chubby child; of his brother Shire, sticking his tongue out; his cousin Harlan, as chubby as Edgar; Uncle Warren, elected Boykin County sheriff twice; and Edgar's stepmom Dottie, Shire's mom, from Biloxi. In a skimpy polka dot bikini, laughing, and holding a bottle of bourbon.

"She was a wild one, too," said Edgar. "Lost her and Walt C. in a car accident."

"I'm sorry," said Ginger.

"Drinking and driving is a real bad mix."

"Do you have any pictures of your mother?"

"Only one that I keep special," Edgar replied. "She was never too keen on having her picture taken."

"I'd really like to see her picture," said Ginger.

Edgar flipped to the back of the album and opened a frilly white envelope taped to the back cover. From it he withdrew a Polaroid photo, scratched, and faded and labeled Veronica 'Ronnie' Fenner at Neptune Beach, with no date. A thin, darkhaired young woman in a demure one-piece bathing suit stared uneasily at the camera. Behind her a quilt of stratus clouds filled the sunny sky, but odd, hazy, cloud-like swirls floated in the sky and on the bright beach.

"Your mom was a beautiful lady," said Ginger.

"Yes, he was," said Edgar. Old penumbral memories floated to the surface like risen spirits he didn't beckon, couldn't decipher, and wished would go away back to the netherworld whence they came. Edgar sniffled and wiped his eyes with a hankie.

"Don't be sad," said Ginger. She pointed at the wispy swirls. "What're these?"

"That's why she didn't like to have her picture taken because strange stuff turned up and sort of ruined the photo. Spirits, I reckon."

"Spirits? Really?"

"Lot of them floating around," said Edgar. "People that passed but got stuck in-between. Elvis says they're a nuisance. Like homeless people. Messy and messed up. They don't know where they are or how to move on."

With trembling hands Edgar replaced the photo of his mother and slammed the album shut and replaced it on the dusty shelf in the Jungle Room next to the old never-opened liquor bottles in the shape of Elvis. "Anyways, most everybody's passed. Fenners don't seem to be long-lived people, most of us. It's down to just me and Shire and auntie Kate upstairs, and some cousins scattered about, but we don't see much of them anymore since they got cut out of Gamaw's will and got sore about it. But there's you, honeybun. You're here with me and that makes everything better."

One afternoon they decided to hold hands, stroll through the pines, and have a picnic at Ococonee Spring. They listened to the birds chirping. The *queedle queedle* of the scrub jays, the rough *caw caw* of the grackles. Ginger had no fear of the spring now. She retained only a hazy notion of what had happened there and didn't ask about her boyfriend Josh anymore. They plopped in chaise lounge chairs and soaked their feet in the cool water. They feasted on canned sardines, saltines, honeybell oranges, and a bottle of Boone's Farm Wild Cherry. Edgar wore baggy swim trunks and Ginger shed her dress and, underneath, wore nothing but panties. The surface of the water rippled.

"Elvis," she said, getting her hopes up.

"No, just the wind," said Edgar.

"He hasn't visited." She frowned, lower lip stuck out, like a petulant child. Come to Elvis, and then Elvis disappears, was a cheat.

"No, not lately," said Edgar. Not since her baptism. "But don't fret. He's there. Mysterious in his ways. Keeps to himself for long patches of time. I reckon he's deep in contemplation."

"About what?"

"Heck, hon, I wouldn't know. That's the mystery. But he's there. Until he goes to Graceland, and when he goes, we go with him. That's a promise. Hey, looky here."

Smiling, Edgar stood and waddled into the brush and plucked a fuzzy green prickly caterpillar from a bare branch. It twirled about his finger, and he held it out for Ginger to see. She crinkled her nose.

"Ew."

"Nothing to be scared of," said Edgar. "Harmless little creature."

He dangled it over Ginger's belly button, teasing her. She trembled, her stomach muscles quivered. Then she giggled. The caterpillar sought a hiding place, Edgar reckoned, where it could cocoon. With deliberate care he placed the fuzzy caterpillar in Ginger's navel. It squirmed this way and that, tickling her, but didn't sting. Then, as Edgar watched with wonder, the creature made itself at home.

"It likes it there," said Edgar. "Leave it be. Don't evict the little creature."

"What's it doing?"

"Making silk for a cocoon. A wonderful thing, how they change like that. Promise me you'll leave him there."

"If you want me to."

"Just you wait," said Edgar. "A butterfly is going to come out your belly button. Will that be a wonder, or what?"

***

Edgar, Edgar. Wake up. Wake up.

The roll down blinds in the bedroom window rippled. A blue-green shimmer suffocated the pale grey dawn light that leaked through the shaded windows. Edgar lay in his bed, Ginger curled up next to him. The sheet floated from the bed and rippled. Sharp twinges, like electricity, ran up and down Edgar's bare legs. He sat up. The strong aromas of jasmine and Aqua Velva, Elvis' favorite scents, flooded Edgar's nose, almost suffocating. Elvis floated out of the shimmer, his hand beckoning. Intense blue eyes transfixed Edgar. The electric mist enveloped the bed. He pulled the sheet over Ginger to shelter her.

I've decided to bring people to Ococonee Spring.

"Bring what people?"

My fans.

"Um, all this time, you said we had to keep 'em out. We did some terrible things to people we caught trespassing."

Don't even think about that, Edgar. You and the Diddler did what you had to do at the time. But things change.

"So, now, you *want* people here?"

I will change my mind anytime I want. Problem with that, Edgar?

"Nossir," replied Edgar. "No problem."

Time to restring the guitar. There was the time of concealment but that's over. Finito, the end, arrivederci. Now is the time to reveal myself and gather the multitudes.

Ginger stirred, moaning, trembling, as if having a bad dream. Edgar patted her shoulder while he spoke to Elvis. "That's a real good thing. Good idea."

Elvis extended his arms, like enormous wings, the spangles of his blazing white jumpsuit flaring and flapping. His voice echoed. Edgar listened in awe.

I will pour out my spirit on all flesh. I will gather the people to me. Legions of them. They will know my wisdom and my power and feel my love. I will baptize others like I did Ginger. I have songs still to be sung, Edgar, and I will sing them. Live from Ococonee Springs!

***

When Jason Root relocated to Florida, from East Lothian, New Jersey, many of his friends were appalled. *Why would any decent person be in Florida?*

read one text. *Is this some sort of sick joke, J?* Yet another, *Travel advisory. Hell is empty and all the Devils are in Florida.* Jason received a few IM's of support but most trashed Florida for its retrograde politics. One text provided a summation. *Repug state of fear! Justice served if fascist Florida sinks into the ocean!*

Unabashed and unapologetic, but amused, Jason laughed while reading his email and texts, sipping an excellent cabernet sauvignon, and listening to Verdi overtures. The dark shadows of *La forza del destino* rose in intensity. His reasons for moving to Florida were simple but compelling.

One, his aging father Harve Root lived in Florida and, contrary to the elderly man's assertion he remained in the pink, Jason thought it wise to stay close. Harve was in decline. Age catches up. Infirmity works like the old joke about the two ways you go bankrupt. Gradually and suddenly.

Two, Jason's ex-wife did *not* live in Florida. She absolutely loathed the state and remained in the former marital domicile in leafy East Lothian, pending its sale and fifty-fifty division of the proceeds per the divorce decree; in the interim she subsisted on the alimony Jason grudgingly paid.

Three, snow remained unheard of in Florida. Jason hated snow almost as much as he hated the deer who destroyed his garden in East Lothian.

Four, the absence of state income tax. That money makes everything better remains an indisputable historical fact. Tax avoidance was doubleplusgood, and legal; tax evasion, however, was illegal and had to be adroitly skirted. Several of Jason's clients lived nine months of the year in New Jersey but, on Jason's advisement for tax purposes, claimed their second homes in Florida as legal residence. They approved of his move and wished him well. For them, Florida was golden; a land of freedom, the attainable possibilities freedom bestowed, and perpetual sunshine.

As he drove north on I-75, Jason contemplated the hazards of traffic. Precarity Studies showed, and Jason's lived experience corroborated, that the most aggressive drivers in the U.S. swarmed the Florida peninsula like bacteria in a swollen appendix. Jason drove a Toyota Sequoia; safety is piloting a full-size luxury SUV. He practiced defensive driving, navigating I-75 from Tampa to visit his father Harve in The Villages, only an hour and thirty-eight minutes but a perilous odyssey every mile of the route. Behemoth Peterbilts, Freightliners, and Kenworths clogged the road. Freight, at least, served a vital economic purpose, transporting consumer goods to shelves. But steroid-soaked sociopaths operated many of the other vehicles on the highway. Speeding, careening, tailgating, failing to signal, weaving in and out of lanes. Happily, he egressed interstate for less travelled county roads through the flat and uneventful central Florida landscape. Monotony signaled safety.

Baroque stone signage announced The Villages, swathed in sunshine, the Shining City on the Hill, absent the Hill. Jason drove the gamut of behemoth banks — Chase, Wells Fargo, Bank of America —- and calories —- IHOP, Culver's, Taco Bell —- on wide avenues. Golf carts whizzed by. Reckless and feckless geriatrics, their sense of risk apparently atrophied with advanced age and material security. They all smiled and blazed with suntans and good health, redolent of Eternal Life. Jason smiled back and waved. Two decades younger than fifty-five, the minimum age for residency at The Villages, he probed their turf, and it was only polite to be friendly to the natives of this pleasant Florida gerontocracy.

His father had summoned him for lunch at a seafood grill ahead of their bimonthly schedule. Harve always picked up the check for these lunches and paid cash; Harvey L. Root, III, distrusting banks after an IRS tax levy ripped his accounts, habitually carried a wad of money, like a riverboat gambler, one of his many foibles.

A shimmering string version of 'Beyond the Sea' provided background music as Jason entered the restaurant. He paused, disconcerted by a titanic bronze statue depicting a sinister trio of Cthulhu-like floating creatures; then he realized they were only jellyfish. Ugly jellyfish, a waste of artistic endeavor.

Silhouettes of tropical fish adorned the cyanotic blue walls in the dining room. Harvey occupied a table, solo, no girlfriend this time. A salt and pepper beard sprouted amid the dark spots and verrucae on his face; he needed a haircut too. He wore an electric green polo shirt and dark cargo shorts, black compression dress socks with spotless white Adidas. Harve nursed a Bloody Mary with an elaborate garnish, a jumbled mini garden of olive, celery, asparagus stalk, bacon, lobster claw, and pepperoncini on bamboo sticks.

"How are you going to drink that?" said Jason as he sat down.

"Hello to you too," Harve replied.

"Well, yeah, sorry." He sighed. Jason stood and they hugged. Harve smelled of Old Spice. "Good to see you, dad. You're looking well."

"I'm in the pink!" Harve tap-danced a few seconds before they sat down again. "The gout went away." He sipped his Bloody Mary through a straw and chomped bacon.

Jason ordered decaf and skimmed the offerings on the shiny glazed plastic menu.

"Try the *pescatore* plate," said Harve. "Best deal on the menu. They don't clip you on the portion." His face brightened as a server brought a plate of raw oysters on the half shell. To Jason, they looked grim. Mucus of deathly gray.

"Dad, tell me you're not actually going to eat those."

"Didn't order them for display."

"Have you heard of Vibrio Vulnificus?"

"Wasn't he a Roman emperor between Nero and Biggus Farticus?" An example of Harve's dad humor; he laughed at his own joke as he doused an oyster with Tabasco.

"It's a deadly flesh-eating bacterium that thrives in the littoral waters where oysters are harvested."

"Do tell." Harve chuckled, unaffected.

And Jason did tell, at length. He marshalled facts gleaned from Fatal Florida, the subreddit he followed. Fact: a 71-year-old Sarasota man, younger than Harve, died after eating raw oysters contaminated with Vibrio. The CDC, Jason asseverated, estimated 80,000 people become sick with vibriosis annually and one hundred perished from infection. Sixteen cases in Florida this year so far, according to Florida Department of Public Health, and it was only June. A Pinellas County woman lost a leg, and a Miami man suffered fatal myocarditis. Vibrio illness symptoms include diarrhea, vomiting, abdominal agony, chills, fulminant fever, shock, and hideous skin lesions. Especially at risk were *the elderly* — Jason wagged his finger — and anyone with compromised immune systems, cancer, diabetes, liver disease, or unlucky.

Harve downed another oyster. "I'll play-the-odds."

"Rather you did not," said Jason.

"Killjoy. You worry too much. *That*'ll take years off your life. What did they used to call you in your college fraternity? Risky Root. Because you were always calculating the risks if they did such and such."

Jason ordered baked lemon parmesan trout,

perfectly safe. They ate lunch and chatted in a desultory manner. Fine, fine, both men were fine, fine. No, Jason didn't need money, the previous quarter having milked his client base to the extent their AGI and professional ethics allowed. Yes, Harve admitted without Jason asking, he had another girlfriend. Snagged was the word he used and described Joanie from Indiana as a lively filly, but you really couldn't tell without time in the saddle. Yeah, Jason the opera buff still scheduled a trip to Germany for the Wagner festival in Bayreuth to see a post-post-modern production of *Das Rheingold.*

"What's it about?" said Harve. He had no interest in opera.

"The Real Housewives of the Rhine are accosted by an incel dwarf who rips off their dirndls and knickers and leaves them bare and shivering in *die Luft.* Wotan is pressured into selling his sister into sex slavery by a real estate developer with an orange face and hair like a cirrus cloud, so that Wotan can shutter his annoying bling-bling mezzo-soprano wife in a new mansion. The world ends, but the music is incredible. Wagner was a German prick, and inspiration to the Nazis, but his music is great."

Harve quaffed another oyster. "This story has a deeper meaning for you?"

"The mezzo-soprano wife hits home, but never mind, Dad. Let's get to the real reason for this confab."

"Okay. Let's. I'm worried about your sister."

"*Step*sister."

"Family all the same," said Harve. "I recall you sort of liked her once."

"That's one of the regrets I've buried in Florida. Let's be candid, Dad. Kat Condon is a drain. Don't send her more money."

"Now *listen*," said Harve. "She's acting strange."

"Oh, imagine that." Eye roll.

"She left Gainesville. Dropped out of school. Abandoned her belongings. I had to clean out her apartment and put things in storage. Week ago, she called me. To say hello, chat, didn't want me to worry. She's living in a place called Ococonee Springs."

"Never heard of it," said Jason.

"Nor have I," said Harve. "She calls herself *Ginger*. Like the movie star from Gilligan's Island. No idea why. She's, uh, living out there in rural Florida …

perfectly happy. Several times she repeated this, how *happy* she is. Ococonee Spring is a magical place and she's never been happier."

"It's drugs," said Jason.

"No, she got weaned off that. I couldn't get a lot of detail out of her. She was, uh, kind of loopy. Wants me to visit."

Jason said, "And bring money."

"Money was not mentioned."

"I'm pleasantly surprised," said Jason. "What about Kat's mother?"

"No help at all. Barbara's in Ashville teaching yoga. She and Kat don't get along. It's up to me and you and I'm concerned about Kat."

Of course, you are, thought Jason. Harve had two sons, Jason and his older brother who lived overseas, an expat. Harve had always wanted a daughter; he remained sentimental about and, in Jason's estimation, played the perpetual sap for Kat, and that was unbecoming. Also, expensive.

Harve said, "I don't want to go out there to that Ococonee Springs place."

"But you want me to go there," Jason said,

cutting to the chase.

Jason contemplated a face-to-face conversation with Kat Condon again. He averted his gaze to a silhouette of a soaring sailfish on the blue wall, formulating an answer, and knowing a negative response was not going to sit well with Harve.

"I don't think so, Dad. She's an adult and can live her life in whatever risky-ditzy way she wants. Let's stay out of it."

"There you go again," replied Harve. "You're resentful of her. Irks me when you act this way. Look, Jason. Please. I know you and she got an issue. Bygones be bygones. Not asking you to *intervene*. Asking you to see how things are with her at that place. Do an old man a favor. Will you do this?"

***

Research remained a compulsion for Jason Root. Thursday late-night in his condo, Jason sipped a Chilean malbec, nibbled prosciutto, and sat at his Lenovo desktop, keeping an eye on the forex market while he researched Ococonee Spring and listened to Donizetti. *Eccola!* Lucia goes mad and murders her husband, Arturo. A crimson river when Jason saw a production at the Paris Opera.

Ococonee, a first magnitude spring in the Lacoochee River basin. Privately owned and not at present open to the public. Near Hygeia, a census-designated community, unincorporated and comprised of 284 yokels in rural Boykin County, Florida. Mostly white folks on the bottom rungs of the income scale in one of the poorest Florida counties. At one time the center of north Florida turpentine production, an industry long rendered obsolete.

Jason skimmed its history. The Lacoochee River marked the boundary between the Timucuan tribes and their war-like neighbors, the Apalachee. When Spanish explorers first visited the area in 1530, both Timucuans and Apalachees visited the spring, in the belief the water possessed healing powers. Even in times of war, the sacred ground was respected; any wounded warrior of either tribe could bathe in the water without fear of attack. In the 17th century, Franciscan friars founded a mission, *San Sebastian de Ococoni,* baptized the natives, and claimed many miracles transpired, but the mission was abandoned in 1656 when the remaining Timucuans were forcibly removed to the *San Agustín* presidio to replace native laborers wiped out by a smallpox epidemic. And then they entirely vanished from the historical record.

Jason splashed more malbec in his glass. Feeling tipsy and playful after three glasses of malbec, Jason flipped a Jordan almond in the air and caught it in his mouth. But then he reassessed that action and decided it was too risky. Could choke to death accidentally.

The area remained unpopulated until settlers from Georgia tramped into the area in 1831, known as Ococonee Spring until 1893 when a post office was established. Walter Fenner, from one of the original settler families, was appointed postmaster, and renamed the settlement Hygeia, after the Greek goddess of health. The turpentine industry thrived. The Fenner family owned most of the land. Walter Fenner attempted to develop Ococonee Spring as a resort and health spa, touting the ability of its waters to cure kidney troubles, rheumatism, neurasthenia, and other female ailments. Most of the industry and development in the area was destroyed by a hurricane in 1928.

Jason found an image on the internet. A grainy monochrome photo of Ococonee Springs, circa 1900, attributed to a commercial photographer named Fishbaugh from Tampa. Swimmers in old-fashioned Victorian bathing costumes waded in the bubbling water. Men with waxed mustaches, women with parasols. Smiling for the camera, striving to look sprightly. Bleachers stood in the background amid stately oaks dripping with Spanish moss. In the deep background, Jason discerned the ghostly grey shape of an old Victorian house.

Something caught his eye. He opened the image in a new tab on his desktop, enlarged and enhanced it, and scrutinized. *Uh-huh, yeah, that's weird.* An amorphous, wraith-like figure perched on the gabled roof by a dormer window. Skinny, shriveled with age, possibly female, with long tresses like a veil, like a Miss Havisham cosplay.

Jason yawned. *Well, that's interesting.* He closed the tab.

Google Maps gave driving time 2 hours and 35 minutes from Jason's condo in north Tampa. Jason tippled more malbec and leaned back in his ergonomic chair. He supposed he could make a day of it and, filial duty fulfilled, placate Harve. Comfort the old boy. Drive to the damn spring, try to communicate with Kat, who he did not expect to be responsive or even rational, and then drive home again. Or stay the night in Gainesville. He clacked the keyboard and reserved a suite at the Hilton

Garden Inn, just in case, a prudent move. In that case, return home the next day, Saturday as early as possible before the interstate traffic coagulated and jammed Tampa, and not waste the entire weekend on this pointless errand. He planned to be home in time for pickleball doubles prearranged with friends. Drinks and dinner afterward. Might sleep with Brooke. Nothing serious, merely another *fuque buddé*, a low-risk relationship, no strings attached.

He swallowed the last dregs of malbec and brushed off the focaccia crumbs on his blazing Red Dragon t-shirt. Okay, a surprise visit. Oh, wouldn't Kat be thrilled? Not. They hadn't spoken in a couple of years. In whatever addled state of mind she now existed, would she even recognize him?

In the morning Jason ate a hearty breakfast, filled the Sequoia with gas and shortly after eight set out for Ococonee Spring, figuring to arrive before noonish, and taking an overnight bag, just in case. With hand sanitizer, sunscreen, insect repellent, vitamins, and a first aid kit. Bottles of Perrier Lime chilled in a cooler.

Smooth sailing on the Interstate with road music, not opera. Dire Straits soared from the speakers. *Sometimes you're the windshield, sometimes you're the bug.* Once out of Tampa, the landscape turned into rolling green hills. Scenery flitted by. Motels, Cracker Barrel, Big Daddy Don Garlits Museum of Drag Racing, billboards for an Indian restaurant in Gainesville, Guns Galore. Jason glanced at his Rolex and nodded with satisfaction, making good time on the road.

Driving, his mind drifted. Jason remembered the nuptials. *Harvey Llewellyn Root, III, and Barbara Condon invite you to their exchange of wedding vows at The Seaborne Chapel in Verona Beach.* Ceremony performed at a rent-a-venue near the Atlantic beach. Windy, the sound of the surf in the distance, tang of salt in the air. A small affair, maybe fifty guests, mostly friends and family of the bride. The groom wore an orange sports jacket and the younger bride in a low-cut satin gown with ample display of cleavage. No sign of botox, Jason noted. Second time around for both, Harve a widower – recently! — and Barbara was divorced twice.

Jason and his older brother attended. Both arrived late. Neither wore a tie or jacket and his brother had not shaved or showered in the last 24 hours and in addition to basal reek gave off the skittish vibe of a nocturnal creature only reluctantly diurnal. The birth of Harvey Llewellyn Root Version 4.0 had been intended as a one-off nativity, an only child and, propitiously, a son to continue the Root name, the American lineage of which traced to 18th century New England and before that to the village of Wroot in Lincolnshire, England. Jason had popped up inadvertently several years later. He regarded his older brother as brilliant but aloof. Harve Four pursued the solitary occupation of writing code for a software company; code as intricate and perfect as a Bach cantata, he boasted. He worked remotely, in Colorado at the time of the wedding, prancing up the Manitou Incline once a week, and formulating plans to relocate to Southeast Asia. He studied Buddhism, was diagnosed bipolar, professed to be gay but admired asceticism, and remained wedded only to his work and intoxicants, the latter usually imbibed in binges. The Fourth Harvey Root foreclosed the possibility of the Fifth. The brothers, their differences aside, remained close. They sat together and whispered during the marriage ceremony like two accomplices in crime.

"Rather soon to remarry," said Harve Four.

"He was there for mom during the chemo," said Jason. "It was an ordeal. Barbara was his grief counselor."

"They might've waited The Decent Interval." Harve Four's eyes drifted. "What on earth is that?"

A girl with green hair and black mascara around green eyes. Tattoo of a wispy feather on her arm. Gold hoop earrings dangled from lobes. Clad in black. a tight corset, clingy blouse, no brassiere, short black pleather skirt, and sheer black nylons, with long symmetrical runs along both thighs. Did they sell them like that? Jason wondered. He wasn't apprised of current fashions. The girl had arrived late and sat alone.

"Barbara's daughter, Katherine," said Jason. "Goes by Kat. Only child. She works in a vintage clothing shop or something. She's on TikTok, too. She *influences*."

"Quite the spectacle," Harvey Four said. "Goth, I assume. Or Addams Family. Are you sure her name isn't Wednesday?"

When the blonde, suntanned chapel officiant pronounced them man and wife, Barbara let loose a piercing cry of joy and threw her arms around the groom. He tottered but retained his balance. They kissed.

"What a banshee," said Harve Four.

"Reminds of your wife."

"Ouch," Jason replied. Sore subject. Marriage on the proverbial rocks. "You're in goblin mode today. Dial it back."

"Colitis," replied Harve Four. "Brings out my bitch."

The Seaborne Chapel of Verona Beach offered an all-inclusive wedding package. Vows completed, husband and wife and their guests debouched through sliding doors into the spacious reception area. The chapel officiant doffed his Anglican-style surplice, untied his man bun, shook his golden blonde hair loose, transforming from the Right Reverend John Duhamel into Doc Jay Dee, the hip deejay in an embroidered purple guayabera. A cold buffet was served, the cash bar open. Doc Jay offered an *insalata mista* of Oldies, Classic Rock, EDM, and retro Malt Shop Favorites. He dedicated a slow-dance RB love song to Harve and Barb. First dance as Man and Wife.

Jason devoured smoked salmon after inquiries to determine if its source was farmed or wild. Harve Four sucked down G&T, colitis notwithstanding. He rarely ate. Food annoyed him. Harve Four regarded mastication as messy and atavistic, as he regarded most human functions. Kat Condon approached them, ice clinking in her drink. Her second already.

"You're the bros," she announced, sizing them up.

"Yes, we are," replied Jason, thinking *let the games begin.*

"I'm Loki," said Harve Four. "He's Thor if you're looking to get hammered. I'm given to understand that is customary at wedding parties."

"I'm Kat." She brandished her iPhone. "One of you is a Buddhist and the other isn't. So, like, which is which?"

"I am the enlightened being," said Harve Four.

"Awesome." Brandishing her Google Pixel.

"If you please, I'd prefer not to be part of your TikTok."

"Why not?" Disappointed and a tad sullen.

"Social media is insidious, addictive, and brings out the vipers."

"Okay, cool, yeah, whatevs." Kat lowered her phone. "By the way, I'm off TikTok permanently, switched to Rvrrr, it's new, and it's edge, way cooler. And, anyway, this deejay is fucking lame, but I want to dance."

"I only dance when in stupor or possessed," replied Harve Four.

Kat made a fishface at him and turned her attention to Jason. "What about you? You're Jason, right?"

"I'll dance with you."

Kat proved an incredible dancer, feline on her feet, awing Jason. They drank. And drank. Jason dropped his Amex Platinum card at the bar for an open tab. Kat introduced him to Deep Eddy lemon vodka mixed with hard lemon seltzer and a dribble and swirl of cherry juice, and Jason Root pronounced it *good*.

"I'm happy to see you made a new friend," said Harve Four while Jason refreshed their drinks at the bar.

"One big happy family," said Jason.

"How convenient that Lady Drusilla couldn't be with us today."

Jason's wife, Drusilla Catriona O'Donnell. Theater arts degree, classical training in voice, polyamorous pansexual Anglo-Irish drama queen. Unable to attend the wedding due, ostensibly, to a scheduling conflict; she was in rehearsal for a production of *Cosi Fan Tutte* as conniving Despina, the maid. Of course, Jason knew, she was about to be bounced from the production due to 'artistic differences' with, well, everybody involved in the production. Harve Four often kidded his brother that Drusilla should give up opera altogether and pursue her true vocation as a pro domme.

"Big D on the horizon. In pre-stage now."

"Am I not surprised," said Harve Four. "I noticed you're not wearing the ring."

"My finger turned purple," said Jason.

"Must be an omen."

"There you are!" Elfin Kat swooped in, elated, grabbing her vodka and Jason's arm. "I still want to dance!" The Cranberries' *Dreams* blared from the speakers.

"Let the revels continue." Harve Four raised his glass. He stood rigid, as if anchored. In a stupor now, Jason surmised. His brother had the ability to drink to excess but never appear drunk, never stagger, or slur his words, or become belligerent. Bitchy, yes, but belligerent, never. Harve Four smiled like a porphyry Buddha, enigmatic, detached, and knowing.

But at that moment his brother didn't

concern him. All Jason could focus on was Kat Condon, contemplating her dark, green eyes, and getting lost in those eyes. The deejay played Blondie. Deborah Harry sang Follow Me. *To a world young and free, we shall fly, follow me.* Jason pushed everything else aside —- his failed marriage, the humongous credit card debt Drusilla had accrued, his financial finagling, his compulsive risk factoring, his mother's recent death, his dad's hasty remarriage. He focused on those bewitching green eyes. And the rest of Kat Condon along with them.

Then Doc Jay Dee spun an Elvis Oldie. *I'm in love, I'm all shook up.*

They slipped away from the party and dashed to the beach, wading in the soft sand as the waves crashed. They wandered barefoot; they played in the surf, running, prancing, splashing, a frolic. Kat pirouetted on incoming waves. She confessed to dropping out of ballet and dance lessons. The sunlight faded and in the soft grey twilight the hotel lights came on along the coast as far south and as far north as the eye could see, like a fallen constellation.

"What hotel are you in?" Jason asked her.

"I don't plan that far ahead."

"Where did you plan on staying tonight?"

"In my car," Kat replied. "It's a Subaru."

"I have a suite at the Atlantic Royale Resort. The bright one there." He pointed. "Four stars. An oceanside paradise in sunny south Florida. Concierge service. Private beach, a thousand linear feet of alabaster sand. The Breakfast and Brunch rated an outstanding culinary experience."

"Do you, like, memorize brochures?"

"I got OCD for Christmas last year."

Kat Condon pursed her lips, playing coy, but considering. "I suppose it's …it's sort of … a luxury experience."

"Never scrimp," Jason said. "Only live once."

"So, show me. Before I change my mind. I love my Subaru."

They zigzagged down the beach to the Atlantic Royale Resort and dashed through its susurrating automatic doors, through the lobby and crashed into an elevator. They ascended, arms wrapped around each other, lips to lips. Almost missed the fifth floor.

A short time later Jason found himself in his hotel suite with his face between Kat's legs, lapping at her like a thirsty man at a spring. Her spidery fingers stroked and pulled his hair while she moaned.

"Don't stop, don't!"

Jason remembered reading somewhere that women are wondrous, mysterious, and magical creatures, worthy of awe, if not worship. Jason decided at that moment, this resonated with absolute truth, and he loved her. Passionately, profoundly, proverbial head over heels. He doted on the tattoo of a delicate petaled flower gracing her magical mons, her intimate tat. That few are privileged to see, she told him; count yourself among the blessed that you have seen the sign.

"It's my enchantment," said Kat. "Like in a fairy tale."

"No, no, no, don't say that. Fairy tales end badly. In the original German, I mean, the Brothers Grimm version, not the anodyne Disney. The happily-ever-after part, no way. Like in opera, everybody dies at the end."

She laughed and tweaked his nose and pressed her breasts against his chest. "You don't have to worry. We'll survive."

The next morning, Jason awoke with a start, as Kat pinched his nipple. Ouch! She giggled. He sat up in bed.

"Hi," she said. Alert, awake, smiling. An adoring smile. She had scrubbed her face. Make up gone, she was pretty. But merely pretty. Young and fresh, just out of her teens. A twenty-something kid, not a siren, girl not goddess. His father's new wife's daughter. Regret hit Jason like a sledgehammer. *Oh, fuck me, I've made huge mistake.*

"Hi," Jason said. His mouth dry as concrete, his head ached, and he was stricken with sudden-onset photophobia. Vodka hammered the day after; he should've known better. He shielded his eyes from the excruciating light searing through the window.

"I'm still here," Kat said.

"Yeah, I see that," said Jason. He stumbled into the bathroom, closing the door, urinated with care to avoid splashing the rim, washed his hands, splashed his face with cold water, and guzzled the tepid remainder of a bottle of San Pellegrino from the room's mini fridge. Then, with a deep breath, he emerged from the bathroom to see Kat Condon perched on the disheveled bed, smiling, and wearing his maroon Miskatonic University T-shirt.

"So, did you want to have the outstanding

culinary Breakfast and Brunch first, or fuck some more and then have the Brunch and then more fucking until checkout time, or the maids come around and we yell *más tarde?*"

"I don't know if that's a good idea."

"The breakfast or the fucking?"

"Um, well, sort of a tossup." Jason flopped into a chair. "I need coffee. Caffeine and aspirin. No, I need more sleep. I'm sorry. I really feel like death warmed over. I don't usually drink liquor. And especially not to such excess. For evident reasons. I like my wine. Especially pinot noir. I confess, I'm a wine snob. Sorry, I'm babbling."

"Okay," she said. She peeled off the T-shirt, gathered her clothing, and dressed. "If you're not up to it, I'll get myself off. I love my Subaru. Did you ever see a French movie, *Titane?*"

"I'm not trying to be rude or throw you out."

"I'll go. Alright? We're family now. Family forgives everything. Yeah, so, uh, everything's cool."

Jason wrapped a sheet around his torso and stood, feeling sheepish, like a college frat boy at a toga party gone wrong. "Truly nice to meet you. Sincerely. Thank you for, um, a fun evening."

Kat shrugged. Blasé. And a more than a tad sullen. "It was okay."

That afternoon in a rush Jason Root was driving his rental car to the airport to catch his flight back to New Jersey when Jason's phone vibrated. He answered.

Harvey Four said, "You've been tagged."

"I feel like shit and I'm in traffic. Can I call you back?"

"I must apprise you. As you know, I deplore social media."

"Cut to the chase," replied Jason.

"Kat Condon posted a video, and you're in it."

"In it?" Sudden trepidation gut-punched Jason. Risk factors, previously ignored, leaped out of their dark crevices like hissing serpents.

"Featured performer, *you*, dancing, drinking, snoring in bed the morning after and getting a wake-up titty twister. She emailed everybody on the wedding party chain."

Jason swerved, after drifting out of his lane. Another vehicle honked. "What?"

"Prepare for impact. Peace. Goodbye." Harve Four ended the call.

No, this could not be happening to him. Jason looked at his phone and discovered a crescendo of rage-filled text messages from Drusilla. "Oh, shit," he said aloud. "Shit, shit, shit."

***

At Gainesville, Jason exited interstate and cruised secondary roads. The landscape reverted to forest, oaks shaggy with Spanish moss, and plumosa palms. Signage announced walled communities, Gainesville suburbs, retreats for the tenured cognoscenti at the University of Florida, places with names like Villages of West End and Steeplechase. After that, rolling hills, pasture, and pine saplings, and another world, disconnected from the university haven. Small town and rural Florida. The Abiding Savior church stood white and pristine in front of a screen of slash pines. *Repent,* a billboard above the church adjured. *You can never know the hour.* Pavement narrowed to two lanes. Squished bloody carrion dotted the shoulder, fresh and yet to be discovered by scavengers. The highway meandered into Boykin County. GPS in Jason's dashboard ceased to function. Finally, a roadside sign peppered with bullet holes announced Hygeia, a dismal cluster of rattletrap houses and a gas station. Shielded by the pines, as if hiding, Jason spied a shuttered church; whitewashed walls dingy, windows boarded; gabled roof shedding asphalt shingles; its steeple absent a cross. In front of the gas station he spotted a sign, *Elvis Tribute at Ococonee Springs*. Crude, hand lettered on cardboard, the sign had been tacked to a stick. Jason chuckled. He'd heard of Elvis tribute artists, never seen one, of course, and regarded the whole phenomenon as gaudy and naïve; an exercise in nostalgia. He opted to stop for directions, a stretch, a pee, and something to munch on, and rolled into the gravel of the X-Press market. An oblong box of stucco with gas pumps outside and defunct, padlocked ice machine on the curb, *We Appreciate Your Business* stenciled over the frame door.

"Hi, honey!" The stout woman behind the counter said as Jason entered. Silver-blue hair, celery green smock, sparkling rhinestone glasses dangling on a chain. Her name tag read Ardell. "How are we doing today?"

"Uh, fine. Washroom?"

Ardell pointed. "Tinkle, tinkle, this way."

The washroom. Wet floor, cracked mirror,

an unflushed commode, mucus wiped on the dingy tile walls. Nasty graffiti. Jason cringed, urinated quickly, and sprayed his hands with sanitizer. He strolled the aisles of the store.

"Help you find something?"

"I'm alright." He selected a package of mixed nuts and tossed it on the counter.

"Tiny bag of nuts, not enough to eat." Ardell pointed at the foods behind the glass, simmering under heat lamps. "We got tamales, pepperoni pizza, chicken fingers."

"I'm not that hungry. Can you tell me how to get to Ococonee Springs?"

She brightened. "You here for the Elvis Tribute?"

No. my stepsister is staying there." He offered an ATM card.

"We're not set up for plastic," said Ardell. "Banks charge a merchant fee, and that's a squeeze on a small business."

"Okay. I get that." From his wallet, Jason slipped two dollars on the counter.

Ardell handed Jason his change. "Who's your

sister?"

"*Step*sister. Calls herself Ginger."

A dimpled smile inflated Ardell's face. "Ginger is your sister! You don't say! She's a real sweetheart! Edgar's girl."

"Who's Edgar?"

"Edgar Fenner. The Elvis Tribute is all his doing."

"I see," replied Jason. Thinking Edgar Fenner must be a local promoter of sorts, an entrepreneur hustling out here in the boondocks. Well, whoop-de-doo for Edgar. More power to him. "You were going to give me directions?"

"Ococonee Spring," Ardell said. "Keep down this road until you get to the old Fenner farm. Can't miss it! Turn right. Dirt road. But be nice. Those boys get tetchy if they don't know you."

"Thanks." Jason munched on mixed salted nuts. Tasted stale.

"You're welcome! Come back and visit the Hygeia Xpress again real soon and you have yourself just the most wonderfulness-filled day, darlin'."

Jason stepped outside, munching mixed nuts, and dropped the crumpled package in the trash bucket. He glanced toward the derelict church in the pines. A tall man stood outside the doors of the church, glaring at Jason. An older man, face the color of mahogany, dressed in a loose white tunic and black pants, his bushy white hair a wild explosion from his head. Church deacon or caretaker, Jason supposed. Or a ghost, giving off a definite minatory vibe. Jason waved. The man waved back, then turned, moved stiffly, and shuffled back inside, slamming the church door.

Jason drove down the highway.

Ococonee Spring? Couldn't miss it. A larger-than-life bronze statue of Elvis stood in a shrine constructed from cinder blocks painted purple and adorned with gaudy, glittery shower curtains. A two-lane dirt road led into pine woods. Jason wheeled the Toyota and bounced over the rutted road. He didn't proceed ten yards before a scrawny blonde man stopped his car, waving his arms and shouting.

"Private property, private property!"

Jason braked. The blonde scarecrow scrambled to the side of the Toyota as Jason lowered the window. "This is Ococonee Spring, right?"

"Who's asking?"

"My name is Jason Root. I'm looking for someone who lives here. Her name is Kathleen Condon."

"Nobody here by that name," the scarecrow replied.

Liar. Being a successful financial advisor required the ability to read people, and Jason read this country cretin in an instant and the beady-eyed cretin irritated him. "She calls herself Ginger."

"What's she to you?"

"If you must know. Family. My stepsister. She didn't know I was coming. Surprise visit."

"We don't like surprises. I'll ask you straight out. Are you one of *them*?"

What? The fuck? Jason's irritation quadrupled. "One of who?"

"Enemies would do us harm if they got inside."

"Inside what?"

"This is a sanctuary." The other man made a circular motion with his hand, indicating the thick pine forest around them. Jason only then noticed the orange sashes knotted around skinny tree trunks, and orange traffic cones spaced at intervals, marking a perimeter. His Toyota had been halted just outside the circle.

"Look, I'm here to see Kat Condon, or Ginger if you call her that. That's all. I'm not an enemy and have no ill intent. Are you Edgar Fenner?"

"Edgar's my brother. I'm Shire Fenner. I'll allow you entry. Park and wait in your vehicle until I talk to Edgar and Ginger. Follow me."

Shire Fenner strutted down the road, waving Jason on. Jason levered into drive and navigated the Toyota over the dirt, angling to avoid potholes. To his dismay, he spied a semiauto pistol tucked beneath his belt at the small of Shire's back. Cretins with guns were a hazard. The number of accidental shootings in Florida soared in the last few years. Through the trees to his left, Jason could see the old Victorian house to his left, the same as he had seen online doing research. Shire directed him to an improvised campsite and parking lot scraped out of the pines and marked with flags, wire and more orange cones, a caravan already parked there, several campers, tents, RV's, cars, a silver bullet of an old Airstream. Asian girls, barely out of their teens, in shorts and skimpy halter tops lounged in folding chairs under a drooping canopy attached to an RV. Jason parked and got out of the Toyota.

"Stay," said Shire, and trotted down the road.

Jason leaned against the Sequoia, uneasy. They watched him. The Asian girls, doe-eyed and listless but curious; and several men, rough-looking guys standing around a beer cooler, looking bored and belligerent. He could smell the rankness of the men and the too sweet perfume of the females. One of the former, bushy red beard, dark piercing eyes under the bill of a baseball cap, nodded to Jason. Jason nodded back. Red Beard spit tobacco juice. Jason, in turn, cleared his throat and spit saliva. Red Beard averted his gaze. The knot of plug-uglies continued chatting,

"You want massage?" One of the Asian girls called to Jason.

"No, thanks."

"First one free. Courtesy massage."

Jason pretended to consider. "Thanks, but no thanks."

"Think about nice massage. Maybe change mind."

Cicadas buzzed. Grackles cawed. Baleful

birds hopped about, flitted between tree branches, and shat on his Toyota. A disheveled, plump young man with mutton chop sideburns got out of one of the cars, waddled to the RV, chatted with the girls, struck some sort of bargain, and went inside with one of them. Red Beard kept his eyes glued to Jason. The other men talked in low, twangy voices and hocked tobacco juice into the palmetto. Jason fidgeted, uncomfortable in the humidity and feeling edgy. A strange energy permeated this place. Discernable, almost palpable. Jason looked at his phone. No bars, no reception, a black hole.

Half an hour later Shire Fenner came striding down the dirt road. "She don't know you," he said to Jason, and jerked this thumb in the direction of the main highway. "Get out."

"What?"

"Did you hear me? Ginger don't want to see you, so you might as well get in your vehicle and vamoose. Arriva-derchee."

"That's not right," said Jason.

"What the fuck's not right about it?"

"I've driven a long way. From Tampa."

"Ain't that fuck'n far," Shire said.

Jason wagged a finger. "Now you listen. I'm

here to talk to Kat Condon. Or Ginger, whateverthefuck. *Okay*? I've driven all this way and I'm not leaving without talking to her."

Shire bristled, like a small suspicious terrier about to lunge and bite. "*Told you*. She don't want to talk to you."

"I want to hear her say it. I want her to tell me, face to face, that she doesn't want to talk to me. So, *Shire*, toddle along and relay the message." He crossed his arms and leaned against the Toyota. "I'll wait."

Shire glared at Jason, reeking of malice, his breath stinking like stale sauerkraut. "This is private property, and I'm telling you *to leave*."

"After I talk to her."

Jason's courage began to wane, and he wanted to jump in his Toyota and dash, but he refused to give in to the impulse and allow this moron the satisfaction of intimidating him. Never a good idea to show fear or let hoi polloi win. He'd bluff, bargain, and play the alpha dog. "You know, there is a Missing Persons alert filed. Making this a legal matter. You should know that Harvey L. Root, her stepfather, is a man of means. Money, in other words." Jason wanted to connect the dots for the cretin. "Money buys lawyers. Now, do I talk to her, or do I have come back here with a court order and a SWAT team?"

Shire Fenner didn't budge. He smoldered in angry silence; Jason could almost smell the fumes. The men around the beer cooler started moving toward them, menacing. The unnerving thought occurred to Jason that he'd underestimated the risk.

"Back off, Shire!" A booming baritone cut through the humid air. Loud and commanding. A six-foot bulk in bib overalls and a denim shirt strode out of the palmetto to confront Shire.

"I got this, Edgar," said Shire.

"I say again," said Edgar Fenner. "All of y'all, back off."

"Am I in charge of fuck'n security nor not, Edgar?" Almost a tantrum. He stomped on the ground. Like a twelve-year-old denied a pony ride.

"Leave this to me, Shire, and mind your dirty mouth. I can't count the times I've told you about that. That is no way to speak."

Shire skulked away. Red Beard and the others deferred to Edgar, turned away and clustered around their beer cooler again. Shire joined them.

"I am Edgar Fenner. Privilege to make your acquaintance." He extended his huge hand to Jason. They shook. Edgar's grip made Jason wince.

"Oh, sorry. Didn't mean to hurt you." Genuinely abashed.

"It's okay. As I told your brother, Kat Condon is my stepsister."

"Was," said Edgar.

"Excuse me?"

"Things change." Edgar put a brotherly arm around Jason's shoulders. Like being embraced by friendly grizzly with a mellifluous baritone and evangelist demeanor. "You see, things are different now."

"What's different?"

"Everything." Edgar smiled. "I know you are her kin, and I respect that but understand that we all grow. Evolve, you might say. But you will see with your own two good eyes. Come along, Mr. Root. Walk with me."

Walk with me proved sort of a command. Edgar herded Jason toward the old house. He morphed into tour guide.

"Ococonee Spring was sacred to the Indians," said Edgar.

"I read about that."

"It was a sanctuary respected by all, a place of healing. The Spanish built a mission here but there's no trace of it now. Miracles here documented too by a Spanish priest, but they thought he was crazy and defrocked or unfrocked him, however it's called."

"I read about all that too," said Jason, though he hadn't.

"You done your homework." Edgar nodded, impressed, smiling, and benign. "Been Fenner homestead two hundred years. We Fenners came from Georgia and put down roots here. I was born in Florida and lived my whole life at Ococonee Spring. Well, so far, that is. Not done living yet. You from Florida?"

"From New Jersey originally," said Jason.

"I won't hold that against you," said Edgar. "Only teasing you. You got some Florida sand in your shoes and had to stay and that's alright."

They approached the old Victorian house, adorned with a fresh coat of paint, pink and black. An elderly woman with a long train of ragged silver-white hair protruded from a dormer window like a deranged

Rapunzel. She cackled and, seeing Jason below with Edgar, pointed a bony finger and cawed like a crow, until someone inside pulled her away and slammed the window shut. With a sudden frisson of apprehension, he recalled seeing her before but, no, no, no, that wasn't possible.

"Pay her no mind," said Edgar. "That's Auntie Kate. Near and dear to me but she's not quite right in the head and that's a darn shame."

"*Jason*?!"

Jason had no time to react before his stepsister, bounding from the porch, leaped upon him, wrapping her arms around his neck and her legs around his middle. Jason staggered backward and would have fallen had not Edgar acted as backstop. Kat, in gingham blouse, bare midriff, cutoff jeans and flipflops, hugged him and planted puppy kisses on his face.

"So good to see you!"

"Whoa," said Jason. He peeled her off. "Kat?"

"No, no, no, no. *Ginger*."

"Um, okay. Sure." He noted the frenetic gleam in her eye, the huge smile, her hair growing out mousy brown, armpits unshaved. Okay, she was Ginger now; he'd play along. "Ginger it is. How are you, Ginger?"

"Fine and dandy!"

Edgar ushered them into the house and into a garish, green-carpeted parlor he called the Jungle Room, adorned with Elvis-themed baubles and brass lamps. Edgar and Ginger cuddled on a leopard skin couch. They nuzzled each other and, for refreshment, sucked down root beer floats with vanilla ice cream, maple syrup, a cumulus cloud of whipped cream topped by cherries. Jason, situated on the edge of an oversize leather recliner, declined the concoction. He drank Diet Pepsi instead and watched the lovers as the ice in his glass fizzed, inwardly appalled, deciding they were looney tunes, but content in mutual delusion. More than content. In rapture. A daffy rapture. Completely detached from reality and making out like teenagers.

"Harve is worried about you."

"He shouldn't be," replied Ginger. "I'm fine. Never been so happy in my whole life! This is where I belong. Did Harve, for real, file a Missing Person on me?"

"No," Jason admitted. "I invented that on the spur of the moment."

"Huh," Edgar said. "Shire was fit to be tied. You rattled him."

Ginger scolded Jason. "Shouldn't tell lies! And don't make Shire mad, he gets ornery. But Edgar can put him in his place, can't you, Edgar?"

"I sure try," said Edgar.

"You're not mad at me still, are you, Jason? About your wife. Tell me you're not mad at me."

"I'm not mad at you. Dru and I divorced. That's finished."

Ginger leaned closer to him and whispered. "She's the b-word, isn't she?"

"Yeah, she is," Jason said.

"So was I, but I'm a different person now! A happy person! I *evolved*. Didn't I evolve, Edgar honeybunny?"

"Yes, you did, my own true love," replied Edgar, and they nuzzled each other as Jason averted his eyes, staring at a chintzy white porcelain monkey on a coffee table. The obsidian-eyed monkey grinned back at Jason, a creepy mocking knowing lascivious little bugger. Jason wanted to smash him.

"Ococonee Spring is magical. Miracles happen here. Every day, miracles happen. A bright orange butterfly flew out of my belly button."

"Is that so?" Jason said. Hmmmmm …

"You doubt," said Ginger with a frown. "Doubt is in your eyes. And I can read it in your aura. Your aura's green like algae and that's not good."

"No, really," said Jason. "My aura's fine and dandy."

"No, it's not. Edgar, honey, Mr. Smarty Pants here doubts that miracles happen at Ococonee. He doubts Elvis."

"Jason only just got here, sugar. He will see the truth of it. That is, if he stays for the Tribute."

Ginger clutched Jason's hand. His warm, hers clammy. "Stay for the Elvis Tribute. Please. Pretty please. Stay for the Tribute and stay for the night."

"We can put you up, no trouble," said Edgar.

"Oh stay, oh stay, oh stay," Ginger warbled. 'You'll have the best sleep of your life here. And the Tribute will *change — your – life*!"

"We have us a big old' picnic before the Tribute," said Edgar. "Best darn BBQ you will ever have."

"Well," said Jason, with a nervous laugh. "Can't miss that, can I?"

***

"This is the best BBQ I've ever tasted," said Jason. He meant it too. The BBQ was so good you could start a religion with it.

"Edgar never lies," said Ginger. "He has a pure heart and it's not in him to lie."

"Where is Edgar anyway?" said Jason.

"Getting ready for the Tribute."

Water rippled and bubbled in Ococonee Spring. The congregation, local folks, happy and expectant, gathered in a picnic area around the spring, with food in Biblical-strength abundance, like loaves and fishes. Everybody ate, gorging on BBQ brisket, pork, and chicken; hush puppies; slaw, tater salad, and fried okra; thick shingles of crispy bacon; fried PB and banana sandwiches; gallons of ice cream, and deep-fried Mars bars. And a mushroom casserole called Velvet Elvis that Ginger insisted Jason try.

"Just a tiny little bite," Ginger said.

"Not bad," Jason admitted, savoring its delicate, sweet, nutty taste. He ate another forkful, and then another.

The whole town of Hygeia, which the locals pronounced *high-juh*. turned out, Ginger bragged. Well, with one or two holdouts but Ginger dismissed them with a wave of her hand, adding that people came from further away too. From Newberry and Steinhatchee and a few from Gainesville. And when they went home again after the Tribute, they all took a little piece of Elvis home with them. Ginger's wide eyes beamed 120 watts. Wasn't that wonderful?

The younger Fenner brother, Shire, in charge of 'security,' slinked among the crowd, reminding Jason of a rodent. Every time Jason turned his head or glanced, Shire lurked, often close to him. The creepy little redneck is shadowing me, thought Jason.

"You want massage now?" Lotus, the Asian girl asked, popping up at his elbow. "Massage after eating good way to digest. Massage and green tea. And we can talk. I am a good listener."

"No, thanks," Jason replied.

"We should talk. I'll be back." Lotus scurried away.

The Asian girls from the RV worked the tables, offering massages. Lotus flitted away, passing, in the deep shadow of the oaks, a clutch of yahoos orbiting around Shire. They whispered, as if conferring. Sinister, Jason thought. Didn't like the looks of them.

"Who are those guys with Shire?" he asked Ginger.

"His posse," she said. "His, like, security detail." Ginger pointed them out. "That's Palatka Red, and Chucky Fike, and Skeeter, and the new kid named Bobby something, and Wide Boy with the sideburns, he's Edgar and Shire's cousin Harlan, and Bourbon. Bourbon's a dyke, but everybody's equal in the eyes of Elvis."

"The mustache deceived me."

"It's painted on," said Ginger. "Henna, I think. Because she's in, like, *transition*. Bourbon used to own a bar in Ocala where Shire and Palatka Red used to hang out. Bourbon's girlfriend was in prison there. They call it the Florida Women's Reception Center, but it's a prison. They broke up. She's from Pensacola and her name really is Bourbon. Eloise Bourbon or something, but she wants to start calling herself Elliot, or maybe Elmer.

I can't remember."

As Ginger rambled, Jason watched Shire Fenner out of the corner of his eye. "You know, I get the impression that Shire doesn't like me."

"Oh, you're new here, he doesn't know you, and Shire – he's got, like, a sort of suspicious nature — just keeps an eye on things."

"I'm not a thing. I'm a guest."

Ginger planted a kiss on Jason's cheek and whispered. "Shire's troubled. Edgar's trying real hard to bring him along. They didn't have the same mama and Shire's mama was a real doozy, Edgar says. She worked in a casino in Biloxi where she drank and did drugs and even while she was carrying Shire."

"Edgar and Shire are half-brothers?"

"Half or whole, family's family," said Ginger. "Edgar feels he has an obligation. But never mind. I shouldn't have said anything." Ginger kissed him, a demure peck on the cheek. "Don't you worry. Just watch the Tribute and let Elvis' spirit move in you and everything will be okay."

A solo trumpet pierced the air. A ripple of excitement buzzed through the audience. Then came a scratchy recording of *Viva Las Vegas* in continual loop blaring from the loudspeakers amid the scruffy pines and lofty, twisting oaks. The congregation cheered as Edgar Fenner emerged from a conical tent. In costume, crimson aviator glasses wrapped around his head, clad in a white spangled jumpsuit with bell bottom trousers. A shiny black pompadour wig adorned his head. Fringe and tassels flapped when Edgar bounced along like an unmoored parade float.

"That's my man!" Ginger whispered. Her erect nipples almost poked through the thin gingham blouse.

"Edgar is an Elvis impersonator?"

"No, silly!" She punched Jason's shoulder. "Edgar is the Receiver. We don't need an impersonator. We got the Real McCoy! I know you don't understand yet but please be patient. Just wait and see. Gonna be a miracle!"

No Jason didn't understand; he remained baffled. Receiver? The Real McCoy? Miracles? None of this made sense. He felt strangely lightheaded, disoriented. Shire Fenner, an obvious example of fetal alcohol syndrome, lurking and watching him, kindled paranoia. And then the Tribute commenced.

"Howdy!" Edgar bellowed to the crowd. "How y'all doing?"

They answered as one. "Fine!"

"Good, good, good." Edgar paced. "Well, here we are again! At Ococonee Spring. Where You-Know-Who resides."

This elicited laughter and delighted smiles. Ginger giggled and wiggled. Jason shook his head, bewildered. His stomach ached with little twinges and cramps. He turned and saw Shire Fenner glaring at him, the only person not watching Edgar.

"We," Edgar's baritone boomed, his arm sweeping the crowd, "are the people Elvis has been waiting for. His loyal legion of fans."

"Yes, we are," they shouted. Heads bobbed, stupefied. They warbled. Somebody whooped. Raucous laughter and garbled voices rose like miasma.

"He's here," said Edgar, motioning with a sweep of his hand over the spring. "His mighty spirit dwells herein. Ococonee Spring, his sanctuary. Because before, in his other life, things didn't turn out so well. No, no, we have got to admit that. Accept that. It's a tragical story. He messed up bad, went astray. Drugs and such. But he was already a legend. He poured his spirit into his music and sacrificed himself for his fans, and went down, down, down. *But now he's back.*"

Cheers erupted. Amen, someone cried, overcome. Amen, amen, amen. Several others joined the chant, raising their hands in the air.

Edgar preached. "Ococonee Spring is where Elvis' troubled spirit, wandering between worlds after he died sitting on the porcelain throne, found sanctuary. *Sanctuary.* That's a place where you are safe. Stuck here in a form not of his choosing, no, in sort of a punishment, but here he healed, ready for another Comeback, and he is going to do it right this time. Going to gather his fans and lift spirits. And he will take us to a better home … you all tell me where Elvis will take us!"

"Graceland!" All voices joined the enthusiastic response.

Except Jason Root. Jason responded with an eye roll.

"Yes!" Edgar leaped high in the air and, to Jason's surprise, touched earth again with preternatural grace and balance, astounding. Like a great inflated Thanksgiving Day parade float. He bounced along the shore and continued to preach.

"That's right, that's right, right as rain. Graceland! This is a broken world, can't be fixed. But in Graceland, there are many mansions, everybody gets one of his own, and the Path to Graceland starts right here at Ococonee Spring!"

The audience chanted. Graceland, Graceland, Graceland. Edgar turned his back to them, his arms raised above his head, palms toward the water. The chant echoed in the pines. Bugfuck insane, thought Jason. They really believed this shit. He began to sweat. His pulse raced and the stomach cramps worsened. Vaguely nauseous and nervous as a cat, he thought about fleeing …

"We shall all ascend to Graceland!" Edgar roared, swiveled, and pointed into the crowd. "Do not *pretend* you do not *comprehend*, you must *ascend!* Repeat after me! *We will ascend."*

"We will ascend! " Everybody stood. Ginger grabbed Jason's arm and pulled him up. With reluctance, he joined the chorus, but only mouthing the words, wondering how he could escape.

"We will ascend!"

"That's good, that's beautiful," said Edgar. " Now, Elvis requires you to work too. Work your butt off. You got to give up your old life, like a butterfly out of its cocoon."

Edgar paused to catch his breath. His chest heaved. He wiped the sweat from his face with a silky red scarf he drew from his pants pocket. The scarf whipped about leaving contrails in the humid air like wispy red ripples and watching the contrails made Jason dizzy. *What the fuck am I seeing?*

"Once you Come to Elvis, it's a new life. He will never allow you to backslide. And now, folks, it's that time. Time to bring new fans to Elvis."

The crowd about Ococonee Spring became silent and in the hush the waters began to stir. Gently at first. Percolating, bubbling. Then, as if swept by an invisible wind, water splashed. Waves rocked the sandy shore. As Jason watched, an eerie, gold-green shimmer shined upon the water and as the adherents gasped, yes, yes, *something* appeared, rising out of Ococonee Spring.

Five new fans in loose fluttering white robes trotted down to the river like a scrimmage line. Men and women, one a girl barely in her teens. Shire's posse escorted them. Like herd dogs, Jason thought. Rough canine looks that alarmed Jason. The Five waded into the spring. Doffed their robes. Naked underneath. This one skinny, pale, and white; another chubby and pink; a stout, potbellied man hairy as a chimp. The girl's dainty breasts were barely bigger than pears and she shivered in the water up to her thighs and the water lapped around the bramble bush between her legs. The Five remained in a line, on each face a faraway look, rapture. They waded until they stood waist deep. Shuffling sand into a cloud. Blue-green electricity buzzed over the water. Ooh and aahs from the congregation. Gasps. Tears. An image materialized, floating on the water. A tall wispy white figure like strands of cirrus strung together. Then a long, armored creature cut through the surface of the spring, its mouth agape. It sliced the churning water and floated, spewing a white cloud.

"What is that?" Jason stared. Gobsmacked. Horrified.

"His seed," Ginger whispered.

The five inductees in the spring immersed themselves in the cloud, splashing, gulping, swallowing, gurgling. Drowning! The posse assisted, holding them under. Until the cloud dissipated, and their escorts plucked them out of the spring and dragged them back to the shore. While the audience went nuts. Cheering, hooting, clapping, guffawing like primates. Like some crazy coven, Jason thought. A witches' sabbath, that kind of dark mad shit. Goyaesque in the Florida humidity, with a monster fish in place of a he-goat. Then, as the fish submerged again into the depths of the spring, a blue-green haze rose and swirled above the water and solidified like a nimbus cloud. The audience murmured, rapt in expectation, as the outlines of a man emerged, like a ghost.

"Omigod, omigod, omigod. This is nuts!"

"No, it's not!" Ginger scowled at Jason "It's beautiful. It's Elvis! He's here! Can't you see him? What is wrong with you? Don't be such a buzz kill!"

"Fuck the spirit. That's, that's something weird and evil. I'm getting out of here. Come with me." He wanted to take her away from this craziness. She wasn't Ginger; that was absurd. She was Kat, whom he had been smitten with at a wedding in Verona Beach and could never quite get over.

"No! I'm not leaving! I belong here! You're ruining things again, like last time. You're so *ungrateful*!"

He grabbed her arm; she recoiled. "Earth to

Kat, listen to me, listen! Your name is not Ginger. You're Kathleen. Kathleen Condon. Kat!"

"No! I'm Ginger! Ginger! Ginger! Ginger! Ginger!"

Her face contorted, turning red. She shrieked, keening like a banshee. Jason cringed; her breath stunk of sauerkraut, sulfur, and BBQ sauce. Chewy bits of Mars bar and hush puppy issued from her mouth with a shower of saliva and bile and blood and baptized Jason. Her eyes bulged. She pounded her head with her fists. Until Edgar came rambling into the palmetto and hugged her.

"It's alright, it's alright," he said to her. Turning to Jason, his expression baffled and hurt, he said, "What did you do?"

Ginger shrieked. "You always were asshole! Jason is an asshole! Asshole!"

The cloud over the spring dissipated. People were staring. Some were confused. Some glared at Jason. He heard ominous whispers. The red-bearded man called Palatka herded people back toward the picnic area. Jason ran. Atop the roof of the old house the old woman Edgar called Auntie Kate had escaped out the dormer window and squatted naked and prune-wrinkled on the roof under her long wispy veil of white hair, like a gargoyle. She crackled, screamed, babbled, and pointed at Jason below. Running down the road until his lungs ached and his side felt pierced, and cramps pinched his stomach, he pinballed among the vehicles parked askew in the makeshift lot under the pines and found his Toyota amid the jumble of cars. Jason fumbled with his key fob.

A tap on his shoulder. "Where you think you're going?"

Jason turned. Another member of Shire's posse confronted him. A slovenly old man, shirtless and scrawny in bib overalls, thinning grey hair on his noggin and scrap of salt and pepper beard clinging to his chin and jaw. At his side stood a gangly redheaded girl barely out of her teens with a face full of copper freckles, an expression of placid stupidity on her face.

"I'm leaving," said Jason.

"Nope," said the old man. "I got orders that the driver of this vehicle, and I deduce that is you, doesn't leave the premises."

Genuine morons, both of them, Jason concluded. He assumed a fighting stance, his fists up, ready to rumble, and fixed the old man with a steely stare. The old man didn't flinch. He scratched his scruffy chin. The girl hiccupped.

"I've got a black belt in karate."

This, however, was another strategic fiction. Though Jason had taken martial arts classes, his skill level remained rudimentary; he qualified only for a yellow belt. But he reasoned this feeble old fart didn't present much of a threat.

The old man guffawed, coughed, and spit a glob of phlegm. He pointed at his shoes. "Black belt? Is that so? Well, see here, I got neon green shoelaces."

Jason looked. Glowing green laces like wriggling worms fastened the man's cheap sneakers, so wondrously bright Jason had to squint. The old man slugged Jason between the eyes. Hard, a torpedo, the sucker punch of doom. Jason reeled. A coppery taste filled his mouth. He slumped against the driver door of his Toyota, and the old man then slammed his knee deep into Jason's groin. Jason groaned and doubled over in agony.

His assailant motioned to the slovenly girl who stood gawping and giggling, boobs bouncing under her T-shirt. "Bring me the bat, bitch, and be quick about it."

The long-legged girl sprinted away, fetched an

aluminum baseball bat, handing it to the old man. He brandished the bat and turned to Jason.

"Whack him, papa. Do it!" the simpering girl said, delighted.

"You ain't a-going nowheres." He swung the bat. *Whack.*

Sometimes you're the Louisville slugger, and sometimes you're the ball.

***

Edgar carried Ginger, screaming and convulsing, to the house where the twin sisters, in matching polka dot bikinis, sat on the porch with his cousin Harlan, whom everybody but Edgar called Wide Boy.

"Edgar," said Wide Boy. "What happened?"

"I don't know!" Edgar rushed inside the house, the screen door slamming behind him, the twins and Wide Boy following. He raced through the house and deposited Ginger on the sofa in the Jungle Room and covered her with a blanket up to her chin. He ducked when she sat up and spewed vomit, barely missing him but showering the white porcelain monkey.

"Take care of her," Edgar told the twins. "I

got to get back to the Tribute and see to the folks. Harlan, auntie Katie unlocked the darn windows again and got out to the roof. Don't know how she does that! Go up there and get her back inside."

"I'll take care of her, Edgar." Wide Boy stomped up the stairs to the attic.

"Before she falls off the roof and breaks her neck," Edgar called after him.

The twins restrained Ginger, keeping her comfy, and talking her down. One of them fetched a cold compress for Ginger and wiped her face and vomit-soaked clothing. Before Coming to Elvis, the twins had studied to be LPNs.

"Edgar, stay with me," said Ginger.

"I'm here, honeybun." He clasped her hand. "Not going yet."

"Why?"

"Because I love you, sugar booger," replied Edgar.

"No, I mean Jason. Why is he such an asshole?"

"Maybe because he's high-strung and the shock of Elvis for the first time was too much for him. Don't be troubled, honeybun. Everything's going to be okay."

Ginger gulped Gatorade the twins offered her and then buried her face in a satin pillow, still sobbing. But her convulsions had ceased, to Edgar's relief. She lay down again and the twins smoothed the plaid blanket.

"We'll take good care of her, Edgar," said one of the twins.

"You better go back to the Tribute, Edgar," said the other.

They were identical twins; Edgar knew their names but wasn't sure which one was which, and this both embarrassed and confused him, a ticklish problem. Edgar considered name tags or mismatched bikinis. Shire suggested tattoos, or branding.

"Okay," replied Edgar. But he hesitated to leave Ginger.

"Go on, Edgar, go now," both twins said, speaking in one emphatic voice, and shooed him out of the Jungle Room. The screen door slammed as Edgar left the house and hustled to the spring.

***

Shire drizzled the last few drops of chlorofornum into the greasy shop rag as he stood over Jason Root Then took the aerosol can of PAM and sprayed the rag with a thick coating and then hunkered down over Jason's supine body and clamped the rag over Jason's nose and mouth. He and Red had lugged Jason unconscious from the parking area out of sight to the garage under the corrugated tin roof. Didn't want to alarm the audience at the spring. Shire had dispatched the rest of his posse for crowd control and then Edgar lumbered down to the spring to reassure everybody and lead them in a singalong. People began to disperse, going back to their vehicles in the designated parking area outside the orange cones, and driving home. Jason's Toyota remained there.

Jason rocked with spasms under the rag, his eyes fluttered, and his arms flailed. Shire liked a victim with spunk. Made things more fun. Shire applied more pressure and with his free hand slapped him and then jammed his thumb into Jason's ear. Jason struggled, and then he was still. Shire stood, drenched in satisfaction, almost aroused.

"Dirt nap for this fucker?" said Red.

"Not yet, much as I'd like to. Edgar and his bitch would have a hissy fit. He's her fuck'n brother, you know."

"About time she cut some family ties," said

Red.

"Yeah, for sure, but they will take some convincing. You know how Edgar is about that. Besides, I'm nowhere near done with him. He fucked with me when he got here and I'm going to fuck with him, and I mean *fuck with*."

"Remind me to never get on your bad side."

"Don't worry, you're solid with me," said Shire. "Like family."

Red spat a black gob of Copenhagen into the palmetto. "Excuse me for being a weepy motherfucker, but that touches my heart."

Shire tossed the rag, empty brown glass bottle of chlorofornum, and the spray can of cooking oil in the trash can in the garage. He had extracted Jason's wallet, split the cash with Palatka Red, and had riffled through the ID and credit cards. "He'll be out for a while. I want to have a talk with Mr. Jason Root later."

"I'm there if you need backup," said Red.

"Bring pliers," said Shire. "For time being put his ass in the RV. Chinky bitches can keep an eye on him."

***

"Now you want massage?"

Jason woke up aching, his head throbbing, vision blurry. He lay supine, a squishy air mattress beneath him, on the floor of the RV. Lotus squatted beside him, holding an icy compress to his face. In the periphery of his vision, more girls lolled at the dinette, in tight shorts and halter tops.

Jason sat up. He groaned. "Oh, ouch. Fucking ouch."

Lotus gave him a toothy smile and pressed ice to the side of his head. She pointed at the girls at the dinette. "They are Luna, Toy, Ting Bo, and Amber."

"Hello," said Luna with green hair, Toy, Ting Bo, and Amber with pink hair.

"You are hurt," said Lotus. "Sam Fleance hit you with bat."

"Sam Fleance is mean son of bitch," declared Luna, and the girls nodded in agreement and Luna went on about how that mean old son of bitch Sam Fleance, they said it *flee-uhns,* did terrible mean nasty things to the tall, skinny strawberry girl.

"Drink tea," said Lotus. Offering him a cup of green tea and several ibuprofens.

"Thank you," said Jason. He swallowed the

pills and sipped the tea.

She whispered in his ear. "We must talk."

"I don't want a massage," Jason said.

"No, no, I must talk to you. Away from the other girls. It is important."

Jason pushed her away. "Not now. Thanks for the tea and the pills but no, I don't want a massage, and I don't want to talk. Some other time."

The other young women chattered. Resentments bubbled. Other members of the posse were arraigned in an informal tribunal, conducted in English and Chinese. Shire, the girls agreed, set a bad example. Shire has dark heart. Edgar good man but didn't know what was going on, Edgar in another world, Edgar in Elvis World. Bourbon, the dyke, she's mean, too, Luna said; the girls shuddered at mere mention of her name. Bourbon treats girls terrible! Torture! Whip! Hurt! Cigarette burns! Palatka Red, he is mean one too. But Wide Boy, they giggled, he plays nice. Not so bad as the others, Wide Boy is dumb like Edgar.

"I have to get out of here," said Jason. "Where are my pants and shoes?"

He wore only his blood-spattered Weyland-Yutani Corp t-shirt and a pair of navy-blue polyester-spandex Jockey shorts. He tried to stand, shaky on his feet. He wobbled. Lotus caught him.

"Better you do not go." Lotus reached out to steady him. "First, we should talk."

"To stay a while is nice," Luna said.

"No, no, I *have to* get out of here!"

"You want bananas?" Luna motioned to a bunch of bananas in a ceramic bowl on the foldout dinette.

"Bananas? No!" I need my pants and keys and wallet and Rolex and my iPhone."

"We take skins off," said Luna. "Watch how I peel skin." Her delicate fingers slowly stripped the peel away.

"Where are my things?"

"Ah," said Luna, crestfallen. "He doesn't want his banana peeled."

"They take your things," Lotus said. "And tell us to keep you here."

Jason plopped down on the mini couch in the RV and grabbed a pair of pink and black sneakers from the floor and squeezed his feet into them. Tight, but they fit. He looked at Luna, the tallest girl among them. "Give me your pants."

Luna balked. "You don't want your banana peeled but now you want my pants? Make up your mind!"

"Just give them to me! I need pants and yours are the most likely fit."

Luna peeled off her hot pink shorts and handed them to Jason. The girls laughed as he shimmied into them.

"Be careful." Lotus cautioned him as he moved toward the door. "It is dangerous." She clutched his arm and added, in a whisper, "Go to the white church. You will be safe there."

Jason opened the RV door a crack and peered out. Twilight. Darkness creeping over the pines. Parking lot empty. His Toyota remained where he had parked it. He spied the old man, Sam Fleance, and the red-haired girl huddled together in canvas chairs, foreheads pressed together. The aluminum bat leaned on cypress stump with a collection of empty beer cans and ashtray filled with butts. With all the stealth he could summon, Jason stepped out of the RV and took slow, furtive steps toward Sam Fleance. He saw the redheaded girl's t-shirt raised to her collarbones. The repulsive old man fondled her breasts, a cigarette dangling from his lip. The girl saw Jason first. Her stupid smile vanished; she gasped and raised her eyes, signaling the old man, and quickly covered her breasts. Jason grabbed the bat as Sam turned.

"Payback," said Jason, and whacked him with the bat.

The old man toppled out his chair and sprawled under the wheel of the RV. The skinny girl let loose a shrill, five-alarm shriek and rushed to the old man's aid. Papa, oh papa, you're hurt! Help! She didn't stop screaming.

Jason dropped the bat and ran headlong, in panic mode. Past the bronze Elvis to the highway. Hit the pavement and kept going. Heard shouting and commotion behind him. Shire's posse. Jason ran faster. He made it to Hygeia. The tall, black man in a loose tunic emerged from the derelict church, flailing his arms and shouting, a foreboding figure; Jason recoiled, and stumbled into the X-Press store.

"Are you alright, hon?" said Ardell behind the counter.

But her concern quickly turned to a deadly intent, and she wielded an ax. Her swing at Jason failed and shattered the sliding door of the ice cream cooler.

"I'm going to get you, hon," Ardell said, raising the ax again and waddling toward Jason, eyes burning with rage. "I was there! You should not of got Ginger upset like that. You damn near wrecked the Tribute, and we can't have that!"

Jason jumped as she swung the axe. He skittered down the aisle, almost tripping. Ardell pursued him. She morphed into gargoyle now; face distorted, eyes bulging, glowing red. She grunted with each wild swing of the axe, shattering the glass door of a cooler, destroying an aisle of canned goods, spitting, foaming at the corners of her mouth, and cursing with each missed swing.

She roared. "Give it up! You're not getting away!"

Jason fell, twisting his ankle, and Ardell pounced. A kick to his kidney immobilized him. Jason howled with pain.

"Bye-bye!" Ardell raised the blade above her head.

A deafening blast from the muzzle of a shotgun splattered her and sent her bulk reeling to crash into the beer cooler. The axe clattered on the floor. Ardell, now defunct, slid into a heap, a coppery, crimson stew.

Jason retched and then looked up. Two men stood before him. A hulk with shaggy hair and a beard bristly as a broom wielded a pump shotgun.

"Score," said his companion, a thin youth with short dark hair.

"Scratch that hell bound bitch." The hulk popped the orange plugs from his ears and slung the shotgun over his shoulder.

"You killed that woman," Jason said, in shock, his ears ringing.

"In case you didn't notice, pilgrim," said the hulk, "she was about to chop your fool head off."

The younger man hunkered down beside Jason and helped him to his feet. "We're the good guys. Taking you to safety, Jason."

"How do you know my name?"

"Dudek will explain."

They each took an arm and dragged Jason outside to a waiting panel van, its motor idling. A man in a fedora stood by the open side door and motioned for them to hurry. His saviors hustled Jason inside the white van. He skidded and sprawled on the plywood floor cover. The Fedora, presumably Dudek, plopped in a swivel chair beside him and slammed the panel door shut with a sharp chop like a guillotine falling. The other two hustled in front seats, the hulk driving, his shotgun discarded on the console between bucket seats. He clunked the van into drive, swung around, spitting gravel, and upon touching pavement, plunged the pedal. Tires screeched as they sped down the highway, away from Ococonee Spring and into the gathering darkness.

"Had to throw lead on the unholy," the hulk reported in a voice that suggested matter of fact and no big deal. Couldn't be helped. Shit happens.

Dudek nodded approval; his face concealed in dashboard light chiaroscuro. He turned to Jason. "Good evening. You're probably wondering what is going on."

"Yeah, I'm fucking wondering!" replied Jason. "Who are you guys? What just happened back there? How do you know my name?"

"One thing at a time. First, introductions. The belligerent bloke behind the wheel is Cody and that's Mincemeyer riding shotgun. I'm Dudek. In another life, I worked for the IRS. Now, I hunt demons."

***

Ococonee Spring, June 1992

An onerous task lay before them. They realized that direct confrontation with Becky Fenner, the mother-in-law and the boy's grandmother, was inevitable. Bob and Diane Dortch drove four hours from Cassadega, the spiritualist town where they lived, to Hygeia, Florida, in a twenty-year-old Mercedes-Benz with a freshly applied Clinton/Gore bumper sticker to reclaim their only grandson, the boy called Edgar. A rescue, an intervention. They had made their intention known to Mrs. Fenner.

But Becky Fenner wasn't having it. Wouldn't give an inch. They had met only once before at a table in a conference room, seeking to arbitrate the issue, and communicated only through an intermediary. Becky Fenner refused to relinquish custody. Thereafter she wouldn't take their calls —- she slammed the phone down —- or reply to their letters.

The Mercedes bounced down the rutted dirt drive. Becky Fenner, fiftyish and spry, marched out of the house and down the garden path between the azalea bushes as their car approached. She held up her hand. Stop! Bob Dortch braked the Mercedes and Becky, stout and almost six feet tall, strode toward the vehicle, not welcoming.

"Oh, my word," said Diane. "What an awful virago."

As Bob Dortch opened the car door, to his chagrin, Becky slammed it shut. Bob, taken by surprise, stared at her slack jawed. Beside him, Diane emitted a startled cry. Becky pointed to the road. *Go*, her lips mouthed the word as Bob Dortch rolled down the window.

"Mrs. Fenner, please, be reasonable."

"Didn't I make things clear to that cheap lawyer you hired?"

"The arbitration wasn't cheap," said Bob.

"What you paid him is your problem."

"Mrs. Fenner," said Bob. "Listen to us for five minutes."

"You got nothing to say to me and I got nothing to say to you."

Diane Dortch exited the air-conditioned car from the passenger side and stood to face Becky in the withering midday heat and humidity. "You must listen!"

"No, I don't," replied Becky.

"Will you have the courtesy and decency to listen to us for five minutes? Is that too much to ask?"

It was, but Becky reconsidered. The husband was cottage cheese, but his wife was something else Becky sensed, a tornado of a woman who would not be put off. Best to hear them out and then send them on their way. She sighed. "Alright, I'm listening. What have you got to say?"

"Our grandson is a gifted child."

"I know that!" Becky said.

"You have no idea! He has gifts of a spiritual nature. Possibly enormous gifts, equal to or exceeding those of his mother. Veronica was a prodigy. Perfect scores on Zemer card readings and the Voight-Kampff tests. She was clairvoyant. Her son is most certainly an empath too."

Gobbledygook, thought Becky.

Bob Dortch emerged gingerly from the Mercedes. "We think it best if Edgar is in our custody."

"He must come live with us in Cassadega," said Diane.

"That spooky town?" said Becky. "I don't think so. That is not in the cards."

Diane insisted. "It is an enlightened community of spiritual seekers and the best environment for a prodigy like Edgar. There, with the proper tutelage, he will thrive. You must defer to us in this matter. We have the training and experience in these matters. I possess a doctorate in spiritual psychology with Jungian emphasis and Bob is a credited psychical investigator."

"You don't say!" Well, weren't they all highfalutin and looking down their noses at Becky Fenner. Alright, she had listened to them. That was all she said she'd do.

"Hogwash," said Becky. "Edgar's a normal boy. Sure, he's got some problems but what child wouldn't what had lost his mama."

"I'll be frank," Diane Dortch replied, "You are not capable of recognizing abilities that transcend the normative. You are out of your depth here."

"Bless your heart! You come onto my

property, to my home, and talk to me like that? That's some nerve!"

Diane remained adamant. "It would be cruel to raise the boy without the proper training and refinement of his abilities. Without proper guidance, there is no telling what fate may befall him."

"Don't lecture me about what's cruel," said Becky. "I know what you people are like. Ronnie told me all about you. Why do you think she ran away?"

Both Dortch's reacted as if they had been slapped. Bob sputtered with indignation, his wife with consternation.

"Her training was necessarily strict. Rigor is required. Psychical science is a serious discipline."

"Bunk!" Becky Fenner's booming voice ascended to the tops of the scraggly pines. "You call it science! You were 'training' her to talk to ghosts and spirits and boogeymen and whatnot and that is a buttload of bunk. The poor girl was wasting away under your so-called training. Ate like a bird, had no appetite, starving in more ways than one. Only real fun she ever had was with my boy Walt. Nobody but yourselves to blame for her not wanting anything to do with you."

"Veronica was willful," said Diane. "She rebelled, as teenagers are prone to do. She failed to mature and was foolishly infatuated with your son. Now Veronica has died, and the father has abandoned the boy."

"Don't badmouth my son," said Becky. "Walt hasn't abandoned Edgar. Walt is not that sort. Edgar is safe and sound right where he is here at Ococonee Spring with his Gamaw and his auntie taking care of him while his daddy is working in Biloxi and sending money on a regular schedule. We love Edgar while *you people*, well, I will you give my unvarnished opinion. For you, Edgar is just another quack science experiment. A guinea pig."

"How dare you!" said Diane.

"That isn't so," her husband said. "Simply isn't so."

"Oh, hush, both of you. You folks have driven a long way for nothing. Edgar stays here and you won't get near him as long as I'm breathing, and I'll thank you for getting your butt off my property before I call the sheriff. Who is also named Fenner, by the way. It is a respectable name hereabouts." She turned and strode away.

The screen door slammed as Becky reentered the house, leaving Bob and Dortch exasperated and dumbfounded. Diane plopped down on the seat. Bob rolled up his window, started the engine, and dialed the AC full blast.

"I could weep," said Diane.

"We could litigate," said Bob.

"No, that is futile. We do not have a legal case. Sternhagen already told us."

"We could consult another attorney. Get a second opinion."

"One lawyer is enough." The legal profession, like the medical establishment, was grounded in cupidity, skepticism, and materiality, in opposition to the spiritual enlightenment that Bob and Diane Dortch lived their lives for. As her husband put the Benz in reverse and turned around to leave the Fenner property, Diane turned her gaze to the Fenner house and emitted a deep, solemn sigh.

"I feel drained by that woman," said Diane, "and by this terrible humidity and this terrible primitive place. Florida has so few civilized places and so much squalor. There is a dark, ruinous aura about that house. Did you notice?"

"No," replied Bob. "My chakras are out of alignment and I'm a bit slow on the uptake. I must get grounded with gemstones as soon as we're home."

Diane nodded; she retained a firm belief in healing crystals. Then, looking back over her shoulder and disquieted by what she sensed, she murmured. "It lingers, the aura, purple like a bruise. It bodes ill."

***

Becky peered out the window as the dark blue Mercedes coupe vanished down the dirt road. Whew! She hoped that was the last of *them*. Cranks, quacks, not good people. She could see right through that veneer of sanctimony and do-gooder. Edgar was hers, well, hers and Katie's and his daddy's, and those goofy people had no right to him. They were never going to do to Edgar what they'd done to their own daughter, Ronnie. Over Becky's dead body. She returned to the parlor where five-year-old Edgar watched alone, because her younger sister Katie was at work in Newberry at the Family Dollar checkout. Katie worked and Walt C worked because they had to make ends meet until the bankers in Tallahassee straightened out the sale of the old Fenner turpentine farm, cleared the liens and title, worked out the DEP problems, and got the family trust set up. Once established, the trust would pump out money annually to the Fenner recipients. Edgar's future was secure.

Becky had converted the parlor into an Elvis memorial, whom both sisters had loved with an enduring love, a true and pure love, for over three decades. The Greatest Entertainer of All Time. Not even death diminished his greatness. Photos and posters adorned the walls, a wooden bin held Elvis LP records and on the shelves were stacks of DVD Elvis movies and a collection of liquor bottles in the shape of Elvis. And in place of honor on the wall above a bronze bust of the King, was the most valuable mementos of all, framed and displayed. A ragged shred of frilly pink cloth from the shirt Elvis wore at a concert, which had been torn to shreds along with his fancy pink jacket and tie by adoring fans. Becky and Katie, wild and high-spirited kids at the time, had been present at the Beginning of Elvis Mania. Wolfson Park, the new baseball stadium in Jacksonville, Florida, 1955. Elvis wasn't a headliner then, only a feature act on the bill of the Hank Snow jamboree, and old shorty Hank and the other country singers really didn't like or understand Elvis or his music or his style. They denigrated Elvis as an oddball upstart who mimicked colored singers and didn't belong on the stage with the likes of Hank Snow or Andy Griffith. But Elvis struck lightning bolts of greatness and performed with V-8 powered energy and the audience responded. Becky and Katie were there, screaming like the others and fell in love with Elvis that concert, that day, that moment, forever more. Elvis, the great big hunk of forbidden fruit fallen into their humdrum lives, had said to his audience at the close of his act, "Thank you ladies and gentlemen, and girls, I'll see you backstage." And that set it off. Both sisters had been in that throng that invaded backstage in wild maenad pursuit of Elvis. Becky's hand had snatched that piece of cloth. She treasured it and intended to be buried with it. Even now, gazing upon it kindled memories and induced a deep pleasurable sigh. Time didn't mean a thing. She was twenty-one again at Wolfson Park.

"Who was here, Gamaw?" Edgar said from the sofa.

Having finished his baloney and cheese sandwich, except for the crusts, he sat eating Mallomars and a Moon Pie, sipping strawberry milk, and watching a DVD from Becky and Katie's collection. *Charro!* An Elvis Western and not one of those spaghetti Westerns with Clint Eastwood. In the movie, Elvis sported a beard and Edgar at first could hardly recognize the King. He got upset at first but watching the movie a second time, he loved it. At times, Becky had to work like the dickens to keep the boy calm. He got upset often. Couldn't breathe. Got heart palpitations. Imagined he saw scary things. He needed hugs and a shoulder or a bosom to cry upon. Food worked too. So did Elvis movies.

"Oh, nobody, hon. Just some people."

"My name's Wade," the bearded, roughshod Elvis said on the screen, a tough hombre in a cantina, the handsome stranger who rode into town, scowling as if afflicted with flaming saddle rump. "Jess Wade. Mean anything to you?"

"No, Charro," replied the Mexican bartender.

Edgar didn't lift his eyes from the TV screen. He chewed on a chunk of Moon Pie. "They wanted to take me away with them, didn't they?"

"Don't talk with food in your mouth, Edgar. That's uncouth."

"I'm sorry, Gamaw. Did they want to take me

away?"

"Wherever did you get that idea, Edgar?"

"I don't know," replied Edgar. "Sometimes … "

"Sometimes what, sweetheart?" She sat next to him on the lumpy sofa and draped an arm across his shoulders. She tousled his hair. The boy had secrets and Becky made it her business to pry them out of him. "You can tell Gamaw."

"Sometimes people talk to me inside my head."

"What people?"

"They don't tell me names."

"Well," said Becky, "you don't listen. That's not real, hon. Lot of things might seem real, but are not. It's like old Bill Shakespeare said, the stuff dreams are made of. You got to know the difference and not be afeared of things that aren't real and can't hurt you."

"Those people who were here want me to live with them in that town with the funny name and teach me to talk to people … who passed." The boy shivered. He couldn't speak of death. Not since its cold touch, his mother's passing.

Becky hugged him, smothering him with her ample breasts. "That is not going to happen. Don't you worry, dumpling, nobody is taking you anywhere. You're staying right here at Ococonee Spring."

"Okay," said Edgar, reassured. He watched the TV. "If I talked to people who passed, I'd like to talk to Elvis."

"Elvis isn't dead," said Becky.

"He's not?"

"No, he is not. You know why? Because love is more powerful than death and millions of people love Elvis. Passing doesn't mean the end of us. You're alive so long as somebody remembers and loves you or you have family to continue after you. That's the secret. Don't ever forget. Promise your Gamaw who loves you, precious, promise you won't ever forget."

"I promise," said Edgar.

***

Shire Fenner paced and forth in the Jungle Room and ranted.

"If you'd listened to me," he said, "we wouldn't have this problem. Never should of let her call that old man. Never should of let that brother of hers stay for the Tribute. Didn't I tell you? Didn't I, Edgar?"

Edgar made a calm and forthright reply. "It was the right thing to do." He still wore his Tribute MC threads, now stained with blood and vomit. "Now stop making a fuss, Shire. You're getting Ginger even more upset, and we can't have that."

"Fuck her," Shire said under his breath.

Edgar snapped at Shire. "What did you say, Shire?"

"Didn't say nothin'."

"You had better watch it, Shire. Or you and me will go to the woodshed."

"The woodshed?" Shire laughed. "I don't think so, Edgar."

"I'm warning you, Shire."

"Shut up, Edgar. Tell you what. I'll talk and you listen for a change."

But Edgar's attention immediately diverted to Ginger, who lay on the couch wrapped in a blanket like a mummy, her head in Edgar's lap, her face red from bawling and sobbing, her eyes glassy. It had taken an hour and the combined efforts of the twins and Edgar to ratchet down her rage and stop her puking and then she lapsed into a crying jag. Edgar stroked her hair to console her.

Kat Condon had abandoned her former life when she Came to Elvis but hadn't cut all the strings. Edgar had tossed her driver's license and student ID and everything else from her purse but kept the iPhone. She had wanted to contact her family. She begged. Didn't want them to worry, wanted to let them know she was alright and happy in her new life at Ococonee Spring. That was only fair, Edgar agreed. Uh-uh, Shire had argued otherwise, but couldn't convince Edgar. Family remained family, Edgar insisted. Ties that bind. Ties couldn't be severed so drastic like, Edgar had insisted. Snip, snip, snip, retorted Shire. But Edgar allowed that she ought to call her stepfather, who cared about her, and the mother in Ashville she didn't have a good relationship with and who, it turned out, wasn't all that concerned anyway. Now Shire blasted his brother with *I told you so!*

"She wanted to call the old man," said Shire. "And like a pussy-whipped sap, you let her, and that uppity sneaky stepbrother showed up, and here we are."

"I thought there was a chance that he would Come to Elvis just like she did."

Ginger wailed and then sobbed. Edgar comforted her. Tried to shoo away Shire but Shire, adamant, continued pacing, indifferent to both Ginger and Shire. His mind cogitated. Dark suspicions surfaced. Some concocted on the spot and accepted by Shire as incontrovertibly true. Jason Root was in cahoots with that roving pack of Elvis killers. Had been the whole time! Bloody goddam mess in the X-Press proved it. Shire's posse was there now, cleaning up. A sign in the window read reopening soon under new management. Going to plant Ardell in the boneyard behind the old shed with the corrugated tin roof. Getting crowded there. Shire shrugged. So what? Worms got to eat. Ardell died for the cause, a martyr to Graceland, but what the hell, can't make an omelet without breaking a few, and anyway, Shire had to focus on the problem at hand. He stiffened, backbone straight and strong as steel. Hey, he thought, there might could maybe be a way to seize advantage out of this. Had to a be way and Shire Fenner would find it.

"Up to me to fix things," Shire announced.

"Shire," Edgar said, "please don't do nothing without talking to me first."

"Sure," replied Shire, *thinking like hell I will*. He plopped his butt on an ottoman by the couch and zeroed in on Ginger and shook her shoulder, not gently. "Hey, girl. Wake up. Tell me more about your sugar daddy."

Ginger stirred. Opened her teary eyes, sniffled, swallowed, and wiped her nose on the sleeve of Edgar's shirt. "I don't have a sugar daddy. I belong to Elvis the King and Edgar is my Teddy Bear."

"Yes, you do got a sugar daddy. The old fart in The Villages. Your stepdaddy. He's got oodles of money. Your stepbrother Jason said so. He flashed a wad of money and wanted to buy one of the chinky girls. To do nasty things to her."

"No, he didn't." Ginger, sniffled. "Jason wouldn't do that."

"I saw for myself. Him flashing money. He wanted five girls, now that I recall. One for each limb."

"You're making that up," said Ginger.

"Leave her be, Shire," said Edgar.

"I get a little cooperation here, and you two can go back to playing house and smooching. Tell me about daddy's money, girl. Talk to me!"

"Yes, Harve's got money!" said Ginger.

"In a bank? What bank?"

"Harve doesn't trust banks. He has a safe in his house."

Even better! Shire stroked his chin. Now he was getting somewhere, making real progress. Here was something to make a go of. "So, he's got a big old safe and it's chockful a green cash money. Is that what you're saying? I like the sound of that, I surely do. Upwards of how much?"

Ginger fidgeted. "I don't know!"

"Probably enough, huh? Tell me where old Harve lives. His street address."

"No," said Ginger.

"It's okay, honeybun," said Edgar, "Give brother Shire what he wants, and he'll go about his business and leave us alone."

Ginger told him. Shire rummaged through a drawer and found a scrap of paper and a pencil stub and had her repeat while he chicken-scratched the address. He grinned, inspired. Gleam in his eye. He unsnapped the pearl button of his shirt pocket and crumpled the paper inside.

"Okay, Edgar, I got this."

"You got what?"

"A fuck'n plan," said Shire.

***

Jason said, "IRS? Really?"

Dudek said, "Who would claim to work for IRS who did not?"

Jason huddled on the floor of the vehicle, sipping hot coffee from a thermos Mince handed him from the front seat. "Okay, I'll concede. IRS, that's credible. But hunting demons?"

"You've already witnessed," replied Dudek.

"I'm still processing."

"You can't unsee what you saw in the spring. But we'll save further conversation for after we arrive at our destination."

"Where is that?"

"What he means," the gravelly-voiced Cody said over his shoulder, "is you should shut up for now."

Dudek's phone chimed. He drew it out of his pocket and glanced at the screen, his face hardening into consternation. He then swiped the screen to delete the message and jammed the phone in his pocket again.

"I didn't think you could get service out here," said Jason.

"No, you can't," Dudek said.

The van scudded along dark two-lane county

roads. Slash pines and grotesque oaks draped with ghostly moss flitted by on either side of the road. Jason's rescuers, now his captors, did not speak further. Mince munched potato chips. Offered some to Jason, who declined. Cody slurped Mountain Dew. He clicked on the radio, a Classic Rock station out of Tampa. *Sweet Home Alabama* blared out of the speakers. Followed, ominously, by *Hotel California.* A song Jason disliked by a band he disliked but that you had to be living in a mine shaft or a missile silo in North Dakota for the past half century not to have heard a thousand times. The cryptic lyrics sharpened Jason's unease. Damned synchronicity. Jason too was trapped, in a world suddenly ominous and surreal. The relentless dual-guitar fandango that concluded the nightmare, and foreclosed any escape, made his head throb. Relieved when it ended, he wasn't reassured by the next tune on the station playlist, Ozzy Osbourne going off the rails on the crazy train.

Off the grid was not a preferred destination however safe it might prove. Jason had no idea what direction they were travelling, and in the pitch dark no landmarks were visible, nothing, a bleak stygian airless void. But these men had, after all, saved his life. Jason allocated that to the plus side. On the minus side, however, they remained strangers, *weird* strangers pursuing unknown objectives, armed and dangerous, holding him a de facto prisoner, and they smelled of sweat, body odor, and halitosis. Arrival at Ococonee Springs had plunged Jason into a murky world. *Abandon all hope ye who enter*, like that, reality gone pear-shaped and malignant. Jason was along for the ride, and not by choice, on a crazy train. Where was the off-ramp?

The van slowed, turned sharp left, and rumbled down an unpaved road. Jason craned his neck to peer out the windshield. A ramshackle Cracker cottage with a screened front porch materialized out of the darkness on a spit of land, surrounded by thickets of mangrove and sea grape. Dim lights glowed inside. Cody parked the van in a row of vehicles and all of them trundled out. Moths fluttered in the cone of light from the floodlamp over the porch.

"Welcome to our hideout," said Mince. "Off the grid, and safe."

"Great to be here," Jason replied. "And meet new people."

"Nobody likes a smartass," Cody huffed.

They went inside through the rickety screen door with screaming hinges. The cottage was redolent with incense; cedar, citrus, and patchouli to mask the odor of cooking oil, sweat, and musty furniture. Jason almost gagged. He surveyed the interior. Wood paneling, a sagging parquet floor, windows boarded over or covered with tarp. Crucifixes hung on the walls, along with parchments upon which words were scrawled in what looked like Greek or Latin or Hebrew. A primitive kitchen, gas stove and battered microwave. Black cast iron skillets and pans. A gun cabinet and crude, cinder-block-and-pine-plank shelves with ammo boxes and votive candles in glass cups. Tattered chairs with multifarious stains and burns, an overstuffed sofa, and a spool table formed a parlor. Mince and Cody retreated to the kitchen to feast upon White Castle sliders heated in a noisy microwave, its faulty magnetron in its death throes. They provided Jason clothing; khaki pants in place of the tight shorts he'd taken from Luna in the RV, that Cody remarked made him look like a sissy. White gym socks, and work shoes, brand new and stiff, replaced his footwear. Jason plopped on the couch. Dudek brought a white swirl coffee carafe to the table and poured a mug of steaming hot black coffee for Jason, then sat in a chair facing him.

Dudek opened his windbreaker, revealing a

black shirt and a dingy white priest's collar around his neck.

"By the way," he said, "it is *Father* Dudek. Vows and all, the whole nine yards."

In good light now, Jason saw the priest was a stocky middle-aged man, blonde hair turning gray and receding over his forehead, hard hazel eyes, and deep pouches underneath them, a trim goatee on his prominent chin. Dudek removed a small pistol, a black Beretta with a threaded barrel, from the shoulder holster he wore along with a laminated scapular on a nylon cord. He ceremoniously dropped the Beretta's magazine, unchambered a hollow point round, and deposited these in a ceramic bowl on the spool table with a loud clink. He replaced the unloaded pistol in its holster. A gesture of good faith, Jason surmised.

"Relax, Jason. You're safe with us. For the time being."

"Am I?" Jason gripped his coffee mug. Relaxation, under the circumstances, remained a remote possibility. Dudek's priestly demeanor and smile did not reassure him.

"I promised you an explanation," said Dudek.

"Captive audience. Start anytime."

Dudek ignored the sarcasm. He lit a cigarette from a loose pack on the table and offered one to Jason.

"Thanks, but I don't smoke," said Jason. "I try to avoid carcinogens."

"You're a sensible young man." Dudek continued. "Yes, I used to be an IRS Revenue Agent, an auditor in SBSE, the Small Business and Self-Employed Division, working out of Tampa."

"Must've been fascinating work. Can we skip ahead to the part where you tell me what the hell is going on."

"Be patient," Dudek said. "Sarcasm I understand. A defensive mechanism. I choose to overlook it. To make a long story short, I was assigned a brokerage firm to audit, an LLC owned by a shady character named Argyron Stavropoulos."

"Sounds Greek," said Jason.

"He was Albanian. actually." Dudek continued. "An ethnic Greek from a region in southern Albania known as Epirus, with a rich history of witchcraft and related chicanery. The audit should've been a routine case. But to my shock and horror, I discovered Argyron

Stavropoulos traded in human souls."

"Huh?" said Jason.

"You heard me correctly," said Dudek. "Imagine my shock. Argyron Stavropoulos sold Satanic subscriptions. He lured, he enticed, and he doomed souls to perdition. A Ponzi scheme of the damned. He worked assiduously to meet his quotas."

"Did he try to sell you a subscription?"

"Blandishments were offered." Ash accumulated on the tip of Dudek's Marlboro Light. The silence grew awkward. "Of course, you're incredulous."

Jason nodded. As any right-minded person would be, he thought. Because this sounded nuts, even if the demeanor of the priest was perfectly sedate and rational.

"My superiors at IRS were also incredulous. They shelved my career. They brought false charges of misconduct against me. Thus, did I leave government service, renouncing Title 26 to pursue a higher calling." Dudek flicked ash. "What I realized is that the Deep State, so-called … and that's merely a tabloid, pulp fiction name … but, by whatever name it is known, it is not only real but deeply infiltrated."

"Infiltrated?" A loaded word. Jason, wary, decided that this was not an opportune time to be a smart ass.

"By occultists," said Dudek. "Those who seek to subvert. Working with secular ideologues who remain none the wiser. I wrestled not against flesh and blood, nor against complacent bureaucracy and run-of-the-mill venality, but against principalities, powers, spiritual wickedness in high places."

"Amen!" thundered Cody from the kitchen, as he chomped on a White Castle burger. He stood with a burst of flatulence and his chair scraped the floor. "It's not just bullshit you find on internet sites."

"So," Jason said. "You hunt demons, You're … like … *exorcists*?"

"As a priest, I do the X-work. But our primary mission is tactical."

Tactical? Jason's gaze drifted to the gun cabinet. "You guys are well-armed."

"In the battle between good and evil," said Dudek, "the archangels are armed. But we are mortal, we're on earth, and don't carry flaming swords. But enough about us. We need to talk about Jason Root. You must be debriefed, Jason." Dudek pulled his chair closer to Jason. "Tell us everything that you witnessed at Ococonee. Everything. Omit nothing, no small detail."

Cody lumbered into the parlor and plopped in a chair beside Jason. He slurped coffee. "We got all night, pilgrim."

***

Hours later, pale sunlight crept over the Florida peninsula toward the cottage and the impenetrable mangrove.

"And you *still* haven't told me," Jason said, buzzing with caffeine, "how you knew my name."

"We have informants inside Ococonee Spring. More than that I cannot divulge." Dudek sipped coffee and plucked another Marlboro Light from the crumpled package. "Now, let's go over it one more time, shall we. Start with meeting your father in the restaurant. When he voiced misgivings about your sister."

"Stepsister," said Jason.

He sat sweating in the overstuffed, tattered sofa, surrounded by his three relentless interlocutors, like cops grilling a suspect, and who seemed to have no need for sleep. Jason had consumed so much thick black Cuban coffee he feared his swollen bladder would burst.

"Is this how you broke people down at IRS?"

"Cigarette?" Dudek shook one out of the pack of Marlboro Lights.

"I don't smoke. But on second thought, oh, what the fuck." He snatched a cigarette, balanced on his lower lip as Dudek lighted for him. Blue flame dancing on the Bic proved startling, a conflagration; Jason stared. He inhaled. Coughed. Exhaled. Coughed again. Remembered he hated nicotine and then, regardless, took another deep drag on the cigarette. The drooping skin under his eyes felt like melted lead and his head reeled. "Look, guys, I've told you and told you, everything that happened, that I witnessed. Will you let me sleep? This is grueling. I'm exhausted."

"Soon you can sleep." Dudek remained an imperturbable, black-frocked block of ice. "One more time."

"No, I can't," Jason protested. He pointed at the boarded-up windows. "Look, for fucksake, it's getting light out."

Towering over Jason, Cody stepped between him and the window, as big as Pavarotti and declaiming in a deep tenor. "Jason Root, do you want to save your sister's soul from damnation, or not?"

"Stepsister," said Jason.

"Save her or not? You *saw* it, slick. The demonic infestation, the beast, the unholy spunk, the beta programming slaves, all of it. You witnessed it."

"You've stumbled into the no man's land between two opposing forces," said Dudek. "One side is Evil. The battle must be fought."

"Boots on the ground," said Mince.

Jason teetered. Head reeling. Disoriented. Caffeine high. A no man's land, alright, a febrile looking-glass world, and these men, the priest in black and his rough-edged cohorts, were sinister smudges on its distorted surface.

"In or out, Jason," Dudek insisted. "No gray areas, no fifty shades. Save your sister or let her, and many others, succumb to evil and die horribly. Or join us. *Elvis delenda est.*"

Fatigue dragged on Jason. Menthol burned. He coughed. He drifted in a sleepless haze. Dudek, Cody and Mince remained silent and stony, gazing at him, like judges in timeworn chairs, implacable, waiting for his plea. As if the fractured hours meant nothing, as if the approaching dawn meant nothing.

"Her name is Kat. Okay, sign me up. I'm red pilled. I'll be on your team."

"Do you swear?" Cody loomed over him.

"Pinkie pledge, whatever you want."

"This is serious," said Cody. "Like a blood oath."

"I'm in! Okay? I swear, I swear. Can I sleep now?"

Dudek nodded, Cody and Mince relented, and Jason stretched out on the lumpy couch and in seconds was asleep.

***

They cruised down the highway in the Pink Cadillac, searching for cell phone reception. Not a Classic Fifties Cadillac with pointy shark fins above its taillights but a more sedate Seville, twenty years old, with bald tires, worn upholstery, and a leaky oil pan. Originally beige, Shire had supervised its paint job. An uneven paint spray had left splotches and drips. Shire slouched on the leather upholstery beside Wide Boy at the wheel, 12-gauge between them in addition to the revolvers they both carried. In the capacious back seat, Edgar cuddled Ginger.

"You got bars yet?" Shire said over his shoulder. "Ought to have bars by now. We're halfway to fuck'n G-ville."

"Watch your language, Shire."

"Bars or not?"

"Not yet," said Edgar, holding Ginger's iPhone. "No bars."

"I want to go back to Ococonee Spring," said Ginger.

"Me too and we will, honeybun, just as soon as we get this done."

"I'm hungry," said Ginger. "Feed me."

"Find some place, Shire," Edgar said.

"I could eat," said Wide Boy.

Shire grumbled. Little bitch ate like a bird, a *vulture*. She was always hungry but never gained a pound, fancy that. She vomited a lot, often projectile, and Shire reckoned that might explain it. Shire tapped Wide Boy on the shoulder and Wide Boy sped up. They drove into Newberry on 232, the small town just waking up on a Saturday morning. Something fast,

Edgar insisted. No time for a sit-down restaurant; they had to make the call and return to the spring pronto to restore Ginger. Edgar directed Cousin Harlan – he never called him Wide Boy – to turn into the Hardee's drive-thru. They ordered chicken biscuits and OJ and then Wide Boy parked the Caddy in the shade. Everybody ate except Shire who slurped black coffee. His impatience didn't abate.

"Got bars?"

"We do at last, Shire," replied Edgar. He handed the phone to Ginger.

"Here's what I want you do say." Shire had already composed the message in his mind. He got on his knees and talked over the seat. "You say that you're happy as can be, a happy little chickadee, and that your brother Jason —- "

"Stepbrother," said Ginger.

"You two had a nice visit, and everything is okay, and add heart emojis and happy shit like that."

Ginger tapped the phone as Edgar looked over her shoulder. "No, hon, not turd emojis! Shire didn't mean that literal. Erase those and, Shire, telling you for the umpteenth time, watch your language. There you go, honey bunny. Now send. Okay. Shire, let's get back to Ococonee Spring, pronto."

Shire slapped Wide Boy's shoulder. "You heard Edgar! Drive! Got to get the lovebirds back to the nest."

Wide Boy bundled his Monster Biscuit in its wrapper, tossed it on the dash and started the ignition. The engine churned and blew black smoke, tires screeched on pavement, and in seconds they were rolling back toward Ococonee Spring.

***

Jason rolled off the couch, landing on the floor with a thud. His eyes popped open. The aroma of coffee and bacon filled his nose; he heard the sizzle. Cody stood over the stove brandishing tongs. He looked at Jason. Jolly this morning, a friendly Sasquatch working as short-order cook.

"You want eats, pilgrim? We're running out of grub so might as well feast while we still got something to eat."

"I'm starving," Jason replied, picking himself up from the floor. He stumbled to the table to confront heaps of scrambled egg, bacon, fried potatoes and burnt toast. Mince blamed the toaster.

Cody transferred bacon from the skillet to a bed

of cozy paper towels on a paper plate and then plopped in a chair and attacked breakfast, spooning scrambled eggs, and dousing them with Tabasco.

"Eat," Cody said to Jason. "Mama Landry didn't raise her boy not to say grace. I said a sort of blanket grace over the stovetop."

Famished, ravenous, Jason ate. He remained dazed, suspicious, and sore, but hunger took precedence. They offered food; he'd take advantage. Hunger improved the taste of anything. Between mouthfuls he said, "You guys are priests too?"

"Hell, no," replied Cody. "I was Southern Baptist, but I quit the Evangelical-Industrial Complex. Too many greed heads and hypocrites and pharisees. But don't get me started on that subject."

"For real," said Mince, chomping on burnt toast. "Don't get him started."

"Mincemeyer was a grunt and earned his battle scars. Two tours in the Stan in the Great Gee-Wot."

"Gee-Wot What is that?" Jason spooned more scrambled egg on his paper plate.

"The Global War on Terror," replied. Mince.

"Or the Gigantic Waste of Time. Take your pick."

Cody snorted. "There's a dog that didn't hunt. Pissed away a lot of lives and trillions of dollars Twenty years trying to fix a place ain't fixable in a thousand years." Then he added, as an afterthought, "Mince fought yeti there."

"Yeti?" said Jason. "Whoa, wait, no, uh-uh, a mindboggling moment here. Don't tell me that because there's no such thing."

"Beg to differ. Yeti killed my squad except for me and my sarnt."

"You're saying you *fought* them?"

"Roger that," said Mince, "and they are bad asses."

"You were in Tibet?"

"No, Afghanistan." Mince slathered orange-jalapeño marmalade on a shingle of blackened toast. "They migrated from Tibet to escape the Chicoms destroying their habitat. My platoon was in the Waadi Valley, narrow strip of Afghanistan between the stans of the Pakis and the Tajikis, like a finger checking China's prostate."

Mince gestured, drawing a map in the air with his toast, and Jason tried to visualize the finger and the

190

prostate but without success. Mince added a strip of crisp bacon to his toast and chomped, chewed, and swallowed, washing down the toast with a gusher of black coffee.

"We were on patrol," Mince went on, "hunting Taliban in the Hindu Kush. Ran into a troop of yetis instead. Grim as all fuck that action. Anyway, the Echelons Above Reality put a lid on it. Enemy combatants mistaken for large primates, the official narrative. Me and the sarnt got medals, medical discharges, disability and all the paxil we wanted and all we had to do in return was not tell the truth. After that I started studying cryptids and other weird phenomena and met Cody and the padre at a convention in Reno and here I am today, eating toast and fighting demons, and you can too!" Mince pointed a carbonized crust of toast at Jason. Crumbs and flecks of marmalade flew like shrapnel.

"Cool," said Jason, hoping to placate them. They were all buddies now, sharing breakfast and war stories that strained credulity. Jason finished eating, sipped coffee blanched with powder creamer, and summoned the sangfroid that he hoped had fully recharged overnight. "Say, how about — if it's not too much trouble — giving me a ride home to Tampa?"

They looked at him askance, in silence.

"Nope," Cody replied.

"Dudek will not approve," said Mince.

"You need Dudek's say so? Okay. I'll talk to him right now."

"No, you won't, pilgrim. He's asleep. Exhausted, man. *Do not disturb.* And let me remind you, you're sworn. You stay with the team until the mission is finished."

Jason insisted. "You know, you guys got no legal right to not let me leave if I decide to leave. You are aware of that, right?" He leveled his *You're not that stupid, are you?* look at them. To no effect, however. They wouldn't budge.

"Let me show you something," Mince said to Jason. "Come outside. You probably missed it in the dark last night."

Jason followed. They halted a few steps from the threshold of the cottage. Cool outside in the morning light; slow, feathery cirrus strayed over a blue sky; the Gulf of Mexico glistened beyond the tangle of mangrove. Cody pointed at a white line in the dirt, several inches thick, circling the cottage.

"What am I supposed to be looking at?" said

Jason.

"Protection," Cody said. "Don't step over the line."

Mince said, "Salt, crushed coquina, alabaster, and some stuff we can't tell you about and you probably wouldn't believe us if we did. Anyway, it forms a barrier. Concealment. It's sanctified."

Jason stepped to the edge of the line. "Sanctified? Did I hear you right? What is this? A magic show?"

"Operational security," said Mince. "Inside the circle, we're safe. We're cloaked. Outside the circle, you could find yourself in a world of shit. Evil won't pounce immediately, it bides its time, cruising like a shark searching for blood in the water."

Jason stared at the holy chalk-shell-alabaster-secret-ingredient consecrated circle in the Florida sand. A tiny lizard skittered over the line with impunity, reptiles perhaps not a participant in the Manichean battle between good and evil. Jason noted the Chevy van and other vehicles parked *outside* the circle, but he refrained from inquiring if Evil could mess with the ignition system, clog fuel filters, or steal license plates.

Cody grumbled. "Don't believe it if you don't want to. Just two things. Don't wake Dudek and stay inside the circle."

***

Luanne and Lynette, the twin sisters who'd Come to Elvis and recruited for household duties scurried around the house in matching polka dot bikinis, flipflops flapping, matching rhinestone barrettes adorning their blonde hair. They cooked, cleaned the old house, did chores, fetched, entertained, and took care of Ginger and Auntie Kate too, a real difficult job. Wide Boy assisted them with Kate, standing guard in case the crazy old auntie became unruly or combative. At night, the twins curled up like house cats and slept together in chairs or on the sofa or in Shire's bed, always on call, 24/7, never leaving the house except to go to the spring. They watched Elvis movies in the Jungle Room during their few off hours, drinking Cheerwine Cherry or ginger ale with maraschino cherries bobbing in the fizz. They did whatever they were told, even wrestling together in nothing but white panties, and remained pleasant and starry-eyed Elvis fans. Shire liked to boss, tease, spank, and torment them but he didn't have the time today.

Because *Shire Fenner had a plan.* He chased out the twins and took Edgar aside to confer in the Jungle Room and lay out his plan.

"I can't approve of that," said Edgar.

"Sure, you can," said Shire. "It's a cinch to pull off, and it's fair."

"No, Shire. It is thieving."

"Things have changed, Edgar! That filthy old man sent his flunky son to take Ginger. Tried to snatch her happy ass right from under you. Reason enough right there. Not to mention both the son and the old man are in cahoots with *them.*"

"We don't know that for certain," Edgar said.

"Yes, we do," said Shire. "He told me. The brother told me and had the nerve to *brag* about it."

"When was this?"

Shire, having a gift for the impromptu lie, didn't hesitate. "When I questioned him. Before he escaped, which was no fault of mine. That was the fault of people I thought I could trust but you know, Edgar, want a thing done right, you got to do it your own self. Anyway, I gave him a right good third-degree and. man, did he talk! Spit in my face too.

He hates us in case you didn't know. Hates you, hates me, hates Ginger, hates Elvis. They were waiting to pick him up in Hygeia. You think that was a coincidence?"

Shire saw that Edgar teetered, and he relished his big brother's pained expression and weakness. All Edgar needed was a good push ...

"They were waiting, and they drew blood too. Poor Ardell. You should've seen the mess at the X-press. A real *bloodbath*."

Ever squeamish at mention of blood, Edgar shuddered. "Don't say no more about it. Don't want to hear about it."

"Don't think about it," said Shire. "Don't think about all that blood and gore and awful stink, Edgar. Don't think about Ardell, her innards slopped all over the floor."

Edgar seized a waste basket and doubled over, dry heaving. Shire, suppressing a grin, patted Edgar on the back.

"Thinking about it is my job. Doing something about it is my job too. Got to retaliate! That old man, with all that money lying around, he's behind all this. He's paying those people!"

"I don't know," said Edgar. "I better ask Elvis."

"Okay, ask Elvis," said Shire. "Don't be chickenshit. Let's go! Right now."

They left the house. Edgar traipsed to the spring, Shire prodding and badgering him all the way from the house like a chihuahua nipping at a lumbering sheepdog. Then Shire skittered away. Edgar fretted. For sure, he could and should invoke Elvis and seek his counsel. That door remained open, always. But lately Elvis had changed. His greatness and abounding love never diminished, no, never, but he was moody. Under pressure, pouring out soul for his fans. Less approachable, didn't like to be disturbed, an attitude of don't-call-me-I'll-call-you. His aura became a bruised, deep purple. But this problem required resolution and Edgar remained confused, shaken with uncertainty. Unleashing Shire might not be such a good idea.

Alone by the spring, Edgar concentrated. Elvis' power surged with each new person brought to Him; waxing like the moon, Elvis proclaimed. But Elvis was harder to summon now, and more likely to be peevish. Edgar closed his eyes so tightly his face hurt. His body tensed. Words sprang out of his mind and plunged into the chilly, percolating depths of Ococonee Spring. *Excuse me? Elvis? Need to talk to you.*

And Elvis answered. *What is it now?*

Sorry to bother you. I was talking to brother Shire —-

I know you were talking to brother Shire, and I know about what. Nothing is hidden from me. Here's the answer you seek. Take care of business.

"Huh?" Edgar replied aloud, unsure how to interpret this.

I don't like repeating myself. Then Elvis commanded, *Look upon me.*

Edgar opened his eyes. A stormy purple mist hovered over the spring, swirling and coruscating. In its midst, Elvis manifested himself as a dark shape with piercing red eyes. Not Happy Elvis, not Rockabilly Elvis; this was Karate Elvis, on the warpath. Edgar shivered. Elvis commanded him to kneel. With a grunt Edgar planted his knees in the soft sand.

Anybody hurts me, I hurt 'em right back, twice as hard. Tell Diddler to get on it lickety-split and to play rough, like a tiger. Take the old man's treasure and hurt the old man. Tell Diddler, my power will guide him.

Well? You heard me, didn't you? Why're you still standing there like a block of wood? Get cracking. Chop chop. Go tell Shire ... no ... wait ...stay right where you are, lard boy. I will tell the Diddler myself. About time me and him got better acquainted.

***

Shire sat on the commode in the downstairs bathroom. His bathroom breaks were few and far between but usually consumed considerable time. He paged through a back issue of *Guns and Ammo*, admiring the AR-15 Bushmaster; he wanted one to augment nis arsenal of handguns, AK's, and shotguns. Shire listened to the sounds of the old house. The ominous creaks of old wood, scraping sounds, water gurgling in the pipes. Auntie Kate babbling and moving about upstairs. The clink of ice cubes in her jar of rock and rye. The twins prancing down the stairs, pinballing off the walls, giggling and chattering. Snapping the elastic of each other's bikini bottoms, playing. Wide Boy rummaging through the kitchen. Wide Boy slurping milk. Wide Boy burping.

An electric green-blue mist sizzled behind the dingy shower curtain in the old, chipped tub.

Shire's mouth dropped open, his scalp tingled, and an icy streak ran up his spine. His butthole tightened. He dropped the magazine, hands shaking.

Shire Fenner, the apparition whispered. *Are you ready to receive, Diddler?*

Shire fainted, slumped on top of the commode. He drooled and his distended penis popped over the edge of the toilet bowl. The porcelain rim of the tub dripped with purplish drops of sizzling ectoplasmic goo The mist expanded, reaching toward Shire, enveloping his face, streaming into his mouth, nostrils, and ears. Shire jerked, staggered like a billygoat, gasping for breath. His eyes popped open. White and blank.

Shire uttered incoherent cries. *Ugh! Uuuuuuuuuuh! Whaaaaa?*

Elvis hovered. With simmering patience, he waited for Shire to regain consciousness. Finally, Shire responded. He gurgled. His eyes popped open.

Now that I have your attention. You don't receive as strong as Edgar, but you will get there because we're on the same wavelength. I got a motto. Do unto others as they would do unto you, only do it first and do it hard. I like your plan. But I want to add an angle to it.

"What angle?" said Shire, unafraid to speak now. He and Elvis had a new bond.

Fixing to tell you. Pay attention.

***

Shire found Wide Boy asleep in the RV, snoring, drooling, and clutching a ceramic titty bong like a child clinging to a teddy bear. Shire slapped him awake. Wide Boy's eyes popped open.

"Get your pants on, porker," said Shire. "We got work to do. You and me are going to The Villages."

"Why go *there*?" Wide Boy rubbed his eyes. Luna lay in bed next to him, face buried in a pillow, loose seaweed strands of green hair streaming. She clung to Wide Boy like a vine and didn't stir.

"We're going to break into Ginger's sugar daddy's home," said Shire. "Rob him blind and hurt him bad. It'll be fun."

"Ginger coming with us?"

Shire snickered. "You better believe! She's the bait."

***

Father Stephan Dudek lay on a canvas cot,

immersed in a dream. The dream proved beautiful and pleasant at first. Under an azure sky he strolled within a quadrangle-shaped Renaissance Garden, amid its green and orderly symmetry. Pale roses swirled like clouds; stately cypresses stood in rows; and upon pedestals of white and roseate marble, vases overflowed with golden ivy.

A flicker of movement told Dudek wasn't alone.

Someone – *something* - approached. A dread something, to despoil the serenity, like a Venus Flytrap, luring its prey with sweet-scented nectar and then snapping shut; a grim repulsion, presenting a false face, and a stolen identity. A youth with a wave of black hair above a pale, pouting face. He wore a mocking smile. A sizzling blue-green haze enveloped him.

Did you get my text, priest?

Driving back to base after they rescued Jason Root in Hygeia, Dudek's phone chimed, and Dudek read the message before deleting it. *If you're looking for trouble, you came to the right place because I'm evil, don't mess around with me I'm evil!* A blatantly in-your-face, typical demon tactic, an adolescent taunt. Dudek had instantly erased the text. Demons adapted to technology, using ubiquitous smart phones the way they once used Ouija boards. They infiltrated social media too. Chat rooms, many subreddits, X, and Facebook.

Dudek had trailed this waterborne demon for several years, its name unknown to him. It migrated. Caused damage, incited madness, ruined lives, and moved on, as demons are wont. It always appeared in or near water. Lakes, wetlands, swamps, even a retention pond. It had corrupted Ococonee Spring and knew Dudek was in the vicinity, but didn't know his physical whereabouts, not yet anyway. Frustrated, it chose to confront its pursuer on psychical terrain.

Old man. Old shitforbrains. Old shaman. Old wheezer geezer. You are rotten meat. Maggotty. Oozing. You stink of death, priest.

In a microsecond, the garden dissolved, the fabric of the dream melting into a vast hyperbolic shape; an inverted, non-Euclidean nightmare. Black clouds smudged the trough of sky beneath Dudek's feet and slithered along the rocky precipice in torrents. Fissures opened above, belching smoke and a rotten cadaverous sulfuric stench. Grimy water flowed overhead. Bodies bobbed to the surface. Briny, bloated and ghost pale; garlanded with brown strands of foul-smellling kelp. Empty eye sockets; cavernous holes that had been noses; mouths agape, teeth clattering; severed limbs and fleshless bones white as salt. Dudek fought to repress his revulsion and fear. Instead, he commanded the apparition. *Show me your face, not the face you use to deceive, but your true hideous face, and tell me your name. Your name!*

To no avail.

No, I don't think so, priest. The demon cackled, then blew raspberries. *Don't even think about giving me that power-of-Christ-compels-you routine. Your tired old shibboleths are dead and defunct. Don't you know the band is getting back together? Scotty, D.J., Ba'al, Big Mama Cybele and the Corybantics. The comeback tour of the ancient ones. Soon you will look up and see a sign above heaven and earth. Under New Management. We'll run the show.*

Dudek shook with anger. *That is not so. Never! Liar!*

In response the apparition emitted more razor-sharp cackles. Mocking. Supremely supercilious and confident. *No, you are the liar, old christcuck. Want to see my face and know my name? Visit us at the sanctuary. No reservations required, open 24/7, and bring your friends too. Let's rock, everybody, let's rock.*

Nothing would be more pleasing to us. We will enjoy ourselves immensely. You, priest, on the other hand will suffer torment upon torment. I will gouge out your eyes and skull-fuck you.

The demon then hunkered down, dug its hand in a cloud of ash and yanked out a wizened skein of dry skin, that of an elderly man, liver spots on its pate, genitals shrunken, and a white tag pinned to its chest. The demon balled up the skin and tossed it to unfurl at Dudek's feet in a pile of orange-glinted embers.

Then, howling with laughter, the apparition receded, making a slow zigzagging exit, waggling legs, butt, and hips. It chanted something in an ancient language, wheezy and assonant, that Dudek did not comprehend in discrete sentences, but he understood its meaning. *Die, you lump of shit on a stick, I will impale you on my enormous thorny cock.* Or words to that effect.

Dudek looked at the skin as it roasted on the embers. The half crumpled white paper. A parking permit. For *The Villages*. In the name of … that part curled with bright orange flame.

Dudek woke with start, his heart pounding. He gasped for breath and sat up on the cot. Cody stood over him. Reliable, as always, his face grave with concern.

"You good, Dude?"

"Yeah, I'm good," replied Dudek. "Bad dream, that's all."

Memory dissipated, flitted away like sand in a strong wind. His dreams, no matter how vivid, urgent, or minatory, always proved fleeting, often to his frustration. Dudek sat up and accepted a mug of strong black coffee from Cody.

"Talk about it?"

Dudek nodded. Drank coffee. "I was somewhere, Italy, I think, where I haven't been in more than two decades. I can't remember."

"You awake now?"

"How long was I out?"

"All day," said Cody. "Like you were in a coma. Now that you're awake, padre, we got a little problem. Root wants out."

Dudek nodded. This was not an unexpected development. The predictable, pusillanimous, and proverbial cold feet. Alas, typical of young people these days, the lack of commitment. After vetting the young man, Dudek had intuited that Jason Root, in the cold light of day, would seek to rescind his participation and require further prodding. Another matter to be dealt with.

***

"No." Dudek stood firm. "You can't leave, Jason."

Minus his priest's collar, wearing only a military green T-shirt and grey cargo shorts, Dudek looked unpriestly. Rumpled, unshaven, weary, bleary-eyed. He sat at the table and smoked a Marlboro Light over black coffee and a chicken empanada. He listened politely, face impassive, and then responded to Jason's importuning. "That's out of the question."

"No, it's not," replied Jason. "Absolutely not."

"You joined the team," Dudek pointed out. "You swore an oath."

"Under duress!"

"Sorry, Jason," Dudek said. "Sorry we had to put you through that, but we had to ascertain your bona fides and extract information. That was, I admit, rough." He sipped his coffee, unperturbed, and took a drag on his Marlboro Light. "Be that as it may, the oath you took is binding."

"Wouldn't hold up in a court of law."

"We're not in a court of law," Dudek said. "We're operating under circumstances outside any conventional definitions of —-"

"I'm not your guy."

"I consider myself an excellent judge of character," said Dudek. "Rarely mistaken."

"This time afraid so. Look, I'm not a zealot." Jason looked at Mince and Cody. "No offense, guys. But I'm not even religious, I'm agnostic, and I'm not a soldier. Never shot anything except skeet with a Benelli shotgun that I don't even own anymore. Sport shooting. Clay does not bleed or shoot back. I won't lie. I've got a highly refined sense of risk and discretion is the better part of valor. Physical courage is not one of my attributes. I am the wrong guy in this situation. I'll only get in your way."

Dudek's hard hazel eyes fixed on Jason. "You cannot renege on your oath."

"Agnostic," said Cody, "don't work no more, pilgrim."

"Jason," Dudek cautioned, "they know who you

are. They have your vehicle. They will find where you live. They will come after you. That puts you and people close to you in jeopardy. Wait." Dudek paused, suddenly distracted, wheels clicking in his mind, images resuscitated. "Where did you say your father lived?"

"The Villages. Why? What's he got to do with this?"

***

A quiet Saturday night in The Villages, Florida's premier Active Adult Retirement Community. His new girlfriend was out of town, visiting family in Ohio. Or Indiana, Harve wasn't sure. Harvey Root stayed home in his bungalow, tired after an afternoon table tennis tournament. That evening, he received another text message from Kat. *Hello daddy I visit 2nite.*

Odd, mused Harve. She had never called him daddy before. But he rather liked it. Felt genuinely affectionate. OK, he replied, his stiff fingers slowly tapping on the phone. *When?*

No reply was forthcoming. Harve sat in his new Barcalounger and grazed the cable channels, Fox Business to Bloomberg to sports to a Fifties black-and-white movie on TCM. Richard Widmark, oily and creepy, as a small-time grifter named Harry Fabian in London. Harve dozed. His phone chimed with another text message. Harve balanced his reading glasses on his nose.

Love U daddy almost there I need your help!!! With a crimson string of emoji hearts and kisses and a teddy bear. Harve thought this excessive and embarrassing, even a bit salacious, but texted her back. *What can I do to help?*

She answered immediately. *Bthr4me.*

A line of squalls blew in from the Gulf and scudded over The Villages with wind gusts and intermittent rain. Harve sipped his biweekly tumbler of Woodford Reserve, neat, only one and a half ounces, no more. He dozed again until he heard a gentle rapping at his townhome door. He ejected from the Barcalounger and walked, stiff and slow with the thinning of synovial fluid, to the window. Parting the curtains, he peered outside. Rain spattered the dark, slick street. He spied a dark Dodge Avenger parked at the curb and Kat in a vinyl raincoat, hoodie over her head. Her tatatatatat at his door persisted. He opened the door.

"Kathleen?" he said.

She turned. Wasn't Kat Condon. An Asian girl with green hair and a black glitter eye mask. She jammed her foot against the door, pushing her way in.

"Who are you?" Alarmed, Harve tried to push her out.

Shire and Wide Boy, wearing scary Halloween masks and blue nitrile gloves like a pair of deranged trick-or-treaters, sprang out of the bushes, forced their way inside and tackled Harve, knocking the wind out of him, and pinning him prone on the living room floor, his face in the carpet. Luna closed the door and locked it, clanking the dead bolt.

"I can't breathe," said Harve. Wide Boy sat astride the old man, pinning his arms. Harve gasped.

"Don't make noise," said Wide Boy under the gruesome zombie rubber mask he wore. "If you can talk, you can breathe, so calm down and be alright."

"You be okay." Luna patted Harve's cheek. She wore blue gloves too. Shire insisted; leave no fingerprints. Luna squatted and clamped her knees around Harve's head. She tousled the fringe of wispy white hair on the back of his head and giggled.

"Let me up, please!" Harve said.

"Just lay back and enjoy the pussy in your face," said Wide Boy. "I know I sure would if I was in your situation."

"Take little breaths and you be okay," said Luna.

Harve took shallow breaths. "What do you people want?"

Nobody answered him. Shire searched the house, finding the safe in an adjoining room. He whooped, thrilled. He removed a wide-mouth glass jar from the rucksack he'd lugged inside and unscrewed its metal lid. Ococonee Spring water filled the jar. Fleshy, pulpy white chunks swam in the water. *Alive*. Every drop of spring water and each morsel of fish milt was sacramental. Shire held up the jar against the lamplight, swirling the water. He could feel Elvis now, and wasn't scared, no way. They were buddies now, Elvie and Diddler; Edgar wasn't the only one; Shire received too. Not as strong a signal, not yet, but he'd get there. Elvis guided him. There with him now, a tingling on Shire's scalp and hackles. Elvis whispered in Shire's ear. *Take care of business.*

"Flip him over," Shire said, and Wide Boy and Luna rolled Harve on his back. Wide Boy straddled him and pinned his arms. Shire stood over the supine victim on the shag rug, holding the jar. "Got this little elixir for you to drink. You heard of the Fountain of Youth? Ponce De Leon, and all that. Well, this is the stuff. No shit. Got a little additive too, to give that extra kick. See them beauties swimming around in there?"

"No," said Harve, horrified.

"It a delicacy, a treat." Luna pinched Harve's nose. "It is good for you. You must drink all up."

"It's Essence of Elvis," Shire hunkered down and pinched Harve's nose. "Glug, glug, glug," Shire said, pouring.

***

They discarded the masks. Wide Boy sat in a living room chair, peering through the drapes, on guard. "These gloves are tight, Shire. Cutting off my circulation. Can I take 'em off?"

"Fuck'n deal with it." Shire occupied the Barcalounger and sipped Harve Root's bourbon. Good bourbon too; the old fart didn't scrimp on booze.

Wide Boy grumbled but remained silent. Luna knelt on the floor, next to Harve who now lay prone again. She massaged his temple shoulders and back, but Harve Root did not respond. Luna searched for a pulse in his neck.

Luna said, "I think he dead."

"No, he's not," replied Shire.

"Barely breathing!" said Luna.

"He'll snap out of it."

Luna accused him. "You drown the old man!"

Shire pshawed the idea with snort and a smilesmirk. Lotus was as annoying as Wide Boy and Shire's patience wore thin, their whining irritated. Like a couple of damn kids. "You are about as dumb as a bucket of grout, girl. Had to get every drop and every morsel down his gullet for him to get the full effect. He'll be fine."

Harve Root moaned. He shivered. Made gurgling sounds. Blue lips moved as he tried to speak but he emitted only a froggy croaking sound from deep in his throat. He belched water and saliva and coughed. Harve tried to raise his head and then raise his body to roll over, but his elbows and skinny arms failed him. Luna helped him.

Shire sprang out of the lounger. "Get him up."

Luna spoke softly to the old man, coaxing him, lifting him to his feet, her arm around his waist. At Shire's direction, she planted him on the couch. He flopped, as if deflated, staring. Pale and docile. Shire leaned over, slapped his hand on top of Harve's head and turned the old man's blank gaze to Shire's face.

"Can you hear me?" said Shire. "Say you hear me. Say it."

"Yes, I hear you," Harve whispered.

"I want to open the safe in the next room. For Kat. Your baby girl. Kat needs the money. Needs it bad. Give me the combination. Do that, and we will go away and leave you alone and everybody's happy."

Harve mustered a feeble smile that quickly faded. He made motions for something to write on and to write with. Shire provided a post-it notepad and a pencil. Harve wrote the combination to the safe. Shire snatched the note and galloped into the next room. Wide Boy and Luna followed him. Harve remained slumped on the couch, pale, apathetic, and forlorn. He looked drowned, his shirt and hair damp with sweat and spring water. Shire squinted at the note, spun the tumbler with nimble fingers, and opened the safe.

"Well, look what we have here." Shire said, elated. He emptied the contents of the safe into a black duffel bag. Jackpot! Cash, coins, gold. He tossed Wide Boy a Saint-Gaudens gold double eagle. Wide Boy gawped at it and turned in over and over in his blue-gloved hands. "That's worth a couple grand."

"I want one too!" said Luna.

Shire tossed her a coin. He marched back into the living room and confronted Harve, slapping the old man's cheek to get his attention. Harve rubbed his stinging cheek and stared warily at Shire. The dead-eyed old man remained in shock, under the influence. Suggestible, that was the word. Shire grinned. A little dose of Elvis did that. Old man's brain was putty. Harve slumped on the couch like an animatron Boomer, its power source cut off.

"We weren't here," said Shire. "We. Were. Not. Here. You got that? Don't nod. I want to hear you say it. Say it."

"You're not here," said Harve.

"We weren't here. Ginger, I mean Kat was here." He pointed at Luna, who curtsied on cue. "You opened the safe and gave the money to her. No forced entry, no coercion, nothing. None of that happened. You gave her the money because you are a generous old fart and would do anything for her. We clear on that?"

"Yes," said Harve.

"That is all you remember. Nothing else. Okay?"

"Okay." Harve nodded and Shire patted him on the head, like a dog.

"Can we go now, Shire?" Wide Boy sounded whiny. Shire hated whiners and wanted to slap his cousin.

"Yes," said Luna. "Let's go now. Too long here already. Too long!"

Another whiner, and worse than Wide Boy. These chinky women with slant eyes and small titties and high-pitched voices. Shire wanted to bitch-slap her too and put her ass in the trunk of the Dodge, bound and gagged with a plastic bag over her head. He didn't tell Wide Boy and Luna that they weren't going back to Ococonee Spring yet, and probably not for hours. They didn't need to know.

"We're done here," Shire announced.

They skulked to the Dodge, stuffed the loot in the trunk. But Shire still had business to take care of, according to Elvis' plan. They remained on stakeout.

"Why're we hanging out here?" said Wide Boy.

"Part of the plan."

"What plan?"

"Shut up," said Shire.

Their parking spot offered a view of Harve's house. They waited, Wide Boy behind the wheel, Shire in the passenger seat sipping bourbon from the bottle, and Luna asleep in back, snoring. Shire remained vigilant. Wide Boy fidgeted.

"What're we waiting on, Shire? You mind telling me?"

"Yeah, I fuck'n mind, but I'll tell you anyway. They are going to show up." Elvis had assured him of that. The plan was foolproof, only needed competent execution.

"Who?" said Wide Boy.

"*Them*," replied Shire. "The priest and his posse who killed Ardell. We gonna get them. Now shut the fuck up."

Wide Boy had fallen asleep and was snoring too

by the time the white van cruised down the street to Harve Root's townhome, just as Elvis had predicted. One man stayed in the van, three got out, including the priest who wore the fedora. Jason Root rushed into the house. Shortly the three of them emerged, helping the feeble old man to the van, pausing as the old man doubled over and vomited. Shire thought about picking them off right then and there but decided against it, not in the middle of The Villages. Too populated, and no good escape route. Shire opted to wait and catch them on a country road later and move in for the kill. He shook Wide Boy awake.

"Follow that white van. Don't let 'em spot us. Don't fuck this up."

Wide Boy moved slowly, still half asleep. He fumbled with the keys but started the Dodge and dropped the trans into drive. "Is this gonna take all night?"

"If that's what it takes," said Shire.

"Gonna need coffee," said Wide Boy.

"I want coffee too," said Luna, awake now and sitting up in the back seat. "And something to eat. I'm so hungry!"

"Zip it," said Shire. "I *do not* want to hear any more bellyaching from either of you bitches. Now follow that fuck'n van!"

*****

"If it is any consolation," said Dudek, "I sincerely wish we had gotten here sooner and been able to prevent this. I blame myself."

"I blame you too," said Jason, as they left the hospital, walking toward the van where Cody and Mince waited.

Harve Root suffered contusions, bruises, and a fractured rib. He wasn't coherent, couldn't remember what happened. He had given money to his stepdaughter, Kathleen Condon. Because she asked him for it. *Needed the money real bad.* Harve didn't know how he sustained his injuries. Household accident perhaps. A fall, common among the elderly. Yes, Harve admitted he had been drinking. Not sure how much. And, apparently, he ate something that disagreed with his stomach.

Jason said, "I should stay with him."

"Too dangerous for you," said Dudek. "Your father will be safe at the hospital. But you're not safe anywhere but with us."

They piled into the van. Cody drove with Dudek in the front passenger seat, smoking a Marlboro Light, the window open to flick ash. Cody cruised I-75 to Ocala, then exited eastbound on a dark two-lane state road. After a few minutes, Cody glanced at the rearview mirror. "Somebody's following."

"You're sure?" said Dudek.

"Sucker's coming up fast."

Objects in mirror are closer than they appear. Dudek heard the high-pitched scream of the engine as the Dodge Avenger torpedoed in the outside lane, skidding on the edge of the pavement, to overtake the van. A man popped out of the rear passenger window like Whack-A-Mole, only this grinning mole was doing the whacking, and wielded a Bullpup. The 12-gauge peppered the side of the van. Cody shouted and hit the gas pedal.

Dudek drew his Beretta. When the Dodge roared alongside again, Dudek fired. Wildly, unsure his bullets even pinged the Dodge. In back, strapped in the swivel seat with Glock in hand, Mince slid the side door open and fired at their pursuer. The Dodge swerved. Brakes squealed. The vehicle came to an abrupt stop on the shoulder of the road, almost veering into a ditch. The small man in back leaped over the seat, pushed the driver aside, and took the wheel. With a roar of the engine, the Dodge spun around, smoking tires in the opposite direction, and vanished around a curve in the road.

Cody braked the van and stopped on the shoulder of the road. He swiveled in the seat. "Everybody cool?"

"I'm good," said Mince.

Jason picked himself up from the floor. His heart pounded, his head spun, and cold sweat chilled his armpits and forehead. He remained uninjured but had banged a knee in the adrenalin rush for cover. "No, I'm not cool. How can I be cool? I'm a little *shaken up*, okay? We just got shot at!"

"Your first time, huh?" said Mince.

"Nobody's wounded." Dudek said, replacing his Beretta in its holster. He exited the van to examine its side and tires. "Only superficial damage. We're good to go."

"Let's go after 'em!" Cody gripped the steering wheel.

"No. Back to base," said Dudek.

Cody's mouth dropped open. "Why for?"

"Now is not the time," Dudek said.

***

An orange haze warmed the flat strips of stratocumulus. Shire chewed gum, a wad of Big Red cinnamon. He found an unopened can of beer lodged under the front seat, popped its tab, and guzzled. It was warm but that was okay. He surveyed damage to the Dodge. Shattered glass sprinkling the dash and bullet holes in the driver's door. A flat tire, and no spare even if Shire had been of a mind to change it. He giggled, shaking his head. *Well, shit fire, the resale value of this vehicle is gonna be squat.* A real shame. Shire liked that car, donated to Ococonee Spring by one of the locals. Once you Come to Elvis, material shit didn't mean as much and Shire was more than happy to relieve people of their possessions.

Then Elvis whispered to him. The silky voice susurrated deep in Shire's ear. Disappointed, but his wrath contained. *Can't help but notice you failed to kill the priest.*

"I tried my damnedest! You know how it is, the best laid plans. Wide Boy just did not hold up under pressure. I would've had the fuck'n priest otherwise. Gave it my best shot, boss. Sorry about that."

Sorry don't get it done, Diddler. You got to improve your game. With that harsh admonition, Elvis withdrew, shifting away from Shire like an outgoing tide.

"I will. I will," Shire murmured.

"Who you talking to?" said Luna. "Are you crazy?"

"Nobody. None-uh your beeswax, bitch."

After seizing the wheel and making a retreat, Shire found concealment behind the ruins of a demolished motel on an abandoned stretch of pavement, the weedy premises redolent with the stench of mildew, decay, and a ruptured septic tank. In the early morning light, a noisy flock of iridescent grackles dotted the telephone wire above him and filled the air with raucous cawing. He had dragged Wide Boy out of the Dodge and, leaving a bloody trail, and deposited him among the tall weeds and purple thistle. Bleeding out, a wave of blood soaking into the sand. Luna kneeled beside him.

"Help him! Help Wide Boy!"

Now Elvis faded completely, leaving Shire to his own contrivances. Shire sauntered toward Luna.

Wide Boy, his eyes grey and blank, lay on his back. Like a stranded beached manatee. That amused Shire.

"Why you laugh? It is not funny!"

Luna had stripped off her blouse, balled it, and pressed it against the bullet wounds in Wide Boy's shoulder to stop the bleeding. She looked sort of cute, topless, her peach-color titties like little round moons. But the compress wasn't working. Shire's nose twitched at the foul coppery smell. His nostrils flared. Nothing to be done about it. Wide Boy's a goner, Shire concluded. Couldn't do nothing for him and that was that. Besides, it was *their* fault Shire couldn't deliver a dead priest to Elvis. Wide Boy fucked up the driving and the chinky girl was no help at all. Should've brought Palatka Red with me, Shire thought. Red's reliable, a *git 'er done* guy.

"Take Wide Boy to hospital!"

"Hospital? Nope."

"Hospital, yes!" She shrieked.

"Hospital's going to ask questions. For a gunshot wound, they call the cops. Besides, what's the fuck'n use? He's as good as dead already."

Luna's face tautened with anger. She waved her free arm, and her breasts tautened too. "What you do? Leave him here? You want Wide Boy *to die*? He your posse. He is your *family*."

Shire glared at her, sick of listening to this little cunt, sick of her shrill, high-pitched voice "Tell you what, little poontang. You stay here with him."

Holding his beer in one hand, with his free hand Shire pulled his short barrel Colt .357 from under his belt buckle and shot Luna twice in the head. Blood, flesh, bone, and green hair sprayed. Luna pitched backwards, flopping on her back in the sandy soil, her mouth gaping open like a largemouth bass out of the water. The reverb from the gunshots scattered the grackles on the telephone wires overhead. Black wings flapped.

Scratch off one of the RV girls. Shire giggled and paused for a moment to stare. Blood gushed from Wide Boy like a fountain. His face and lips grey, eyes blank. Luna sprawled beside him, her berry eyes wide open with surprise, top of her head splattered, green strands of hair coated with blood and viscera, the delicate shell of an ear erased.

Artsyfartsy types would call this a still life. An original work of art created by yours truly, Shire

Fenner. He wanted to sign his creation in some distinctive way but couldn't think of how. He'd best skedaddle anyway. Gunshots might've been heard. Best not to linger hereabouts, just leave the two of them right there where they sprawled. *Turkey vultures got to eat,* he thought as he searched Wide Boy's pockets for the gold coin he'd gifted earlier. *Same as worms. That's the Circle of Life shit right there, that is.* He crushed and tossed the empty beer can and spit out the gum, peed in the weeds, and pulled the duffel bag filled with money and loot from the trunk. He ransacked the Dodge to find the gold coin he'd given to Luna, then stuffed coins and the shotgun in the money bag. He found another can of beer under the seat too, one for the road. He'd hike or hitch a ride back to Hygeia and Ococonee Spring. Maybe cap whatever unsuspecting numbnuts Good Samaritan offered him a ride and take their vehicle. Shire grinned. For no good deed goes unpunished heh heh heh. The newly risen sun baked his back as Shire strolled down the highway, straps of the heavy duffel cutting into his shoulder, warm beer sloshing in his mouth. He whistled a happy tune. *Zip-a-dee-doodah, zip-a-dee-ay! Plenty of sunshine heading my way.*

***

They sat in the kitchen, safe in the house inside the sacred circle, drinking black coffee and eating burnt toast and dry roasted peanuts from a jar. Little else remained of their provisions.

"That was a mistake." Cody grumbled, sounding like an aggrieved ogre. "I still say we should've pursued 'em and gone toe to toe. Right then and right there."

Mince spoke up. "You are total primal war-making neocon, Cody. You want to fight everybody, anywhere, all the time."

"You say that like it's a bad thing."

"You remind me of a battle buddy back in the Stan," said Mince. "Crank, which was his war name. After this movie with the cool Brit actor, Jason Statham. Crank even looked like Jason Statham. Crank had steel core balls. All due respect, Cody, you're a badass, too, and a righteous holy warrior, but we got to pick our battles."

"We don't pick nothin'," replied Cody. "We're called to battle. You, me, Dude. Even Jason. He's not here by accident. This is good versus evil. This strife is ours and we got to grab the dog by the ears." He gestured, lifting the metaphoric hound dog by its floppy ears.

Cigarette smoke wafted in the air. From the parlor, Dudek said, "The man of action takes measure of the constraints placed upon him. Or, in the immortal words of Dirty Harry Callahan, a man's got to know his limitations. With that in mind, we will wait for reinforcements."

"If," said Cody, "they show up."

"Carmen will be here." A rebuke, silencing Cody. Not a splinter of doubt diluted the assurance in Dudek's voice. He rested in an overstuffed chair in the parlor, smoking a Marlboro Light, ash accumulating on its tip, and sipping black coffee. Weary. Having removed his dingy priest's collar and his white Adidas and black compression socks. His eyelids drooped, the bags were under his eyes deep and solemn.

Hunting demons, Jason surmised, was a tough line of work.

"Who is Carmen?" Jason stretched out on the sofa.

"She's bringing people," Dudek replied. "To augment the team. Fighters. And funding. Carmen is our, I suppose you'd call her, the comptroller. We're running low on funds."

"Who funds you? The Vatican?"

Cody scowled. "The anti-pope and the vipers in Rome are all about climate change and global reparations. Those tightwads don't even acknowledge us. At least not officially."

Both Dudek and Mince shot Cody looks that said loose lips. Cody, abashed, nodded. He clutched a handful of peanuts, slurped coffee, and diverted his gaze to the magnets on the old Frigidaire.

Jason persisted. "Well, then, who?"

In his mind Jason summarized. He was part of the team now, committed, accepted by the others, subject to the same risks as the others, had been personally victimized by the assault on his father, and had taken part in a real live firefight. He deserved some answers. The priest owed him. If owed, Jason always collected. The only way to conduct business.

"Who, who? What are you, an owl?" said Cody. Turning, he yawned and shambled down the hall toward one of the bedrooms.

"Can't divulge," said Dudek. "We are a covert operation. Ostensibly, I am a math teacher at a Catholic school. Mince collects military disability, and Cody has a day job. Further I can't say."

"Okay, tell me something else then. How you found Ococonee Spring."

"Florida Man memes," said Dudek.

"Huh? Did I hear that correctly?"

Jason was familiar with the term. Florida Man was the punchline *of a joke*. Memes proliferated about a random male Floridian performing an irrational, absurd, disgusting, or bizarre act, or any permutation thereof, usually but not always criminal. Florida Man charged with picking magic mushrooms in cow pasture while carrying live anaconda. Florida Man caught in prostitution sting on his honeymoon. Florida Man's arm chomped off by gator while peeing in a pond because the men's room line was too long. These memes had devolved into a national mockery of the Sunshine State, referred to by its legion of detractors as Flori-*DUH*.

"Are you serious?" said Jason.

"I scour the media," said Dudek.

"Do demons advertise?"

Dudek ignored the flippancy. "A dedicated researcher can find clues of demonic presence. Paranormal activity, freakish weather, Fortean phenomena, anything anomalous. More chaff than wheat, for sure. But one item snagged my attention. From a Gainesville, Florida, newspaper. *Florida Man believes spirit of Elvis resides in spring on his property.* I delved into the matter. And here we are."

"Yeah," Cody groused. "Here we are, sitting around on our hunkers, broke, running out of grub, waiting on Carmen and the Devil. Which one gets to us first?"

***

A few miles from Hygeia, on a deserted two-lane road beneath a low-lying, lumpy, gravy grey blanket of clouds, Shire Fenner received a Revelation from Elvis.

He swaggered along lugging the duffel when behind him he heard a great voice, like a trumpet blaring. The hairs on the back of neck bristled, his eardrums painfully popped, and a bolt of electricity coursed through his spine. *Aaaaaargh.* Shire cried out and doubled over, dropping the duffel bag. He fell to his knees, his hands clutching his belly. Convulsions shook his body. His bladder emptied, he puked, then lay sprawled on the concrete.

Finished? Upchuck no more. Get up. I am the One and Only, the King. Set your motherfucker to receive, turn and behold!

Shire obeyed. Averting his eyes at first, then gazing upon the glowing emanation. Elvis hovered above the yellow lines on the pavement in a churning purple cloud, clad all in black, the Slick Leather Elvis in legendary black cordovan leather trousers and jacket from the 68 Comeback Special that fit like a second skin of liquid obsidian.

You hear me, Diddler? Are you seeing Me?

"I see you. You are a fuck'n sight to behold, boss." Sucking Shire's eyes right of their sockets.

Damn right I am. Elvis strutted. Leather crackled like dry wood in a fire and glistened like polished armor. *I am the once and future King who was dead and now I live forevermore, and I am everywhere. I hold the keys to Graceland Everlasting. You better believe I do. Jingle, jingle, jingling 'em in my pocket like loose change. Now I need you, Shire Fenner, as much if not more than I need Edgar.*

Elvis needs him, Elvis values his ass, that thrilled Shire. Flattered him; an honor beyond reckoning. The cloud drew him in, like a vortex.

Shire would walk with Elvis, would serve Elvis. He blurted out his loyalty. "Tell me what it is you need, anything at all, and you got it. I am on top of it, like white on rice."

Keep watching and I will show you something. A mystery.

Seven US dollar bills flitted out of the purple haze and fluttered in front of Shire. Seven pyramids detached from the dollars and floated. *Ascendit crudelitas*, coruscating words above the pyramids, and below a wavy banner proclaimed *Elvis Ordo Seclorum*. Atop the pyramids, seven relentless eyes scrutinized Shire, and penetrated his mind with the message. Elvis was that All-Seeing Eye, His coming foretold. Elvis reigned supreme, the apex of the pyramid, with Edgar directly beneath him, a bulge in the bonewhite crumbly limestone. But now Shire stood on equal footing. Edgar had to move over and make room. Edgar Fenner shrank as Shire expanded.

It's lonely at the top. Elvis echoed from the peak of the pyramid. *But it's not crowded. Diddler, listen up, I will give you a new name and put diamonds in your teeth. Your diddling days are done, now you are The Doer. Because you will do things for me. Take care of business, every day, and every way. Edgar doesn't have the stuff that you got in spades. But both of you got to work together to serve me, else I will use both your heads, one to crack the other like coconuts. Here is your job. Slay my enemies. Kill 'em. I want them dead. Do this for me.*

"That fuck'n priest, you mean?" said Shire.

Yes, the priest. Him and all of them, the brother, the fat Cajun and the soldier. I want 'em dead, dead, dead. The task is the same as it's been since the beginning. Guard my sanctuary. Punish those who violate it. They are coming to destroy me. Get your posse ready for battle. They got to kill. Got that? Am I making myself clear?

Tell me what you're gonna do. What's the magic word?

"Kill," said Shire.

Elvis grinned and nodded with satisfaction. He faded, shriveling into a purple trickle between yellow lines and the flat, pulverized roadkill on the pavement.

Remember! Who comes to me must bleed for me and must shed the blood of my enemies. Whoever comes to me must give their soul to me. For no one who holds back, and cheats on the devotion owed to me, can enter Graceland. They will be cast out into the wasteland of bones and rotting flesh. Now be on your way. Whip that posse of yours into shape. Cattle prod up the ass if that's what it takes.

"I will, I will, I will." Shire swore, his heart throbbing. His eyes burned and his vision blurred, pupils dilated and dark. A purple, tar-like goo dripped from his eyes, and ran down his cheeks. He licked his lips, savoring the sweet and coppery taste. Picking up the duffel bag, Shire continued his stride down the road toward Ococonee Spring. Stepping cautiously, almost blinded, and wiping his eyes with a bandanna from the pocket of his blue jeans.

***

Dubbed Palatka Red when he rode with the Maggots, a biker club out of Jacksonville, before they kicked him out, his real name was Lyman Haire; he preferred his old biker name even though he hadn't ridden a Harley for years. At Ococonee Spring, Red had graduated to Shire's second in command. He nailed a red and white tin sign to a wooden post facing the highway at the entrance to the Fenner property. *No Trespassing. We're Tired of Hiding the Bodies.*

He took a few paces back to admire the sign, stroked his bushy bronze beard and grinned. No joke!

The Colt .45 on his hip wasn't there for show. If he jerked that pistol from its holster, Red meant business.

"Hey!" Someone shouted.

Red crouched, swiveled, hand to the checkered grip of the pistol like an Old West gunfighter. He saw Shire Fenner swaggering toward him on the road, sweat-soaked and lugging a duffel bag.

Red relaxed. "Why're you walking?"

"Because I can't fuck'n fly," said Shire.

As Shire came closer, Red squinted like Clint Eastwood in a spaghetti Western, and his brow creased. "What's the matter with your eyes?"

"Nothing's the matter with my fuck'n eyes," said Shire.

"They're kind of dripping with glop."

Shire quickly wiped his eyes with a bandanna from his pocket. "Nothing's wrong with my eyes! Allergies, that's all."

"Okay, brother. Don't blow a gasket. What happened to the Dodge?"

Shire plopped in the canvas chair under the

sagging canopy that served as the guard station. He dropped the duffel and grabbed a beer from the Styrofoam cooler and popped its tab. Foam spurted. He gulped and dug his hand into the bag of potato chips by the cooler.

"It got shot up. Total loss."

"That's too bad," said Red with regret. "That was a nice car. What about Wide Boy and whatshername?"

"Double-D dead defunct," Shire said.

"No! God damn! Wide Boy?"

"The priest killed 'em. Didn't give them a chance, just shot 'em down like Bonnie and Clyde. Me, he missed. Because I am quick and got a strong survival instinct." He chugged more beer, ate more chips, and burped a tiny burp. "Fuck'n priest will get his. I will see to that. Where's my posse?"

"Scattered around," said Red.

"Scattered? Did I not leave you in charge? You should know exactly where everybody is and what they're doing."

"Bourbon's in the RV putting the girls through their paces. Bitches been slacking lately and needed a good talking to. Chucky's running errands for Edgar and Ginger, and I don't goddam know long that'll take. The others are around somewhere close by. I will find them if you need 'em. What's in the duffel bag?"

"Loot," said Shire. He lifted the bag and plopped it in his lap, draping his arm over it. "Where's the bombs you told me you'd make?"

"Working on 'em."

"Get on it. And did Sam change the oil in the Pink Caddy like I told him to?"

"Ask Sam about that. I'll get your pipe bombs, Shire."

Shire stood, tossed the beer can into the saw palmetto and picked up the duffel. "Guess I'll go check on that old fart Fleance since *you don't know*. Maybe next time I should leave booger-brain Skeeter in charge instead of you. Dumb as he is, Skeeter does what you tell him to do."

Palatka Red fumed. "Don't give me shit, Shire."

Shire grinned. He concluded Red was now sufficiently roused and mean and ready to take care of business. He wanted his posse to stay frosty, wanted them ready to taste blood. Shire looked over his shoulder above the slash pines at the hazy sun in the sky, watched the sun for several seconds without blinking, wiped his eyes again, and turned to Palatka Red. "Got to get me some shuteye. Get the word out, the posse meets in four hours. Everybody's ass better be at the Airstream."

"I'll get 'em there," Red replied.

Shire ambled off toward the old Fenner house. In the shell of his ear, he could hear the wind rustling the leaves of the oaks; he could hear scrub jays queedling, squirrels chittering in the brush, twigs snapping, and horseflies buzzing. Passing by the RV he heard the snap of Bourbon's bullwhip and the cries of the Asian girls. Every sound reported with sharp clarity. His vision was enhanced too. He possessed Elvis Vision now, like some kind of superpower; a whole new world of sight and sound opened for him. The black velvet Elvis art decorating the rickety porch converted to 3D. Elvis the Gunfighter, six foot tall and laminated, greeted Shire as he approached, six-shooter in hand, his dark eyes raptor-like, the cardboard cutout breathing like a living icon.

Images of Elvis adorned the Fenner acres. A resin and fiberglass Elvis here, a glossy porcelain Elvis there. Plaster Elvis busts, painted gold, sat atop fake marble pedestals. Elvis garden gnomes guarded Edgar's tomato plants. Elvis bobbleheads bobbled and hip-gyrated in the windows of the old Fenner house. A laser-cut Vegas Elvis silhouette, its cold carbon steel edge razor sharp, defied touch at the base of an ancient laurel oak. Dried blood the color of rust smeared the metal.

Behind the veil of slash pines, Ococonee Spring glowed. A satiny mist of power hovered over the water. Shire could discern this now after being touched by Elvis on the road to Hygeia. Shire could *see*. He need not envy Edgar anymore. His vision penetrated the percolating depths of the spring where, amid the limestone crags, the armored behemoth dwelled, the spirit within it beckoning.

"What's wrong with your eyes?" Ginger said.

Shire looked up at the ruby red rhinestone in her navel, too big to fit. She stood on the porch with Edgar, his arms around her bare shoulders. Both gave him quizzical looks.

"Nothing wrong with my eyes," said Shire. He wiped purplish glop from the corner of his eye with his finger and flicked it like a booger into the hibiscus bushes.

"What's in the bag, Shire?" Edgar said.

"Decapitated heads. Want to see?"

Ginger and Edgar grimaced. The rhinestone popped out of Ginger's belly button and bounced along the porch. She scrambled to retrieve it, then retreated inside the house, slamming the screen door.

"You upset Ginger," said Edgar.

"What if it was true about the heads in the bag." The idea of collecting the heads of Elvis' enemies appealed to Shire. Going medieval like that, yeah, oh boy, that'd be fun. Putting heads on poles like in Game of Thrones, cool. Yeah, he would do that.

"I know it's not," said Edgar. "And it is not funny. What is in the duffel bag, Shire. The money?"

"See for yourself," Shire said, tossing the duffel to Edgar.

Edgar grunted catching it, almost losing his balance. He unzipped the duffel and poked through its contents. "Everything went okay?"

"No, everything did not go okay. It was fucked up to a fare-thee-well."

"Huh? What happened?" Edgar fretted.

"Old Harve cooperated, no *problemo.* But

afterward *they* were lying in wait for us. Like the vultures they are. The priest and her brother. Ambushed us on the way back." He took off his cap and placed it over his heart, in mock mourning. "It's my sad duty to report they killed Wide Boy."

"Harlan's dead? Oh, no, no, no!"

"Casualties are going to happen in war, and we are in a war. It's to the death, like they say. Us or them. They killed one of the chinky sisters too after they done some nasty things to her that I will not relate the dirty details of because I know how sensitive you are, Edgar, and don't want to hear about a mangled pussy."

"No, no, I don't want to know."

"I barely got away, thanks for asking. Wrecked the car and I had to hoof it. Hey! Pull yourself together, Edgar."

"Harlan was kin." Edgar blubbered. "And that poor girl."

Shire punched Edgar's shoulder and slapped the side of his head. "Stop it right now! Stop!"

"Don't do that, Shire. Don't hit me."

"Got your attention, didn't I?" Shire said. "Nothing to be done for Wide Boy or that girl now

except get revenge. You got to keep it together —
Edgar."

"I will," replied Edgar. "But you better not hit
me again."

"I promise not to." Shire hopped onto the porch,
resisting, for the time being, the urge to slap Edgar
again. Wood creaked. He pushed Edgar aside like a
weightless balloon man and, hunkering down and
unzipping the duffel, helped himself to a wad of cash
and several coins, stuffing his pockets and declaring he
needed money to pay his posse and for this-and-that.
Edgar said nothing. Then Shire picked up the shotgun,
held the stock, the barrel resting on his shoulder.

"Now if you don't mind, I will toddle off. Got to
get some shuteye and things to do before I sleep. One of
us has got to manage things around here. And, you
know what? I am the Doer. Because I get shit done." He
toddled off.

***

Sam Fleance, a mechanic by trade, occupied a
Casita camper next to the garage with a corrugated tin
roof. Shire had delegated vehicle maintenance to Sam.
The lanky, cinnamon-freckled girl everyone called
Junebug shacked with Sam in his camper.

Despite fingers gnarled with arthritis, Sam remained handy with carpentry and rope too. He sipped homemade wine from a Mason jar while he tied Junebug to a pole after divesting her of her clothes. A perpendicular beam under her crotch forced Junebug to stand on tippytoes, her calves already starting to cramp. He lashed her skinny wrists to a cross beam behind her shoulder blades and wrapped coarse, itchy rope around her middle and chest, thighs, and ankles.

"Why papa?" She sobbed.

"Why what?" replied Sam.

"Why're you being mean and doing this to me?"

"It's your comeuppance." An unfiltered cigarette dangled from his mouth. "That guy who whacked me with the bat would never have got the drop on me if you hadn't distracted me like you did."

"I didn't mean to!" said Junebug.

Fleance pshawed her plea, wagging a finger at his helpless, half naked captive. "Don't matter you didn't mean to. You caused me grievous injury." He pointed to the purple bruises on his arm and head. "That's *your* fault!"

Tears welled in her eyes. "I'm sorry!"

He stuffed a rag in her mouth, tossed the cigarette, and took a spool of monofilament fishing line and lead sinkers from his pocket. Junebug moaned. Sam meted out her punishment on a regular basis and the girl proved a glutton for it.

"You were supposed to change the oil in the Pink Caddy."

Sam, startled, turned; Shire confronted him. Sam stared. "What's wrong you're your eyes?"

"Nothing wrong with my eyes! Did you change the oil in the Pink Caddy or not?"

Sam shuffled his feet. "I will get to it."

"Get to it now," said Shire. "I'll stay right here while you work."

"Well, uh, Junebug here has some comeuppance due —-"

"She's not going anywhere," said Shire. "I'll keep an eye on her while you do the work you were supposed to have got done already and ought to be doing instead of diddling this skinny bitch."

Sam replaced the monofilament line and the

sinkers in his pocket. He looked at Junebug, squirming, her eyes wide as saucers, her legs tense. "I'll get back to you later."

Mmmffffppppppuhpuh. She nodded.

The Pink Cadillac was parked in the garage next to the John Deere Gator. Sam changed into oily coveralls, worn through at the knees. He jacked up the Pink Caddy and rolled underneath in a creeper with a ratchet wrench, rags, and an oil drain pan.

Sam chatted as he worked under the Pink Caddy. "Palatka told me about Wide Boy. Bad news travels fast." He clucked his tongue. "I will miss Wide Boy. That Chinese girl, well, they are pretty much replaceable parts."

"Got more of your homemade wine?"

"In the fridge in the Casita," said Sam. "Help yourself." He cursed, scraping a knuckle. He blamed Junebug, and heard Shire enter the Casita.

When he finished draining the oil and surfaced again, Sam saw Shire had filled a cardboard box with Mason jars of Sam's wine. His zesty orange blossom wine, his tangy key lime wine, his sweet strawberry wine.

"Didn't say you were gonna take all of it!"

"I need the jars." Shire drank from one jar and opened the others one by one, pouring out half the contents into the sand.

"Don't do that, Shire! That's a damn waste!"

"You can make more." Shire glared. Purplish-black goo accumulated at the corners of his eyes and dribbled down the side of Shire's nose.

Sam did not dare utter a word about it. He muttered as he poured fresh Valvoline into the Pink Cadillac, then stripped off the coveralls and strode toward Junebug lashed to the pole. "Changed the oil. Now do you mind if I get back to what I was doing?"

The girl moaned again, as if on cue. Her calves and arches of her feet ached. *Mmmmffffffnnnn.*

"I need shuteye," said Shire.

"Well, good idea," Sam said. "You look like shit, Shire. 'Scuse me for saying. You could use you some rest."

"Baptize her," said Shire. He jerked his thumb at Junebug.

"Say what?"

"You heard me. Baptize the bitch. Take the oil

you drained and pour it over her. Make her all black and slick. It'll be fun."

"That's not what I had in mind —-"

"I don't care what you had in mind. Do it, old man."

"It'll make a mess," said Sam.

"Make a bigger mess if I take a shotgun and blow both your fuck'n brains out."

Sam conceded that was not arguable. Junebug shrieked and made plaintive noises with the rag in her mouth, its loose ends fluttering like petals. Sam picked up the black plastic oil drain pan and carried it to her. Junebug flinched. She stood taller than Sam by a few inches and Sam was stooped with a bad back. He held the oil pan with both hands, stood on an overturned bucket, and balanced the pan above her head.

"Pour," Shire commanded, and Sam poured.

***

Shire Fenner didn't sleep. Leaving the garage, he locked himself in the shiny silver Airstream, a Flying Cloud model, which served as his office and arsenal. The posse clustered at the appointed hour, waiting outside in the humidity, sitting at the redwood picnic table or on patio chairs. Chucky Fike, the last to arrive, came loping through the saw palmetto.

"Under the wire," said Palatka Red.

"Wasn't my fault," Chucky said. "Had to put crazy Katie back in the attic and that's a chore, let me tell you. Where's Shire?"

"Inside," said Palatka Red. He motioned toward the Airstream.

"Hot as Hades out here. What's he waiting on?"

"Damfino. Why don't you knock on the door and ask him."

"Nope" Chucky said. He found a folding chair and sat among the others. Sam Fleance, looking glum, mounted a cedar stump. Bourbon plopped on a sagging chaise lounge, her bullwhip on a leather holder on her belt, Indiana Jones-style. Her mustache was freshly inked, but already runny in the humidity, and she smoked a clove-scented cigarillo while idly plucking chin hairs. At the picnic table, Red passed around a container of Copenhagen dip. Each man dipped; Bourbon demurred. Occasionally, they turned to spit into the palmetto.

Red turned to Chucky. "Word of advice. When

you see Shire, don't say nothin' about his eyes."

"Something wrong with his eyes?"

"Just don't say anything. And don't stare."

A few minutes later, the door of the Airstream swung open, and Shire emerged. He carried a cardboard box. Marching to the picnic table he laid the box down and then surveyed his posse, as if taking attendance and mumbling under his breath. Dark, purplish goo lumped in the corners of his red-veined eyes.

"What're you staring at?" Shire snapped at Chucky Fike.

"Nothing, Shire." Averting his gaze from Shire's purple-pus-oozing eyes.

"Who the fuck is he?" Shire pointed at a lanky kid on the periphery.

Palatka Red replied. "That's Bobby Shattuck."

"Who?"

"You remember, Shire. Kid wants to join the posse. He was at the Tribute. We talked this over already, Shire. You gave the okay."

"I do not recall," said Shire.

"Well, you did," said Red. The others corroborated. Red motioned the kid to stand up and step forward.

Shire eyed the kid and considered the matter. With trouble coming, and everything hanging in the balance, an extra trigger puller in the posse would sure help. There was that. And, besides that, he wasn't a bad-looking kid. Wiry, with meaty biceps. Blonde hair the color of straw, a sallow face, ice blue eyes. Pretty mouth and good white teeth. Reminded Shire of someone but it didn't matter who. Shire concluded that this kid made a good addition to his posse. Might even occupy a special position. If he earned it. But that remained to be seen.

"Alright. He's in. What is your name again, kid?"

"Bobby Shattuck from Carrabelle, Florida, up in the Panhandle."

"Didn't ask where you're from. I don't care where you're from. You got to listen to what I say if you want be part of my posse."

"Yes, sir, Mr. Shire," replied Bobby Shattuck.

"Every fuck'n word. You listen. And don't call me mister and don't call me sir."

"Okay, Shire."

"There you go," said Shire. "Siddown, Bobby Shattuck."

Shire let his silent gaze wander over the posse, looking each one in the eye. He had to harangue them, get the message through their thick skulls, and administer the loyalty test. What Elvis called it. A ritual of sorts. *A binding.* Shire had received specific instructions from the King. Things had to be done Elvis' way. That was the pecking order. Elvis was the biggest pecker of all. But Elvis was – what was the word? Incorporeal, a highfalutin word that meant Elvis had no physical body, like a ghost. The fish didn't count, and Shire hated fish, but anyway Shire Fenner was the biggest pecker in the posse, and he had no qualms about throwing his weight.

"Now, hear me," said Shire. "Listen up. It's that fuck'n priest! The priest and his 'congregation.' Them sons of bitches are double-D determined to bust into Ococonee Spring and do harm. Harm to Elvis, harm to Edgar, harm to me and all of us. What we do is guard the sanctuary. Is that right, Chucky?"

Fike nodded, agreeable as a spaniel. "That's

right, Shire."

"Is that right, Red?"

"Hundred percent, Shire."

Shire made the rounds, calling out an affirmation from each member of the posse. Lastly, Bobby Shattuck.

"If you ain't right, Shire," Bobby said, "grits ain't groceries." That got a laugh all around, easing the tension. Then Shire took a breath and got rock hard serious again.

"They are coming soon. Maybe tonight. Maybe tomorrow or the next day. We got to be ready. Show 'em no mercy. Make 'em bleed! *Kill. Them.*" He paused to let the words sink in. "Is everybody cool with that? Anybody goes chickenshit, I will cut your heart and feed it to the fuck'n birds."

As if on cue, grackles lighted on the Airstream, iridescent blue-green heads bobbing; dark greasy purple wings fluttering; each minatory bird slicing the humid air with its beak. Shire chuckled. He turned back to the posse and opened the flaps of the cardboard box on the picnic table. The Mason jars inside clinked.

"We going to drink on it," said Shire. He selected a jar, unscrewed its lid, and held it up. Every jar contained a few remaining ounces of Sam's wine, diluted with spring water. Fleshy, pulpy white chunks danced in the sacred spring water. Every morsel alive, every morsel magic, every morsel Elvis.

"Everybody takes a jar out of the box," said Shire. "Bourbon, get your big ass off the lounge. Sam Fleance, you old fart, hobble over here. What're you looking so glum about? That oily girlfriend of yours? She'll clean up."

"We're short one jar," said Red.

"I will share with Bobby Shattuck," said Shire. "Now, first off, watch me and do as I do. This is a serious fuck'n ceremony. Straight from Elvis. Yeah, me and Elvis are *talking* now. We got a working relationship."

Shire swaggered, thinking I wowed 'em with that bit of info. It's a new deal now. He took a penknife from his pocket, unfolded the blade, cut the tip of his finger, and squeezed a few crimson drops into the jar. The posse copied. Shire took Bobby Shattuck' soft white hand, sliced his middle finger as the boy grimaced, and added blood to their shared jar, then wrapped the boy's bleeding finger in a bandanna.

"Now, you all drink up. I want to see those fuck'n jars empty."

***

This weekend has gone to hell, thought Jason. Literally.

Outside, moonlight painted the ramshackle house and mangrove silver. Inside the house, they waited. Dudek dozed in a chair. Cody occupied a cot and snored in the next room, a symphony of cavernous sinuses. Mince, alert, sat by the window on a folding chair, on lookout. Their reinforcements hadn't arrived. Jason occupied the couch and grew increasingly impatient. He resented not being given salient facts. He shook the priest awake.

"I assume," said Jason, "that once Carmen arrives with your backup, that there's a coherent sort of plan."

"That's correct."

"Want to share it with me?"

"No," replied Dudek. "Not at this time."

"I think that's fair that I know the game plan. I have a part to play in it."

"Jason's right," said Mince. "He's signed on to

the mission. You already gave him plenty of biscuits to chew on. Give him the whole loaf, Mike."

"Alright." Dudek sat up, rubbed his forehead and the bridge of his nose. "Demonic entities search for a means of entering this world. A portal. Sounds hackneyed but it's true. They never rest. The essence of a demon is to never relent."

"Can we skip ahead to the plan?"

"Let me finish," said Dudek. "An entity found a portal at Ococonee Spring. Why there, you ask? Because some places, for reasons not understood, are natural conduits. *However.*" He lit another Marlboro Light. "Demons require the services of the very humans they abhor and seek to destroy. Call it irony. Demons are aided, enabled, colluded with, summoned, or invoked by humans, the wicked or unwitting. At Ococonee Spring a demon found such a *Receiver.*"

"Fat Edgar," said Jason. "Which category is he?"

"Unfreakingwitting," replied Mince. "Short on bandwidth but for reasons God only knows, Edgar Fenner can pick up *signals*. Good signals, bad signals, he doesn't have the sense to tell the difference, and he got played by Pleased-to-Meet-

You-Hope-You Guessed-My-Name."

"Unfortunately," said Dudek, "Edgar Fenner may be too far gone to redeem. We will have to enter the premises. Meeting resistance, that's certain. What we must do, after overcoming that resistance, is repristinate Ococonee Spring."

"Repristinate?" said Jason.

"Restore Ococonee Spring to its original purity. Disincarnating that which pollutes the water, the demonic entity in the grotesque form it has taken."

"The ugly armored monster fish thing?"

"It was a sturgeon, probably," said Dudek. "The demonic entity, in possessing it, effected physical changes. We must destroy it and remove the Receiver too."

Remove? A euphemism, its implication clear. Dudek sounded matter of fact and purely objective and that irritated Jason. "What you mean is killing Edgar Fenner."

"Distasteful but we can't shirk from what must be done."

"Edgar's shitty little brother too," said Mince. "Probably some of his posse. Hey, man, Jason, we're the *slayers*. We are warriors, soldiers. I wouldn't be here if I weren't convinced beyond doubt what we do is righteous."

"But not Kat," said Jason. "She's off the hit list."

"Look, man, we don't aim to hurt innocent people but the padre, Cody, and me, we got a Mission-from-God. It's heavy lifting. It gets messy. Collateral damage happens."

"That's not good enough." Jason stood and paced. "I don't care about Edgar or the rest of those morons, but I don't want Kat harmed. She's, um, fucked up maybe, but not evil."

"Salvation is possible," said Dudek. "The beguiled unbeguiled."

"You're saying that to placate me."

"No, I am not," replied Dudek.

"Chill, bro," Mince said to Jason.

The sound of a vehicle approaching silenced them, cutting the conversation short. Mince peeked out the window. A motor rumbled in low gear; tires crunched gravel; headlamps pierced the darkness. The vehicle stopped, motor idling, lights cut off. Doors clunked opened. Figures emerged and slowly stepped toward the house.

"Anybody home?" a female voice called.

"It's Sister Carmen," Mince announced.

"About freaking time," said Cody as he stumbled into the room, tightening the drawstring of his baggy grey sweatpants.

***

Shire sat on the porch swing in the heat and darkness and listened to the frogs croaking in the pinewoods. He hadn't slept except for a couple quick catnaps, less than an hour total. His mind roamed. Bobby Shattuck, thought Shire, probably got a nice tight little ass. Like the bikini girls' asses, yeah, like that, those peachy twins, and that's good, got to like that. Bobby Shattuck looked like a young Brad Pitt, the actor. Same color eyes, piercing blue and pretty, like a purring blue-eyed cat. Shire fancied he'd party with Bobby and the twins, sometime later, when the trouble had passed, and the priest took a dirt nap in the boneyard amid the dogs, the trespassers, and fat dead Ardell, and troubled Ococonee Springs no more. Shire fancied the girls, stripped down to only panties, wrestling on the shag carpet in the Jungle Room and then, at Shire's bidding, making out with each other for his amusement while Bobby Shattuck sat beside him and ...

"Anything you need me for, Shire?"

Like a specter, Bobby Shattuck materialized on the porch next to Shire. Shire hadn't even heard the screen door slam. Shire shivered with surprise, and his heart did a flipflop. "Uh, no. Not now. I'm good."

"Sorry to startle you, Shire."

"Startle me? No way. I'm always on the alert! Never underestimate Shire Fenner."

"Last thing I'll ever do is underestimate Shire Fenner."

Shire approved with a vigorous, jerky nod. "You got that right. I fuck'n *know* what is going on around me. At all times." Shire karate-chopped his hand for emphasis. "It's called situational awareness, and I got it."

"You're sharp as a tack," said Bobby. "Mind if I go?" He owned a pickup truck with a camper top and bunked on an air mattress on the truck bed.

"Stay hereabouts. At the house. If you're okay with that."

"I'm okay with that," Bobby Shattuck said ."Want some company?"

A nervous tic jolted Shire's cheek. His pulse quickened. Not the time now, outside late at night on the porch swing, no. Maybe later. For sure, later. "Sometimes, a man needs to be alone with his thoughts. I got a lot on my mind. Did you eat?"

"I'm good. Had BBQ ribs and a fried PBJ and banana sammich, heap of potato salad and okra, and two Moon Pies, one banana and one caramel."

"You ate all that?" Shire looked at the boy, his lanky frame and flat belly under a tight cotton shirt. "Skinny kid like you, where you put it all?"

"I got a speeded-up metabolism and burn through calories."

"You don't say! You look sleepy. Comfy couch in the Jungle Room. Nice satin pillows. You're welcome to crash there."

"Sounds good." Bobby shuffled toward the screen door. "Mind if I uh … if you don't want company."

"No, go ahead, get some rest. I might catch some winks in the Jungle Room with you. If you're okay with that."

"Sure, that'd be okay," Bobby turned on his bootheels. Hips swiveled. Shire watching him, sidelong glance. Scuffing sounds, porch wood creaking, the screen door slamming. Rusty porch swing chains squeaked as they scraped inside S-bolts. A barn owl screeched in the treetops. *I'm here. This is my territory, and I will take what I want.*

***

Half asleep, Edgar heard voices on the porch. One was Shire's. The other he recognized as the new kid, Bobby, who had a beat-up old Chevy pickup truck and slept in the truck bed under a camper top. Usually with one of the Chinese girls but Edgar couldn't remember which one. Edgar had seen them together.

The screen door slammed. The eerie cry of a screech owl made Edgar shiver as he lay in bed. *A wise old owl lived in an oak*, Gamaw used to recite to him when he was frightened at night. *The more he saw the less he spoke. The less he spoke the more he heard. Oh, why can't we all be like that wise old bird?*

Awake now, eyes fixed on the peeling paint of the ceiling, Edgar heard Luanne and Lynette chatting and giggling. Then they fell silent. Auntie Kate, locked in her room, scratched the walls but she stopped after a while. Must've got tired. A terrible burden, that old woman, but she was kin, an unbreakable bond.

Edgar snuggled with Ginger in bed under a thin white sheet. Edgar sat up in bed and watched Ginger beside him, her pretty breasts rising and falling as she gently breathed. Happiest he'd been in this life. He loved Ginger more than anything. Well, except for Elvis. But loving Ginger was different sort of love than loving Elvis.

She stirred, turned, and raised herself on her elbows. She switched on the nightlamp, her face white and pale in the lamplight, the look on her face full of uncertainty and unspoken questions.

"What is it, hon? Talk to me."

"I'm scared," she said.

"Of what?"

"I don't know, I don't know."

Edgar rolled toward her and took her in his arms and gave her a good squeeze. Bedsprings squealed and the bedframe rocked. "Nothing to be scared of. We're safe at Ococonee Spring."

"It's Shire. He's changed. He scares me. Did he hurt Harve?"

"No, he didn't," replied Edgar. "Don't let Shire scare you. He gets mean, at times, I know. Prison made him that way."

"Harlan told me Shire killed a man in prison," said Ginger.

"No, he did not. Never happened. Shire made up that story. Told it so many times that he forgot he made it up and thinks he really did kill somebody." Edgar sighed. "I've tried to bring Shire along, but he's got too big for his britches. I'm his older brother and I will have a talk with him and make things right."

"Uh-huh." The look in her eyes told Edgar she didn't believe what Edgar told her, but she kissed him, rested her head on his shoulder, and clutched a pillow to her chest as if it would keep her afloat. A tiny forlorn sob escaped. Tears welled in her eyes. "My brother … Jason … turning on me like that … the things he said … makes me feel sad and betrayed. And if he's with …"

"He will break with that wicked priest," said Edgar. "Your brother will mend his ways and Come to Elvis just like you did, and everything will be forgiven. Believe it, honeybun."

In a few moments she dozed in his arms.

Having peaceful dreams, Edgar hoped. He stroked her hair. He wanted to assure her that things would be okay. Because everybody in time comes to Elvis. Elvis is always there, waiting. People changed, and might be weak, might waver, and go bad, and do terrible wicked things, but not Elvis. No, never, not Elvis. Elvis had transcended and become a beacon. He was eternal. What's eternal doesn't change. Edgar's heart told him this truth. In the sweet by and by Elvis would lead them to Graceland. Like in the old hymns, to sing on that beautiful shore, their spirits to suffer no more.

***

These are the reinforcements? thought Jason. *Is this fucked or what?*

Three of them. Carmen flanked by two female assistants. They whisked into the house carrying olive drab sling bags. All wore simple light grey tunics and white headscarves, gold crosses dangling. Nuns. Hatchet-faced Carmen tall, thin, and angular; Lita, a dark-eyed Filipina, smaller, almost petit; and olive-skinned Nasha, smaller than Jason. They did not, in Jason's bleary eyes, resemble a fighting force.

Greetings remained cursory. Carmen exuded no-nonsense efficiency; clearly accustomed to taking charge. The nuns addressed Dudek as Father Mike.

They scraped chairs across the dingy linoleum to sit at the kitchen table and share a takeout container of coffee and the Krispy Kreme leftovers they brought with them in the Jeep Wrangler. Carmen and Lita already knew Cody and Mince. She scrutinized Jason.

"Who's this?"

"Newest member of my team," replied Dudek. "Jason Root."

"Is Jason Root sworn?"

"We vouch for him," Dudek said. Mince and Cody both nodded assent.

The answer did not satisfy Carmen. "Is he sworn or not?"

"Yeah, I am," said Jason. "Took the oath, okay?"

Sister Carmen fixed a hard, skeptical gaze upon Jason. Her face was angular, too. Sharp cheekbones, strong jaw. Her brown eyes drilled, like a nun in Catholic school regarding an unruly student. When she finally spoke to Jason, she was cordial and businesslike, "Nice to meet you, Jason Root. Do you have balls?"

He was dumbfounded for a moment. What

kind of nuns talked like that? Jason stammered. "Huh? Well, yeah. Yes, I do."

"Don't lose them," said Carmen. "You'll need them."

"Never mind balls," said Cody. "What about the money?"

Carmen turned to Cody, the faintest trace of a censorious scowl on her face. "And what about the money?"

"What Cody means to say," Dudek said, "is that our funds are depleted."

"You disappoint me, Father Mike. With your fiscal background, I assumed you'd be better with money. Parsimonious even."

"Can't fight evil on a shoestring," said Cody, biting into a glazed donut.

"Indeed not." Carmen removed a black poly bag from her kit and unzipped it, withdrawing a stack of cash bound with a rubber band and an ATM card in a plastic cardholder. These items she transferred to Dudek. "The code is 4747. You can withdraw up to $500 in any 24-hour period. Be apprised, it doesn't work in liquor stores or strip clubs."

Cody grumped. "Am I supposed to be

disappointed?"

"Merely an attempt at humor," replied Carmen. "Directed at no one in particular. Please take no offense, Brother Landry. Now, we need to get down to the mission essentials, taking down the demon and its adherents at Ococonee Spring. We brought the drone. I want to reconnoiter."

"We can give you the layout of the place," said Dudek.

"I must insist on a reconnoiter with the drone. I want my own team's eyes on the place. As soon as it's daylight. Sister Lita, that's you."

"Affirmative," said Lita.

Carmen turned to Dudek. "What is the status of your infiltration?"

"Ongoing. Our people remain in place and are undetected. In a precarious situation, of course. The situation's fluid."

"Of course," replied Carmen. "Getting them out safe and sound is a priority."

"What about Kat?" Jason spoke up. "What about getting her out? Is that among your priorities?"

Carmen cast a disapproving look, as if he'd spoken out of turn, and deserved a rap on the knuckles with a ruler, and then looked at Dudek for clarification. "Who is he talking about?"

"His sister," said Dudek, "is one of the demi-possessed at Ococonee Spring. She lodges there in a relationship with Edgar Fenner, the Receiver."

"She's fucking him, yeah," said Jason. "I'd call that a relationship."

Carmen frowned; Dudek held up his hand for Jason to be quiet.

"Jason tried to bring her out but failed," said Dudek. "He was nearly killed in the attempt. We rescued him and recruited him. *Deus disponit.*"

"You have a knack for recruiting people, ad hoc, Mike," Carmen said. Emphasizing ad hoc and making it sound almost pejorative. Jason sensed she did not approve, and probably regarded him as a potential liability. Weak link of the chain. But this wasn't her show, Jason surmised, not totally. It was Dudek's. She looked at Jason, not without sympathy, but her voice was flat and unemotional. "You've been to Ococonee Spring and witnessed what is there. We seek to cleanse the premises, exorcise its evil, and free the innocent from demonic possession, your sister, among others. All of whom are in peril, grave peril. Body *and* soul. Do you understand?"

"Yeah, I get it."

"I will not lie to you, Jason," said Carmen. "No promises can be made. We do what we can."

***

On reconnaissance, they drove into Hygeia and parked the Jeep Wrangler behind the white stucco church, still sanctified ground, affording them sanctuary. The old white-haired deacon, an ally, stood guard. He cradled a 12-gauge.

"Do your thing," he told them. "Be quick. They could be coming any minute."

"Affirmative," replied Mince.

Lita lifted the black carbon fiber drone from its carrying case and custom-cut packing foam. In a few minutes, its four rotors whirred, and the drone sailed over the pines toward Ococonee Spring. Lita worked the control yoke.

"Here we go," said Mince. "Fly, baby, fly. Fly like an eagle."

Lita and Mince kept eyes on the monitor as the drone soared. The gabled roof of the house came into view.

An old woman in a ragged nightgown leaned out the window and screamed at the drone, balling her fists. The drone passed over the peak of the roof and veered toward the spring. Lita made notes of the activity on the ground. The water shimmered; wind rippled. A corpulent man stood alone on the shore and looked up at the drone, surprised. His chubby face contorted.

"That's Edgar Fenner, the Receiver."

"Hola, Edgar," Lita said, sipping Diet Mountain Dew. "*Muah*, baby!"

Then turbulence rendered the imagery indistinct and staticky. With a sudden dark purplish flash and a high-pitched whine that stung their ears, the drone camera went off-line, dead, the monitor blank.

"Lost it!" Lita shut down the control box. "Damn it!"

"Show's over," said Mince. He added, with a grin, "Nuns aren't supposed to swear."

"Who said I'm a nun?" Lita shot back as they got back in the Jeep.

"I assumed." A bit sheepish.

"You assumed wrong," said Lita. "I haven't taken the vows yet, like Carmen has. Carmen is hardcore. Warrior nun legend. She's ex-military. I am also but I am laity, and we serve too." She pointed at the blue and gold badge sewn on her khaki shirt. "Catholic war veterans auxiliary. A martial order, sworn to protect and fight and serve the Light. Like you."

"Cool," said Mince. Giving thumbs up. He drove. The deacon waved and then retreated back inside the church.

***

You see that? Did you see that, Edgar? They sent their little stealth birdie overhead to spy on me. But I destroyed it!

With a lightning karate chop in the air, Elvis had demolished the drone. Shattered it. Pieces rained over the palmetto. Elvis grinned with satisfaction. He hovered over the water, agitated, spinning little purple funnels over the sand and into the brush. Edgar covered his face with his hand to shield his eyes from the sand and grit in the whirlwind.

"Uh-huh," said Edgar. "Yessir, you destroyed it."

That'll teach 'em to fuck with ME! So, are you through bellyaching?

"I meant what I said," replied Edgar.

But Elvis would have none of it. *You go tell that girlfriend of yours to cool it. She got jitters, that's all, jitters, not important. We got business to take of. We're at war. This is war, dammit. They are out there. Those ninja bitches, those cunts. Joined up with the priest and his goon squad. I have seen them. I can see them right now. They're not even trying to hide from me!*

"Well, um," said Edgar, "if you know where they are, why don't you send Shire and his posse after them? Shire's spoiling for a fight."

You think I hadn't thought of that? Sure, I could do that! But I'm not going to. Tell you why. Shire got more balls than brains and the same goes for the ragged ass losers in his posse. They would fuck it up! No, I have another plan. I will lure my enemies to my ground. I will draw them down into my realm and destroy them!

Edgar watched, dazed, and fearful, as Elvis unfurled his arms like vast wings, the black leather sleeves rippling, spangles shining like onyx, his countenance adorned with aviator glasses fierce and determined. Edgar trembled. This wasn't the same Elvis as before. Ginger had it right. He'd changed. Probably the stress, Edgar reckoned. Had to be the stress of the priest and his confederates besieging Ococonee Spring. After the danger had passed, Edgar pinned his hopes on

Elvis reverting to his old self. His loving and laid-back self, who had first started speaking to Edgar Fenner in gentle murmurs and sweet dreams during Edgar's puberty. In secret. A secret covenant between the two of them, a bond that grew stronger and stronger as Edgar developed his natural talent as a Receiver.

Go now, Elvis ordered, as he shrunk into the percolating depths of the spring. *I am done talking with you. Begone. I'll call you when I need you. And when I call, you get your lardass here fast as you can. Hear me?*

"Yessir," said Edgar. "I hear you." Edgar turned to go.

Wait.

Edgar froze.

Elvis retracted his fearsome wings and instead of vanishing into the spring and merging with his armored fishy host, Elvis lingered and a blue-green haze enveloped Edgar like mist. The light softened. Elvis' voice was no longer feral, but conciliatory, gentle, and silky. *I know what you're thinking, Edgar. Sorry I am so harsh with you. But with reason. I'm under terrible pressure, yes, I am.*

"I understand," said Edgar.

Everything will be better later after the trouble is quashed and that priest is rotting in the dirt with the worms. Then everything will be peach fuzz and peaceful again. And don't forget, Edgar. Graceland is coming. Nearer and nearer. Soon to be unveiled. When Time Comes, Edgar, I will take you there. I will transport you and my loyal fans to peace and bliss everlasting. Promise.

***

"Let me ask you a question," Jason said as he and Cody unloaded the groceries bought on an early morning expedition to Newberry for provisions.

"Shoot," said Cody.

"What's the distinction between demi-possessed and the, uh, other kind?"

"The eyes," replied Cody. He stuffed a stack of Jimmy Dean Breakfast Bowls into the fridge. The freezer section resembled an ice cave. "There's a weirdness, like a sort of shadow in their eyes. Plain and simple, demi-possessed means their souls are still redeemable. Not that fat woman who tried to chop your head off. She was running on high-octane. If you remember."

"Vividly."

"Demi-possessed, you can still reach them," Cody said. "Best case scenario is you expel the demons, cast 'em down into the primal pit they come from and set the afflicted free. Well, that's how it's *supposed* to work."

"That implies it doesn't always work."

"No, no," Cody replied in haste. "Don't get me wrong. All I'm saying is … it's like they're brainwashed. You got to run the rinse cycle. Maybe a couple of times. Until the brain juices run clear."

"I see," replied Jason, but not really understanding the mixed metaphors, and thinking of Kat's goth-tinged brain, thoroughly rinsed, dried, and redeemed into pure vanilla. Was that possible? Jason sighed. "You know, this is not how I expected to spend my weekend."

Cody snorted. "Sorry about your ruined weekend, pilgrim. That's tough, real tough. Could've been worse, a lot worse. Your head is still attached. You want a Hot Sausage and Salsa Verde Bowl? It's good eats. Not mama's home cooking but good enough, and you need to eat. Body needs to eat like the soul needs grace. Got to keep up strength for the struggle."

"I'm not hungry," said Jason.

Cody slurped black coffee, wiped his mouth, and jammed the breakfast bowl into the microwave and pressed the controls. "There's another thing I was meaning to discuss with you. This is good a time as any." While the microwave made its horrendous clanging noise, Cody dug into a pocket on his baggy cargo shorts and extracted a snub-nosed revolver with a thick rubber grip, its chambers empty.

"You'll want to carry this."

Carry? That was risky. Jason looked at the weapon, registering a frisson of disquiet. He calculated the attendant risk factors and decided no, I'm not that guy and this won't work for me. Given his limited experience with firearms, and zero experience with handguns, he'd only hesitate at the crucial moment, or misfire, and shoot himself in the foot or worse.

"No, I'd rather not."

"Think hard about it, pilgrim." Cody said, like a dedicated coach introducing a novice player to the game. "Might prove useful in a clinch. Might be a lifesaver. It's .357 caliber but we'll load it with .38 rounds so the muzzle flip and recoil aren't as bad. Control is the thing. If you want, we can go out to the mangrove for some practice to get you acquainted with the piece."

"If it's okay, I'd prefer not to. Thanks anyway."

"That's unwise. But your choice." Cody's shrug telegraphed *at least I tried*. He thrust the revolver back in his pocket. "Suit yourself."

***

Edgar lumbered up the creaking steps to the attic room where auntie Kate waited for him. He heard her chattering behind the closed door, the twins trying to keep her restrained. She heard Edgar approaching and chittered his name. Edgar sighed. He hesitated a moment. But duty, however onerous, called him. He opened the door, crouched down to avoid bumping his head, and entered the odd-angled room, crinkling his nose at the stench. The odor of camphor, stale air, and pee saturated the room. Katie glowered at Edgar, wild eyes bulging and red rimmed. Wearing only a tattered nightie, she stood between the twins on skinny bare legs, ghostly white and trellised with blue varicose veins. The girls pinioned her arms behind her back with leather straps. Their job was that much harder without Cousin Harlan to help. Both girls displayed fresh bruises and scratches. They greeted Edgar with pleasant smiles, nonetheless. Katie screeched at Edgar. Edgar winced.

"Fuckface! About time you got here!"

"Now, now," said Edgar. "That is no way to talk. Be nice, auntie."

"I'll be nice … if you listen to me!"

"I always listen to you. What do you want, auntie? Why'd you call me up here?"

"Matches! Give me matches! I want a box of matches!"

"Matches!" said Edgar. "What do you want matches for?"

"To start a fire," Katie replied, with a look that said *what else?*

"We talked about this. You don't play with fire, auntie. We can't have that. No, ma'am. No matches for you."

"I want matches!" Katie screamed in a piercing falsetto. "Everything must burn! Burn! Burn! Burn!" She lunged at Edgar, the twins holding her back, forcing her to her wobbly knees and hitting the floorboards with a clunk. "This house will burn! You all are going to burn to a crisp, wait and see!"

"Uh-uh, nope. Graceland is coming, not fire." Edgar motioned to the twins and pointed at the bed in the room. A bare mattress on a wrought iron frame, covered with clean towels, which wouldn't stay clean for long, and a polyester Elvis pillow. Straps for restraint. A pile of sponges, plastic buckets, and a side table for Katie's meds; bottles of rock and rye whiskey and a jar of hemp-infused gummies, cherry flavor, her favorite. The twins picked auntie Katie up, plopped her unceremoniously on the bed and proceeded to fasten her ankles to the bed frame. Edgar assisted.

"Now, you behave, auntie! Behave! Drink some rock and rye and swallow the gummy bears and you will feel better."

One of the twins fetched the bottle. The other threatened Katie with the funnel. Katie suddenly lay still. A chill descended upon the room; the twins shivered. Katie exhaled; her breath condensed into an icy skein. She glared at Edgar, her mouth stretching into a toothy grin. Edgar cringed.

"Doom is coming," said Katie.

"No, it's not," Edgar said.

"Oh, yes, it is! Doom on your doorstep,

coming to breakfast. You'll *die.* Your little bitch Gingy too. And this old house will burn!"

"Shush and eat your candy." Edgar opened the jar and dropped gummies into her mouth, careful lest she snap at him like a turtle and take a bite of his fingers. Katie chewed and swallowed. Asked for more. Please. Oh, pretty please. Calm now, her wizened face peaceful and white as new fallen snow. She sucked down rye whiskey too with a loud *gluuuuuurp,* and crunched sugar cubes from a box on the side table that the twins fed to her, along with vitamins and liver pills, then she took a tiny swallow of spring water from a green sippy cup, little chunks of ice rattling in the little child's cup.

"Okay." Edgar sighed, relieved her hissy fit had subsided. He longed for the *old* Auntie Katie, how she used to be before dementia. Terrible thing, dementia. A person becomes a ghost of who they once were. Edgar owed his upbringing, and his love of Elvis, to her and Gamaw; the two of them together had practically raised Edgar. He thought of both ladies back then, long gone days, and thought of Cousin Harlan, dead and gone, and the lump in Edgar's throat pained him like a tumor, and he wanted to weep, but restrained himself. The twins fed Katie a tunafish sandwich; she nibbled. Calm now. Flicking a dab of tuna from her lip like a cat.

"I will leave you now, auntie Kate. Got to get me some lunch, too. I'm hungry. I love you. Be good."

"Thanks for visiting," Katie said. "You always were my favorite nephew. The good boy, a sweet boy, and the gifted one. Like your mama was, bless her heart. But don't forget what auntie told you. About the fire. It's coming."

"No, I won't forget auntie." Edgar closed the door and, shaking his head, promptly put her dire warnings out of his mind. Too many things troubled him, and Edgar wanted peace. Peace, Ginger's love, and Graceland.

***

Inside the trailer that Palatka Red had converted into workspace, Shire examined the device. "You're sure this'll work?"

"You bet your balls it'll work."

"You *are* betting your balls."

"I ain't worried." Red swaggered and slurped beer. His foul breath was redolent of beer, nicotine, and sulfur.

Pipe bombs, made to order. Elated, Shire held one in his hand and admired the workmanship.

Two short sections of grey steel pipe wrapped in black electrical tape, pipe ends sealed with plastic caps and glue. Copper wires protruded from the pipe ends and connected to a crude electronic device that looked like an egg timer. Red had constructed three of them.

"Where'd you learn to rig one of these?"

"From a demolitions guy I knew when I rode with the Maggots. He had cancer and wanted to pass the know-how down before he croaked. His legacy or some shit. All you have got to do is set the timer and press the button. You can plant the thing like an IED, or you can throw it. There're different schools of thought on steel versus PVC. Steel's got hellacious fragment velocity and throws bigger chunks of shrapnel and that's where you get your maximum damage. Blasts about 1800 feet per second."

"Alright, I'm sold," said Shire. He devised a strategy for use of the ordnance; one each in key locations. "You keep one here. I want one at the house. Under the sink in the kitchen. Third one by the spring. I got a cache of weapons there."

"Will do," said Palatka Red.

"Good," said Shire. "We got to be ready when the shit hits the fan. And that is going to be *soon.*"

The sun at noon shined pure and white and the cloudless sky formed a pure azure canopy. In the daylight, boldly outside the chalk and shell circle, Carmen, Nasha, and Lita drilled, practicing martial arts moves. Intent, lithe, clad in black ripstop tactical pants and clingy t-shirts. Mince sat in a folding chair, watching them, impressed.

Jason sat next to him. "Pretty bold, out in the open like that."

"Advertising," replied Mince. "They're like, hey, you, the Grim Repulsion in Ococonee Spring. We know you see us, and we don't care. We. Do. Not. Care. We *fear you not*. Game on. You will be exorcised." His head swiveled toward Jason, and he smiled with enthusiasm. "Cool, aren't they? Sworn, dedicated, and tasked with fighting demons on earth. The pretty little nun outfits they came here wearing were camo. They train. Hone to the razor's edge. You got to admire them."

"Uh-huh," replied Jason. He could admire the toughness and prowess the women displayed but his mind drifted amid the fever dream unreality of his situation. "What day is it? Monday or Tuesday? I'm not sure. Without my phone, I've lost track."

"People get too reliant on their devices."

"I'll plead guilty to that," said Jason.

"To be honest, I'm not sure what day it is, either. But don't worry, J-man. It won't be long now."

"What won't be long?"

"When we go into Ococonee Spring and take out the beast."

***

A wooden barrier and orange cones blocked the entrance to the spring from the highway with a hand-lettered cardboard sign. *Closed until further notice. Ari ver deechee.* The posse took turns on guard duty. At dusk Bobby Shattuck sat in a folding chair under a yellow striped beach umbrella by the barrier when Shire ambled down the road, carrying one of the pipe bombs.

"Hey, Bobby, looksee here! Check this out!"

"That's right nice, Shire."

"Hey, like they say, it's the bomb!"

Shire cradled the pipe bomb in his arms, like a pet and his good mood bloomed like algae in warm coastal water. "Damn straight it is! Palatka Red put this humdinger together. And two more. Hey, Chucky Fike's on his way down here to take over guard duty. What say, when he gets his happy ass here, you come on up to the house with me. C'mon. Let's get some vittles. It's almost suppertime. Drink some cold beer and sip some Jack. You like Jack? I like Jack. Jack's the best. If liquor is a crutch, Jack's the fuck'n motorized wheelchair. We'll drink us Jack together like pals. How's that sound?"

"Sounds good, Shire," Bobby replied. "But I kind of got a thing to do first."

"What thing is that?" Shire, dismayed, dropped his smile like a lead sinker.

Shire pointed in the distance at the RV where the Chinese girls resided and answered sheepishly. "Well, you see, I sort of made a date with Lotus."

"A date with Lotus, huh." Shire wasn't sure which one was Lotus. He remembered Luna was the one he shot by the roadside.

Bobby grinned. "Made a date with her to get cleaned up and get a massage and, well, you know." He winked. "The Happy Ending."

"Oh, sure, I get it, yeah. Yeah, I, uh, s'pose it's better you get yourself cleaned up and jacked off before you enter the House of Fenner, yeah."

He clapped Bobby on the shoulder, friendly, brotherly. His hand lingered on Bobby's shoulder and pinched, his affability a hollow thing. "That's okay. You do that. Have a good time. You got Shire Fenner's approval. S'what we keep those chinky girls around for."

"Thank you, Shire." Bobby spotted slovenly Chucky Fike shuffling toward them, 30-30 rifle on his shoulder.

"Don't be diddling around all night. And don't get lost between the RV and the house. You hear me?"

"I hear you, Shire," replied Bobby.

"I want to see you at the house. I had better see you at the house."

"You will, Shire," replied Bobby. "I'll be there. Promise."

***

They took turns on guard duty. Dudek, unable to sleep, took over for Lita. He sat by the window, the Beretta in its shoulder holster, and sipped steaming black coffee. The vast dark silence outside simmered with Florida humidity. The dull thud of thunder rumbled, faraway, probably out in the Gulf. Owls screeched. Something barked and howled. Coyote?

Dudek scanned the skies. An array of pinpoint stars in a black velvet sky. Light shines in darkness and the inimical darkness comprehends it not.

Dudek placed his coffee mug on the spool table. He touched his scapular. Flicked its laminated edge idly with a fingernail while his thoughts drifted. This is *that* time. Of encroaching darkness and chaos. Of frenzied assaults on human nature, to overturn its most basic tenets, upon which civilization had been built, and crush all tenderness. Faith is mocked. Insult and ridicule of the Church became de rigueur in popular culture. But when it comes down to a showdown with the demons, it's the guy in the Roman dog collar who is called upon. The ancient Roman army had a phrase for it. *Res ad triarios venit.* That was his job. The Last Resort.

The demons never stop, never sleep, and never quit. Demons descended from angels, a distinguished lineage, created from the primordial divine light, the light they abjured in rebellion. They infest the lower astral planes and scour the earth, hunting for vulnerable humans upon which to prey. In the cosmic hierarchy demons outrank humans, whom demons regard as inferior creations created from dust and carbon. Meatsuits and monkey heads, demons called them, as if the human species had never advanced beyond the depiction of actors in simian suits at the beginning of 2001, the ponderous and opaque Kubrick movie. Demons excel at deception. The greater the deception, the greater their exultation. Fooling the meatsuits at whom they sneer, drilling perverse ideas into human skulls, inducing them to engage in reprehensible conduct that no demon would partake of, considering it beneath them. That is their triumph, to debase humanity; they would eradicate humans altogether.

Ococonee Spring was theatrics, masquerade, an infernal *son et lumière* confected to conceal the true nature and overweening pride of the waterborne demon who had taken up residence there. The more adroit demons concealed their very existence, blending into everyday reality, shadowy, subversive, and all but invisible, but few can master that trick. Or want to. Most are blatant. Supercilious and narcissist. Must romp, must have an audience. But focus your mind, and squint at one, and the mask falls away, revealing a twisted evil visage no mere mortal can mimic.

Thunder rumbled. Closer now. Making the floor and walls shake. Something in the darkness outside caught Dudek's attention. In the impenetrable thicket of mangrove, something moving, skulking, shape shifting. Microsecond flashes of lightning illuminated it. That face. Ancient. Primeval. Unalloyed malice, grinning, mocking. A dark form slinked out of the tangle of mangrove roots, slushing through the black brackish water, and slouching toward Dudek.

Hello, shaman. Filthy old cuckchrist priest. Let's rock!

"Father Mike?" Carmen shook his shoulder.

Dudek's body jerked, jolted, and his eyes opened. He trembled. Saw Carmen standing over him, reassuring, her firm hand on his shoulder.

"You dozed," she said, a hint of remonstrance in her voice.

"I did, I must have."

"Get some sleep, Father," Carmen said. "You need rest. I will take over the vigil."

"Yes, thank you," replied Dudek. He surrendered the chair. "I should sleep."

Dudek flopped on the lumpy couch, and silently prayed for several minutes until the repellent dream images faded; then fell asleep again. He plunged into a dreamless sleep. No mangrove, no dark and sinister visions, no dread, no taunts or infernal challenge, and no chicanery. Just untroubled rest.

In another room, Jason's gut rumbled. His stomach churned. He burped into flames. He guzzled water and chewed Tums he had pilfered from the first aid supplies.

Nasha and Cody had collaborated on dinner with dual frying pans sizzling on the stove to cook the dishes of their respective native regions. This translated into a fiery feast evoking West Africa and rural Louisiana and served with mounds of white rice. A jambalaya-like hash, Jason observed, composed of tomato puree, two-alarm peppers, chicken, eggplant, okra, plantains, and onion. They had all crowded together elbow to elbow at a common table. Dudek said grace. He kept it brief. Jason joined the chorus of amens. Then they ate.

The last meal? Jason thought.

He lay awake on a cot in the room he shared with Cody and Mince. His stomach might settle but not his nerves. Risk factors flitted through his mind like stingrays in shallow water. Stingrays without defined edges, amorphous evil stingrays, stingrays of dire possibilities. The nightmarish situation he found himself in lacked any predicate; Jason couldn't fathom the risks or even fully grasp the reality of Ococonee Spring.

Bedsprings rattled as Cody tossed and turned and then, lying as still as a land mass in the dark, resumed snoring.

"Shit," Jason said aloud.

"Hey," Mince said on the adjacent cot. "Try these." He flashed a penlight and handed Jason disposable earplugs in a plastic baggie.

"Thanks." Jason fished two plugs out of the baggie and popped them in his ears.

"Cody snores like a warthog and farts like a howitzer," said Mince.

"What?"

"Get some sleep."

"Okay," said Jason. He clenched his fists and sputtered whispered affirmations. "Cool. I'm cool. I am cool. I'm going to do this tomorrow. Yes, I am. I am. Yes, I can."

"J-man!" snapped Mince. "Just chill! Sleep. You're going to be fine. You're going to rescue the girl and ride off into the sunset."

***

"Honeybunny," said Edgar. "Honeybunny, what's wrong?"

Edgar switched on the bedside lamp. Three AM according to the Elvis wall clock. Holding the lamp, Edgar hunkered down with a grunt, dropped to his knees with a thud, and that hurt. He peered under the bed. Ginger lay there curled up like a newborn, a ball of Ginger in a pink nightgown open in back amid the dust balls under the bed.

"Honeybunny, talk to me. Please tell me what troubles you."

"It's coming," she announced, twisting her head so that Edgar could see her tear-streaked face in profile.

"Don't you worry," said Edgar. "Everything will be okay."

"You say that, but you know that's not true."

"Yes, it is. You got to trust me, hon. Got to trust Edgar and got to trust Elvis."

"Elvis is dead."

A spike pierced Edgar's heart. "Don't say that!"

Ginger whimpered and scooted away from him toward the wall, shivering, and said nothing. Edgar gave up. Couldn't reach her. He sat up and began blubbering. His eyes burned. Tears trickled. This had all gotten to be too much to endure. He wanted things to go back. He wanted time to stop and reel backward. To when he and Ginger first loved one another. When they lay by the spring and Edgar found a caterpillar. Back even further when Elvis had first made his presence known and shown his love for Edgar. Back, back, back. Time travel in his mind. To when it was just Edgar and Gamaw and auntie Kate watching Elvis movies, the whole galaxy of Elvis in Hollywood, watching together and eating sliders and French fries by the bagful only the three of them happy as housecats before his Daddy came back from Biloxi and brought his new wife Dotty he'd met at the Isle of Capri casino serving cocktails in a spangly silver dress and with them they brought the squalling baby boy whom she had named Shire because Walt C. Fenner, a proud and obstinate man, wouldn't allow her to name a son of his Frodo or Samwise, from the Rings books she read and was downright goofy about. Walt C. Fenner never read a book in his life. Except car manuals, if that counted. Edgar never liked Dotty and neither did Gamaw, but she hid it. About Elvis, Dottie Fenner was so-so. Edgar never forgave her for that. For everything else, he could forgive her, up to and including the drugs and drunk driving, but not that.

But those Good Times at Ococonee Spring

were gone, all gone, all used up, sand through the hourglass. You can never go back, Edgar reminded himself. You have got to live here and now in the present. Got no other choice. Until the ascension to Graceland, of course. But that was a whole other level.

Edgar gathered his thoughts. Ginger was in a bad way, but Edgar knew she'd come through this. She'd be cured, be restored. Edgar would take her down the spring and immerse her in the water and Elvis would touch her and she'd be okay again, his beloved Ginger. Everything else might fall away but not Elvis. Graceland, they would get there, sure as baby rabbits or peace in the valley. Edgar took that as gospel. He'd never turn his back on Elvis. Never. He couldn't! No matter what happens.

***

In the predawn dark, moving like shadows, they piled into vehicles and drove down the rutted dirt road to the highway, the van in the lead, the sisters following in the Jeep. Cody drove. Jason sat numb in the back. They passed the thermos of coffee around. Caffeine provided Jason with a jolt, but his anxiety remained, gnawing. This was unreal, a prolonged waking dream.

"So," said Jason. "This is it?"

Dudek nodded gravely. "This is it."

"The battle is what it's all about," Cody said. "Put on the armor of God and stand firm. We go forth like warriors and at the end of the day, we will stand victorious."

"Amen, Cody," said Mince. He turned to Jason, handing him a thick black stick with a checkered rubber grip. "Take this."

Jason looked at it, puzzled, but the solid heft of the object in his hand was reassuring. "Uh, what is it exactly?"

"Baton," Mince replied. "It expands. Like this. See." With a click of a button, he telescoped the steel, and then retracted it. "Good defensive weapon. Take it."

Cody barked over his shoulder. "You don't want the revolver, and that's okay, pilgrim, but take the baton. You don't want to walk into the pit of hell with just your dick in your hand."

Both vehicles switched off headlamps as they drove into Hygeia, the town cloaked in darkness and silence. The van rolled toward the abandoned church and parked. The Jeep parked alongside.

"Why here?" Jason said.

"It's the outpost," replied Mince.

Jason discerned dim lights inside the church. A dim yellow lamp over the doors popped on, and the church doors opened. A tall, black man with wooly white and wild hair exploding from his cranium waved them inside. They grabbed gear and scrambled. Mince, holding a rifle, stood guard, standing at the door. Jason's eyes adjusted. Only candles and camping lanterns illuminated the hollowed-out interior of the church. Pews were gone, the altar was gone, the windows boarded over. A sleeping bag and blanket on the floorboards comprised the living quarters of the pastor. An open, dogeared Bible on a folding chair, a battered suitcase, a pyramid of canned goods, a propane camp stove, plastic water jugs, a case of Gatorade. A pump shotgun and boxes of ammo.

"Deacon," said Dudek in greeting.

"Father Mike," replied the deacon. They shook hands like old comrades. Hope radiated the deacon's craggy face.

"The time has come at last," he announced.

"Where's your congregation?" said Carmen.

"Gone. Only me, myself, and I. My flock despaired and dispersed. I've been holding out waiting on the day of deliverance and deliverance at last has come."

Jason, standing unobtrusively behind the others, spoke up. "Have you been living here in the church?"

"In the midst of iniquity, this church remains consecrated, and they can't touch me here." He eyed Jason, sussing him. "I know you. Tried to warn you what you were talking into when you walked into the X-press store, but you paid me no mind."

"Sorry," said Jason. "I didn't know."

"All right. Let's not get bogged down over that. You're Jason if I am not mistaken. I am Marvin Luckett, the pastor of this house of the Lord, lately the church of dire straits. Father Mike and Sister Carmen and I are in the same line of work. They do it their way and I do it mine, but we get it done, praise the Lord. And now is the time we dispel the unholy thing that has occupied Ococonee Spring."

Dudek gathered the others around him; bodies crowded together, silent, tense, and attentive in a circle in the dim light in the empty church. Jason stood between Cody's bulk and Lita's lithe frame. He took deep, controlled breaths, trying to stifle the dull apprehension that gnawed at his nerves and gut. Jason folded his arms tight across his chest, clutching his biceps, fingers digging into muscle.

Luckett turned to Dudek. "Sorry I couldn't bring more people."

"You stand fast and that's good enough," replied Dudek. "Eight of us, plus the two inside, should prove sufficient to the task. Lotus tells me she has enlisted the other girls. That's good news."

Jason's ears pricked. "Lotus? The massage girl?"

"Yes," replied Dudek. "We communicate on the sat phone. Ask no further questions, Jason. Not now. All of us know the nature of our foe. We know what must be done. Be alert. Be vigilant. Be aware." He bowed his head. The others also did, including Jason. "Lord, we commit ourselves to expel the horrible Repulsion that festers there, free the souls in bondage, and repristinate Ococonee Spring."

As they trooped out of the church Jason saw another vehicle parked by the Jeep and the van, a dark blue Ford Edge that blended into the predawn darkness like a phantom coach. A man got out of the vehicle and gestured to Dudek. Dudek approached him without any surprise or trepidation as if they knew one another and this meeting had been expected, if not prearranged. Carmen joined them. The three of them conferred, standing apart, out of ear shot, while the others halted and waited. Jason studied the man. Middle-aged, squat, muscled, wavy black hair, probably Hispanic. Wearing dark pants and white shirtsleeves with a tie. Jason noted the pistol in a holster on his belt.

"Who's he?" Jason whispered to Mince.

"Shadow agency. On our side. Clean up after we're done."

Cody tugged Jason's sleeve and raised his index finger to his lips to indicate hush-hush. "You don't need to know. None of us need to know. Like the good angels, they observe and then assist. Get it?"

The convo by the Ford Edge ended and The Man got back in his car. To Jason, he didn't look shadowy; he was a bit corpulent. He didn't look angelic either; his demeanor suggested law enforcement, military, or some form of officialdom. A computer screen on the dash illuminated the man's stony, chiseled face and a radio chirped. He answered. Dudek and Carmen returned to the waiting group, remained silent, and signaled time to move. They stalked through the woods in the darkness. Silent, tense, the women in the lead, gliding like specters through the pines following reflective trail markers nailed to the trees, following a path from the church toward the spring. The priest lugged a worn leather bag, containing all his priestly accoutrement.

They know we're coming, thought Jason in the pale predawn light, soundless, eerie. His pulse raced.

Luckett traipsed alongside Jason, carrying his shotgun. Almost hobbling, favoring his right leg. "Hate to admit it," whispered Luckett. "But I'm getting too old for this. I need a hip replacement. Waiting on Medicare."

Jason could see the camp, the trailers and RV, sheltered under the immense oak trees. He spotted his Toyota where he had parked it a few days earlier. Carmen and her team dashed ahead. Mince and Cody followed. Dudek waited. Jason heard the muffled sounds of brief struggle. Mince appeared and waved them forward. Creeping, creeping along. Only sound the crush of the dry palmetto fans underfoot. Jason kept a tight grip on the baton. Pale dawn light washed the sky to the east behind them. By a Chevy pickup truck with a camper top, the Asian girl, Lotus, waited.

"You're alright?" Dudek said.

"I am okay," replied Lotus. "The bad one, Bourbon, is inside the RV. Tied up. The other girls watch over her."

"Good work," said Dudek.

"Not hard to convince the other girls to rebel. Bourbon abused them so much."

Two of the posse, prone on the ground, flopped like fish, disarmed, wrists and ankles zip-tied, hurricane tape wrapped around their mouths. Lita and Nasha stood over them. Old Sam and the skinny redheaded girl, quaking with fright, stood against the RV, hands over their heads, Cody guarding them. Carmen jabbed them both with syringes. Both let out plaintive cries. They were ordered to sit, then to lie down, and both promptly passed out, side by side.

Cody grunted. "So much for the posse. Weren't worth a darn, none of them."

"Not over until it's over," said Mince. "The prelim bout's over. The real fight comes next. We got an evil entity that won't be a pushover."

A young man wielding a rifle stepped into the clearing. Jason flinched, recognizing him, another one of the louts in Shire's posse. But the youth didn't prove hostile; he greeted Dudek. "Glad to see you, Father Mike," he said.

"Bobby," replied Dudek. "Are you okay?"

"I've been better. I had to take the 'sacrament.' Had to swallow it. Made make myself puke afterward. My stomach is still in knots." He guzzled fresh water from a canteen Cody offered. "Between that and fending off Shire Fenner, been a rough couple of days."

Cody pointed. "The house?"

"Shire and three of his guys are holed up inside. They won't be so easy to waylay. Not like these bozos." He indicated the posse subdued on the ground.

"My sister's in there?"

"Ginger? Yeah. There with Edgar. And the old lady and the twins, upstairs."

"We'll assault the house," said Dudek. "Take its occupants and then proceed to the spring to confront the repulsion. Marvin and Lotus, you stay here and keep an eye on the posse Jason, stay with them."

"No," said Jason. "I'm going into the house."

"No, you are not," Dudek replied.

"Nothing is going to dissuade me. I'm taking my sister Kat out of there."

"Let him go," said Cody. "Jason's got skin in the game. He sticks with me and Mince, and keeps his fool head down, he'll be okay."

Mince, standing alongside Cody, agreed. Carmen's expression nixed the idea, but Dudek relented. Carmen signaled her team; they readied their weapons and began a cautious approach to the house. Dudek followed. Then Cody and Mince moved forward in the pale dawn light, with Jason behind them.

A shotgun blast shattered the silence. Buckshot sprayed, shards of glass flying. Jason flattened himself on the ground.

Inside the house, Shire Fenner screamed; an incoherent string of f-bomb-laced babble, like speaking in tongues, but an obscene tongue. Then he reverted to plainspoken English. "Bobby Shattuck! You little cocksucker. You out there? You fuck'n traitor fucktard. I'll kill you!"

From above, auntie Kate hollered and threw empty bottles and the lava lamp at the assailants below. She pranced about on the asphalt shingles, clad in a ragged granny flannel nightie. She babbled, toothless mouth stretching wide as a bucket, her eyes bulged, wild strands of white hair tossing. Running out of items to throw at them, she clapped her hands. Sparks flew with each clap until flames leaped out of her hands and slithered along her arms. She howled and fled back inside the house through the window. The curtains burst into flames.

"That is one possessed old lady," said Mince, flat on the ground next to Jason.

More gunfire erupted. Mince unloaded a magazine at the house and reloaded. Jason gritted his teeth and dug his face into the sandy soil. Heard screams, shouting. When he looked up, he saw flames engulfing the upper story of the old house. Smoke began to pour. Two terrified girls in bikinis came tumbling out of the house to the porch, waving their arms, screaming don't shoot, don't shoot, and the shooting ceased. Then two men Jason recognized as Shire's posse dashed out of the house, each grabbing a girl to use as a shield as they dashed for cover amid the oaks. Gunfire rained fired from inside the house to cover them, bullets nicking the oaks, dropping branches and Spanish moss, perforating the steel Elvis silhouette at the base of the laurel oak. One of the men, slack-jawed, his Adam's apple bobbing, crouched a head taller than the terrified girl, his arm hooked around her neck while he brandished a shotgun in his free hand. Mince took careful aim and fired, disintegrating a chunk of the man's head. He toppled. The girl screamed, her twin broke free and the other man dashed into the thick palmetto as the twins scurried away and surrendered to the nuns. Looking up Jason saw Edgar Fenner carrying Ginger in his arms and running faster than Jason thought the fat, clumsy man would be capable. Edgar dashed toward the spring. Jason jumped to his feet.

"Stay down!" said Mince.

"That's Kat!" Jason took off in pursuit as the spray of bullets from the porch splattered dirt at his heels.

***

Shire howled with raucous laughter, slammed another 40-round magazine into the AK and, popping up by the kitchen window, sprayed the pines. Almost got that damn brother of hers but the fucker stayed ahead of the bullets, damn, he was quick, and Shire regretted missing him. He ducked down again before his besiegers returned fire. He grinned; he had them pinned down. But the house was filling with smoke.

"Skeeter caught it," said Red.

"That's his fuck'n problem," said Shire.

"They probably shot Chucky full of holes too."

"So?"

"They're dead, Shire."

Shire shrugged. He'd ordered both men to circle around and attack their enemies from behind. "Well, that didn't work out," Shire said. "They were too slow, fuck 'em. Make yourself useful and gimme that pipe bomb."

"It's no good! Wires cut!"

"That dirty fuck'n Bobby Shattuck! I'll cut his heart out! Cut his balls off!" Enraged, he leaped to his feet, thrust the rifle muzzle through the window, and emptied the remainder of the magazine, and then pitched backward, sprawling on the floor.

Red, coughing, looked at him through the acrid haze of smoke that filled the house. "Are you hit?"

"Me? No, I'm fine. Thanks for asking." Blood soaked his shirt. One ear dangled, split by a bullet. His eyes bulged, purple goop dripping. Shire smiled, a wide stone-cold maniacal grin. He pulled out the empty magazine and jammed another into the AK.

"It's no use, Shire," said Red, "we're getting smoked out."

"Hell, we ain't! We're good! Hey, what you think you're doing?"

Red held a bandanna over his nose and mouth. He crawled out of the kitchen toward the Jungle Room, leaving his pump shotgun, but taking his .45 under his belt. Red raised himself on his knees and reached into the Jungle Room to grab the duffel bag that Edgar had stuffed under the sofa and put a silky bow and a tag on it that read *Property of Ginger. Nobody tutch but her.*

"Leave that where it is," said Shire.

"Not staying here to get shot to pieces or burned to a crisp."

"Hell, you ain't. Let that go."

Red paused. "Okay, if you say so, Shire."

He released his grip on the duffel strap, plopped down on the floor facing Shire, jerked the pistol and shot Shire point blank.

The fusillade outside had ceased. Palatka Red stood, crouching in the hallway, and grabbed the duffel, He plodded into the kitchen and skittered toward the back door to escape in the billowing smoke. Coughing, eyes burning, he stood on the threshold, wary.

"Like hell you're going anywhere."

Red squirmed hearing the hideous, throaty voice behind him. He turned. Shire materialized, on his feet and aiming the muzzle of the AK at Red, his glare filled with cold inhuman rage, face contorted, irises of his protruding eyes like black balloons, leaking purple ichor, chin jutting, the corners of his mouth stretching upward to his cheekbones, exposing yellow teeth and purplish gums. Chest bloody, his shirt ragged. He was no longer Shire Fenner, but the dead shell of Shire Fenner inhabited by something malevolent and unearthly. Red shuddered.

"Bang," it whispered. "You're double-D dead."

It squeezed the trigger.

***

The shooting ceased. Voracious tongues of flame licked the Fenner house, ancient wood crackled, smoke billowed, and fire rendered the air acrid, stifling, eye-burning. Lita herded the twins to the RV camp. Mince and the others approached the house warily, weapons at ready. They found a dead body of Skeeter and found the other man, Chucky Fike, unconscious in the palmetto. Nasha secured his wrists and ankles with zip ties and remained guarding him. At Carmen's command, Mince and Bobby circled around the house.

They found another bullet-riddled body amid the hibiscus bushes, clutching a duffel bag with a big red bow and name tag attached.

"That's Palatka," said Bobby, kneeling and turning over the body. A limp arm fell away from the duffel bag.

"Bobby Traitor Shattuck!"

A high-pitched scream. Bobby stood to face the house.

A burst from an AK splattered Bobby Shattuck's face; he sprawled on the ground. Mince unloaded his weapon on the wraithlike figure that had materialized from the threshold of the burning house. Hair burning, scalp sizzling, body aflame. Eyes bulged from the face like ping pong balls, slathered in dripping purple ooze. The apparition howled and danced to and fro, a wild dance, like a marionette with twisted strings. The barrage of bullets crumpled what remained of Shire Fenner. He collapsed into a smoldering heap. Blackened beyond recognition.

"Christ Almighty," said Cody, rushing to assist.

"You're bleeding," Mince said. Blood

colored Cody's shoulder and arm.

"Just glimpsed me, is all. It's nothing."

"Glimpsed?" Carmen strode up beside Cody and examined his wound. "Forget the bravado. Get that attended to immediately. Lita's a medic."

"Where's Father Dudek?" said Mince. "And where's Jason?"

***

Jason had collided with Chucky Fike, heads clunking like billiard balls. They both toppled into the rough palmetto and ferns, then sat up and looked at one another. Then Fike pulled the pistol under his belt, but the weapon snagged, and Fike fumbled, cursing under his breath.

Jason telescoped the baton. He whacked Fike on the noggin and across the nose.

Fike stared at him dumbly. Blood poured from his nose. He drew the pistol.

Jason, leaping to his feet, cracked the baton across Fike's hand, smashing fingers. The pistol went flying. Jason kept hitting. Fike yowled and yelped like a hurt hound. Jason pummeled the man into unconsciousness, then ran toward the spring as flames roared over the house and gunfire crackled. The sparkling water was in sight when something struck Jason, knocking him flat. He lay on his back, stunned. A dark wave had descended over Ococonee Spring. An undulating curtain, cloudy, opaque. A barrier.

What the fuck?

It rippled. Jason sprang to his feet, gripped the baton, lowered his head and, with a running start, crashed into the curtain, hitting what he hoped was a trough, weak enough for him to penetrate. His timing worked. His skin tingled and he stumbled but found himself in the spring, immersed in the icy cold water and surrounded by an ominous, swirling purple mist. Kat sat on the sand, sobbing and Edgar Fenner, in a rage, punched Dudek repeatedly and threw him to the ground. He stripped the priest of his prayer book, vestments, and the Beretta, and bawled in Dudek's face.

"This is all your fault! You should've stayed away from Ococonee Spring! And quit bleeding all over my sand!"

Jason stomped out of the spring and whacked Edgar across his shoulders with the baton. The big man groaned, hunched his shoulders, shook it off like an annoyed hippo. He slowly turned to face Jason.

"You again? You're as bad as the darn priest. That hurt!"

Jason raised the baton to strike again but Edgar's fist slammed into his face and sent Jason reeling. Then Edgar hunkered down to wrench the baton out of Jason's hand and, glassy eyed with fury, proceeded to beat Jason with it.

"Stop!" Ginger cried, clutching Edgar's arm. "Don't hurt him!"

"Huh?" As if he had been asleep, thrashing an enemy in his dreams, Edgar snapped awake. He froze. His hand white-knuckle gripped the baton he had taken from Jason whom he now straddled. Jason lay supine and unconscious. Edgar tossed the baton as if had been a red-hot poker and wrapped his arms around Ginger. The crackle of gunfire from the house made Ginger shudder.

"We're safe," said Edgar. "Nothing and nobody can hurt us. It's a sanctuary."

"No," said the priest. He huddled in the palmetto and balled up a white priestly stole from his satchel, pressing it to his side to stop the bleeding. "It is an abomination."

"Shut your goddamned mouth!"

The priest gasped. "It must end ..."

"What did I say?"

Edgar let go of Ginger and leaped upon the priest, flailing, pummeling him with his fists while Ginger cried out and grabbed Edgar's arms. He turned on her. "He can't say that! There's no end to Elvis! Elvis is forever!"

Edgar.

The wondrous silky voice, *his* voice, a deep bass that rippled the water of the spring. An electric jolt surged through Edgar's bulk; his skin and scalp tingled, his heart thumped in his chest; his scrotum tightened. Edgar realized to his horror that his hands were clamped around Ginger's throat. She choked, her face purple. Edgar released his grip, grabbed her shoulders, and hugged her, her head rolling on his brawny shoulder.

"Oh gawd," he blubbered. "I didn't mean to hurt you, sweetheart."

Edgar, Edgar, leave her be and pay attention to ME. It is time.

"Time?" Edgar's head swiveled. Vertebrae made a cracking sound. Edgar scanned the spring;

Elvis did not yet manifest, but his voice reverberated inside Edgar's noggin. "Time for what?"

For what? You must ask? What have I talked about all this time?

"Graceland?"

Yeah, Edgar. Graceland.

As Edgar watched with awe, a colossal purple cumulonimbus cloud erupted over the spring, coruscating with sparkly light, and reaching toward the sky. A low-pitched thrumming made Edgar tremble. An epic fanfare followed, the signifier of impending glory. Edgar recognized the music, the 2001 theme that opened Elvis' Vegas show. Three crystalline trumpet notes sounded; drums pounded; and in the crescendo, an immense clamor like the buzzing of a thousand cicadas, Elvis appeared center stage, flanked by two alabaster white columns. Edgar Fenner gawped, speechless at the vision of corpulent Vegas Elvis, sporting a sweeping sable pompadour, his black velvet sideburns like a lion's mane, his flared white trousers like shark fins, his immaculate white suit festooned with epaulets and braid and buttons that sparkled like burnished bronze.

Graceland is here! Elvis announced. *Witness its splendor.*

"Wow," said Edgar. "Oh, wow."

But wow didn't come near the experience. There it was, *Graceland* rising from Ococonee Spring. Long promised, now fulfilled, floating in the enchanted air. Black wrought iron gates with sheet music designs inched open. Marble lions flanked the steep stone steps to the portico. Bright pink Tishomingo limestone and radiant rose-colored stained-glass windows adorned the façade of the mansion.

Elvis beckoned. *The time has come to ascend. Didn't I promise? Well, didn't I?*

"You surely did," said Edgar. He held Ginger limp in his arms like a rag doll. She murmured, half conscious. Her eyes barely opened when Edgar told her to look.

"You see, honeybun? It's Graceland! It's here!"

Ginger blinked. "Nothing there," she said. "Nothing there."

"Uh-uh! It's there, it's there," Edgar insisted, desperate that she too should behold what he beheld, Graceland in all its glory, where they would dwell together in love and harmony for eternity. She must see! Edgar shook her. He pleaded. "Open your eyes, hon. Look, look, look!"

"It's not real," said the injured priest from where he lay on the sand. His bloody fingers fumbled with the pages of his prayer book. "It's a deception!"

Elvis flared with rage. *The old priest lies! Make him shut the fuck up! Smite him! Smite that damn priest, Edgar! Hurt him!*

Obediently, Edgar delivered a kick to the priest's solar plexus. Dudek absorbed the kick with a groan and collapsed into a heap in the crackling palmetto.

Edgar, listen to me! Put the girl down.

Edgar obeyed, hunkering down, and settling Ginger's body on the ground in the soft sand. He gave her a kiss on the lips, and then turned his face toward Elvis again, in rapture. He narrowed his eyes to gaze upon the golden glow of Graceland.

Behold it good, Edgar. I have taken you to the Gates of Graceland, and you shall have admittance, but there is one more thing I must ask.

"Ask away, anything!"

Cut their throats.

"Huh?" Edgar responded.

You heard me.

With a wave of his hand, Elvis flipped over the red steel toolbox in which Shire had cached weapons at the spring, spilling its contents, a pocket pistol, brass knuckles, the pipe bomb. A Ka-Bar knife clattered at Edgar's feet. Its razor-sharp edge glinted. Edgar shuddered. His jaw dropped in gobsmacked disbelief.

"Say what?"

What I say? Elvis' puffy face remained blank and pitiless as an alien sun. *You heard me loud and clear. Slit – their - throats. Both the priest and the girl.* He pointed at Jason. *And that sonofabitch to make a trifecta.* He pointed at Ginger, his extended finger like a talon. *Her first. I want blood, the wine of the Spirit. Must have blood. Gobs of it, streams of it, puddles of blood, chalices of blood. Do this for me, Edgar. Your final task. Sacrifice to me that which you love. For this I gave her to you in the first place. Everything has a price, Edgar.*

"But ... but ..." Edgar's lip quivered. "I – I - I can't do that."

Yes, you can. Sure, you can. And you will.

Edgar recoiled. "I can't kill anybody like that! Bloody like that … not the priest nor whatshisname and especially not Ginger! Not my Ginger!"

Don't tell me that, Edgar. Unless you shed blood, you may not enter Graceland. Don't diddle around, do it! You've done everything I've asked of you so don't fuck it up at the finish line. Pick up the knife. Pick it up.

"No, I can't!" Edgar implored, tears welling in his eyes. "I love Ginger!"

You don't sacrifice what you care nothing for. In Graceland I will reward you with acres upon acres of fuckable flesh, a thousand wet pussy bitches at your beck and call, dancing on your bed like a bevy of Las Vegas chorus girls.

"I don't want no thousand acres, or Vegas chorus girls. I want Ginger! I will not do what you ask. I will not! Can't do that, *can't!*"

Obey me.

Edgar sheltered Ginger with his body and kicked the knife away. His legs buckled; he fell to his knees. He wiped away the tears and burning sweat from his eyes with the back of his hand. His throat muscles tautened like steel cable. His brain reeled, feverish; synapses snapping, churning; his perceptions altering. Edgar stared deep into the vision of Elvis and Graceland, squinting at the blazing light.

Edgar Fenner had the epiphany that was long foretold in his dreams.

Edgar ... A creaking sound, as the gates moved, hinges squealing, darkness descending, Graceland hovering, receding. *The gates are closing ... and shall be closed to you forever ...*

"You ain't him," said Edgar.

Elvis chortled. *Ha! You better believe I'm me. The one and only.*

"You ain't him at all. I see that now. I was fooled."

Graceland was phony. Fake. Like the priest said, a deception. The roly-poly creature in a white spangled jumpsuit was fake too. An imposter, an impersonator, a sham Elvis. It had pierced Edgar Fenner's mind, hoovered all his treasured memories of the King, and from them configured its disguise. Its twisted reptilian face shone through the melting dripping steaming Elvis mask. Hideous. Inhuman. And brimming with arrogance. A bitter cold resolution gripped Edgar. He stood, planted his feet firmly, and faced the fraudulent Elvis. "I know you now. You're something butt ugly and mean as shit." He cried out in a plaintive voice, "You fooled me all this time! Shame on me for being fooled and shame on you too, you son of a bitch."

The demon roared. *I will destroy you!*

"No, I'll destroy you!"

Edgar snatched up the pipe bomb from the red toolbox, flipped the switch on its timer the way Shire had shown him and holding it under his arm like a football, lunged into the spring. He flailed in the furious purple cloud, splashing in the now boiling spring, and fell upon the great scaly beast that floated in the water. The sturgeon slashed at him with its tail. Blood spurted. Edgar wrestled it, grabbed its snout. A high-pitched demonic scream churned the cloud, and then the explosion shattered the air, dissipating the cloud. Dissolving Elvis, dissolving Graceland. Smoke and a spout of water and a geyser of sand, grit, bloody chunks of flesh and scaly armored fish filled rained down.

Then … silence.

***

Jason heard the ocean. Waves crashing on a

bright, sandy beach. Verona Beach, the Atlantic Royale Resort, special weekend getaway rate, a capacious suite with an Atlantic view. Satin sheets. Canopy bed with a ceiling mirror. Chilled bottle of Dom Perignon on the nightstand with two slender champagne flutes and a package of American Spirit cigarettes.

Kat sat on the balcony. Jason sat up in the disheveled bed amid twisted sheets and the memory of intense pleasure washed over him like the white sand tossed by the waves. He craved more. His whole body ached for more, for her. He wanted the bliss that wiped away cares.

Then Kat Condon stood at the foot of the bed, wearing only his Miskatonic University t-shirt. It looked good on her, incredibly cute. She tossed her head and greeted him with a sphinxlike smile.

Sleepyhead, she said. *G'morning, lover. Let's play.*

"Wow," said Jason. The sliding glass door to the balcony remained open and the drapes billowed with a sea breeze. Jason tasted salt. But he felt relieved, untroubled, and secure now. The nightmare ended and had been nothing but a lurid phantasm. Kat lifted the t-shirt above her navel.

"You would not believe the dream I had," Jason said. He flopped back on the pillow and sighed.

No, I wouldn't, Kat said, disappointed and a tad sullen. Now she wielded a black bladed dagger and approached him. Something about her eyes, a telltale shadow, provoked in Jason an icy frisson of fear. Then that frisson merged into pure terror as blood dripped from one of her green eyes and from the corner of her mouth …

This *is the dream, lover. You're still at Ococonee Spring.*

"Wake up, wake up," said Mince, standing over him. "Get up, get up, Jason."

Mince pulled Jason to his feet. The ringing in his ears subsided. His blurry vision focused but he remained in a daze, wobbly. Smoke drifted, the air eye-pinching acrid. Chunks of gore sprinkled the sand and palmetto and floated on the water. Some fishy, some human. Dudek stood in the spring waist deep, his back to them, wearing his bloodstained priestly stole, holding a leatherbound book, and reciting Latin. He paused to glance over his shoulder, nodded to Jason and signaled Mince, then continued the rite.

"Come on, get up Jason," said Mince. "You're okay."

Jason surveyed the chaos. "You call this repristinated?"

"Some clean up required." Mince led Jason away. "Let's go. Father Mike's kind of busy. Time for you and the girl to bug out of here."

Sounded like a good idea. "Where's Kat?"

"She's okay," Mince replied. "By the big RV." They tromped together through the smoke toward the encampment, past the blazing house. "We'll get together again some time and destroy more demons now that you got Ococonee Spring under your belt. That sound cool?"

"Fine, cool. Where's Kat?"

"Just told you. By the RV."

"Oh," said Jason. He tried to shake off his daze. "Okay."

Mince delivered Jason to the RV. The Chinese girls bustled about, chattering and coughing, and Carmen and her team stood guard over the posse members now prone on the ground. Kat Condon sat by herself in a folding chair wrapped in a crinkly orange emergency blanket, oblivious to the activity around her, wearing a blank stare on her face. The twins huddled together under their own blanket and shared a bottle of Gatorade. Cody, his arm bandaged, sat on a cypress stump.

"You're in one piece, pilgrim?"

"I'm good," said Jason. "You're wounded?"

"Scratch is all. Nothing serious." He quaffed Mountain Dew, rinsed his mouth and spit, then pointed at Kat. "There's what's-her-name. Your girlfriend. Or sister, whatever. Anyway, grab her, find that Toyota of yours, and get both your asses out of here, pronto. They'll clear the way for you." He slapped Jason's shoulder in a fraternal, guy-to-guy farewell. "Been great working with you. See you later, terminator. Stay out of trouble."

"Who will clear the way?" Jason said.

"The angels," said Cody. "Go now. We'll be in touch."

Jason nodded but was unsure what Cody meant or whether he wanted to be in touch with them in the future; that, however, remained to be seen. Leaving Ococonee Spring, pronto, sounded like a good suggestion. He put his arm on Kat's shoulder. She shuddered. Opened her eyes and looked at him, feral and fearful.

"It's me, Jason. It's okay."

Carmen materialized at his elbow, hatchet face skeptical. "Can you drive?"

"Yeah, I'm good. I'm good. I can drive. Driving is no problem." As much to reassure himself as reply to Carmen.

"You're sure?" she said.

"Absolutely,"

"Then go with God." And Sister Carmen was gone again.

Jason eased Kat to her feet. His arm around her waist, they made their way to his Toyota, parked exactly where he had left it the previous Friday, but in worse shape. White streaks and splatters of bird shit stippled the windshield; the driver side was keyed with a jagged scratch the entire length; the side mirror shattered. The Toyota remained unlocked, the key fob dangling from the rear-view mirror on a cord with a plastic shrunken head. The interior stank of beer, smoke, and urine with a pile of crushed beer cans on the floor, a plastic cup in the cupholder overflowed cigarette butts. Jason leaned Kat against an oak, opened the passenger door, reclined the seat and, catching her just as she collapsed, deposited her in the seat, still wrapped in the crinkly blanket. She shivered. He fastened her seat belt and then scurried to the driver's side, pressed his foot on the brake pedal and pressed the ignition button. The engine and dashboard came to life. Jason ripped the key fob loose and threw out the shrunken head with cup and filthy cigarette butts. He executed a slashing turnabout and aimed for the highway.

"Wait up!" someone called.

Jason slammed the brakes. In the rear-view mirror he saw Marvin Luckett approaching the Toyota, trudging with his bad hip, and lugging a duffel bag with a red bow. He waved at Jason.

"This has got her name on it," Luckett said. He opened the door and dumped the duffel on the back seat and closed the door. "On your way. Let Jesus be your wheels."

"Thanks," replied Jason. "Yours, too. Get your hip replacement."

The Toyota jounced down the dirt road to the highway where Jason turned left and hit pavement and speeded up. Kat stirred in the passenger, then snapped awake, sitting upright. She looked at him. Wide-eyed, dazed, lost.

"Where are we going?"

"The fuck out of here," Jason said. "Don't

worry. You're safe now. Safe with me. Absolutely. I promise."

She stared straight ahead. "I feel … kind of … kind of … I don't know …"

Hitting pavement, Jason accelerated. Zoomed through Hygeia past the vacant convenience store. Then he caught sight of flashing lights. Barriers and patrol cars blocked the highway. Uniformed officers, state police, motioned for him to stop and approached the Toyota with caution. Stone faces, hands on sidearms, some toting shotguns, bullet proof vests.

Don't panic, Jason told himself. Then he saw the Ford Edge by the side of the road. Mr. Edge looked at Jason and signaled the troopers, who waved Jason on through past the barricades. Jason accelerated again.

"We're unstoppable," he said to Kat.

"You didn't say where we're going."

"We're going to my place in Tampa."

Kat cocooned the crinkly orange mylar blank around her. "I feel weird. Brain fogged as fuck. Like I woke up from a weird fucking dream. It's like, you do things in a dream, but you're not accountable because none of it is real."

"Uh-huh, that's all it was," said Jason. "A bad dream."

He eased his foot on the gas and turned to look at her. She stared at him. Her pale face, her green eyes. He searched her eyes for some telltale weirdness, a shadow lurking in her irises, some submerged residue of the repulsion that had inhabited Ococonee spring. Jason's insides churned. A vein in his neck throbbed. Was it there? He couldn't be certain. Not yet. Couldn't even be certain what, precisely, he was looking for. Wait and see, he resolved. He rested a hand on her shoulder. "It's over. You're awake again."

"Okay," she said. Meekly, averting her eyes from his and staring out the window.

He removed his hand from her shoulder and gripped the leather cover of the steering wheel at 3 o'clock. "What's your name?"

"Don't you know?"

"I want to hear you say it," Jason said. "Say your name."

He heard her sobbing, then she took deep breaths, sniffled, and wiped her nose with the edge of the crinkly blanket. Then she spoke as if reciting an intro, first day of school. "My name is Kat. Kathleen Condon. Your name is Jason Root. I liked you. We're, like, related. By marriage. Because your dad married my bitch of a mother. We met at their wedding in Verona Beach. They divorced. Where does that leave us?"

"Wherever we want to be," Jason said. "Perfectly free. Look outside. Beautiful out. Sun is shining. A whole new day."

Sunshine brightened the peaks of the pines. Puffs of cumulus dotted an azure sky. Another beautiful Florida day had begun. Fatal Florida, for all its craziness, for all its legion of risks, hurricanes, sinkholes, gators, vicious rabid otters, flesh-eating bacteria, insane criminal rednecks, hadn't killed Jason Root. He had survived an encounter with a demonic Elvis impersonator and its minions. The thought inspired a triumphant smile. He'd get a custom T-shirt, *I survived Ococonee Spring.* A hero, he'd saved the damsel in distress as well as his own ass.

Safe in his behemoth Toyota SUV, he raced due south toward Tampa on a deserted two-lane Florida highway hemmed by impenetrable forest. He fled from Ococonee Spring, away from the grim repulsion and the voracious flames and the plume of smoke over the pines, away from the nightmare. He heard sirens in the distance. Kat patted his hand on the steering wheel, and let her hand linger on his, with affection, but her hand was clammy. Cold as ice. Jason shivered. She looked at him, a strange, fey smile on her lips, a glimmer deep in green eyes. Hope, or love, or something else, sinister or benign, Jason wasn't sure. But, he realized, you have to take chances. Nothing in life, especially other people, was risk fee.

"Maybe we can start all over again. Like, reset to original factory settings."

"I'd like that, Kat," said Jason.

"Yeah," said Kat. "Let's see what happens. You never can know."

CRITICAL BLAST PUBLISHING
THE MAFIA IN HOLLYWOOD STORIES FROM PRE CODE FILM TO
THE BUFFALO MOB
GODS & SERVICES   Carter
GH057 STORY
GH057 STORY
GH057 STORY
THE BLACK DIAMOND EFFECT
THE BLACK DIAMOND EFFECT by GEORGE PETER GATSIS
GENUINE COMICS — PERFECT 10 ARTIST EDITION
CRITICAL BLAST PUBLISHING COLORS NOT INCLUDED! 01
CRITICAL BLAST PUBLISHING COLORS NOT INCLUDED! 02
THE MONSTERS NEXT DOOR
The Fables Next Door
BULLETPROOF
BULLETPROOF
BULLETPROOF
criticalblast•com